"Do you know where the children are?"

"Oh, yes, I know," Jim replied, and Sarah Burnard thought she detected a note of weariness in his strong, masculine voice. But maybe it was just the phone line. "I've got the kids here with me," Jim went on. "All three of them in my one-bedroom, adults-only apartment."

"Oh, I'm so relieved. I went back to that awful room where we found them—to bring them some Christmas presents," Sarah explained, "and they were gone."

"Christmas presents? They'll love that, and they'll love seeing you again. You were a big hit, especially with Ellie. She calls you 'the princess lady,' and refuses to accept that I don't even know your name. So what *is* your name?" he asked casually. "Why don't we get the formal introductions out of the way and then you can come on over and deliver those presents."

"I—I don't think so," Sarah replied, gripping the receiver harder. No matter how much she liked him, Sarah wasn't going to let Jim Fleming know who she was. Because then he might find out she was pregnant—and lay claim to the child.

ABOUT THE AUTHOR

"A number of recent events in my own life have caused me to think deeply about how precious and fagile our family ties are," says Margot Dalton. "Not too long ago, I lost my father, in fact, during the months I was writing *Three Waifs and a Daddy*. And although this is a happy book and writing it gave me a lot of comfort, I'm sure that the pain of my loss added a very special poignancy to the story.

"I think we should all love each other as much as we can," says Margot, "because in the final analysis, the people we love are our richest treasures."

Margot and her husband make their home in British Columbia's beautiful Okanagan Valley.

Books by Margot Dalton

HARLEQUIN SUPERROMANCE
401—UNDER PRAIRIE SKIES
425—SAGEBRUSH AND SUNSHINE
431—MAGIC AND MOONBEAMS
451—ASK ME ANYTHING

Three Waifs and a Daddy

MARGOT DALTON

Harlequin Books

TORONTO • NEW YORK • LONDON
AMSTERDAM • PARIS • SYDNEY • HAMBURG
STOCKHOLM • ATHENS • TOKYO • MILAN

Published December 1991

ISBN 0-373-70480-1

THREE WAIFS AND A DADDY

Printed in U.S.A.

CHAPTER ONE

DECEMBER SUNLIGHT spilled through the trees, thin and pale as spun gold, creating pools of violet shadow across the drifted trail and weaving a sparkling web of mist between the dark, snow-shrouded pines. The air was keen and vibrant, singing with cold and freshness, so crisp that the tiniest sounds hung suspended in the air like brittle snowflakes.

The double grooves of a cross-country skiing trail curled out through a small clearing and disappeared among the trees, the freshly groomed parallel tracks sharp and inviting in the winter afternoon. Light and shade played across the trail, highlighting each subtle curve and ridge, creating dark pools of mystery in the overgrown areas just beyond the smooth track with its lacy edging of pole marks.

On this weekday afternoon few people were using the skiing trails. The silent forest beyond the clearing seemed to close in upon itself, wrapped in an ageless, ancient sense of privacy and self-sufficiency, excluding outsiders and presenting a cold, impenetrable face to the world. The trail lay still and deserted, going nowhere, washed by the cold, pale light and the eerie, hushed music of the wind in the swaying pines.

Suddenly the spell of silence and mystery was broken. A man appeared around a distant curve, skiing swiftly and expertly into the little clearing. He wore navy blue ski tights that showed to fine advantage the superb muscle structure of his long legs, and a heavy white-and-blue patterned Nordic sweater over a white turtleneck. The rich wool of the sweater rested with casual ease across his broad, flat shoulders and chest, its bright color matching to perfection the deep blue of his eyes.

He was a tall man, with a beautifully formed masculine body and sculpted blond good looks that gave him an almost godlike appearance, mystically accentuated by the silence of the winter afternoon and the graceful swiftness of his effortless flight. He could have been a visitor from another galaxy, a vastly superior being dropped somehow through time and space into this quiet golden winter afternoon in the Canadian west.

But when he paused, leaning back on his ski poles to breathe deeply, and then grinned up at a small black squirrel chattering in a tree high above him, he suddenly looked completely human. His dark blue eyes sparkled with fun, a warm dimple popped into one flat, tanned cheek, and his wide mouth curved upward with sunny good humor. He threw back his head with its smooth, shining cap of thick golden hair and waved one pole at the noisy squirrel.

"Hey!" he called. "Why all the noise, kid? And," he added as an afterthought, "what are you doing up there, anyhow? Aren't you supposed to be hibernating or something? It's almost Christmastime, you know."

The squirrel peeped down at him, bright-eyed and alert, and made no response.

The tall man reached behind his body, fumbling with the fastenings on the small pack he carried around his waist. He withdrew a cardboard carton of apple juice, opened it and drained it while he continued to watch the squirrel, and carefully restored the empty carton to the pack. Then he checked the bindings on his ski boots, flexed his muscular arms and shoulders a couple of times, gripped his poles and bent down to fly away once more along the trail.

Before long he reached the summit of the trickiest portion on this section of the run, his blue eyes shining with anticipation as he checked to make sure there were no stragglers or groups of children blocking the trail.

But, in fact, there was only one person in evidence on the snowy landscape. She rested awkwardly on her skis at the top of the hill, peering down at the steep, twisting trail with forlorn concentration. As he passed the woman, Jim had a quick impression of bulging flesh in bright turquoise jogging pants, of a white sweater straining over an ample stomach and an anxious, grandmotherly face framed by gray curls under a turquoise knitted cap.

Jim nodded, sidestepped past the solitary woman, and dropped into a tuck to negotiate the downhill, edging into a sharp snowplow with the snow hissing beyond his skis. At the curve he swerved perfectly to execute a rapid, graceful step turn, and then dropped into racer position to ride the downhill, his lips parted joyously over his white teeth, his golden hair lifting and stirring as the wind sang in his ears and the trees spun dizzily past him.

The trail finally flattened and smoothed, leveling out and then climbing up into the trees again. Jim skied to a stop, laughing, still exhilarated by the speed and smoothness of his flight. Suddenly he paused, his face clouding briefly, and cast a glance over his shoulder at the double grooves behind him in the snow. He hesitated, looking once more at the empty trail. Finally he frowned, stepped over into the other track and began the long, slow climb back up the hill in the direction he had come.

When he reached the bend in the trail and gazed up the sharp incline, the plump woman was still there at the top, a lonely, silent figure among the immensity of the dark, towering pines.

Jim watched her thoughtfully for a moment and then began a rapid ascent of the hill, setting his skis in a swift, skillful running herringbone that carried him upward with astonishing speed. At the summit he paused, resting on his poles and breathing deeply, and looked over at the plump woman.

She stared back at him, her brown eyes full of sadness, her sweet, wrinkled face puckered with anxiety.

"It's really not so bad, ma'am," Jim said gently. "You just need to snowplow a little at the start, that's all. The part around the bend isn't nearly so steep."

"But I don't *know* how to snowplow!" the woman wailed. "I've only been on skis once before in my life. I can hardly stand up, let alone snowplow!"

Jim stifled a grin. There was something so lovable about her, something touching and childlike in the way she stood there teetering on her shiny new skis, her plump face desolate as she gazed down the hill.

Sternly he composed his features and regarded her. "If you're just a beginner," he said, "you really shouldn't be on this trail, you know. This is rated 'expert,' mostly because of this one downhill."

"Oh," the woman said blankly. "Is it? Isn't this the Chipmunk Trail?"

This time Jim couldn't help grinning. His deep blue eyes sparkled, and his wide mouth lifted to reveal the engaging dimple in his left cheek. "Hardly," he told the woman cheerfully. "This is the Timberwolf Trail."

"Oh," she said in alarm, and then seeing his dimpled smile, her eyes widened suddenly with the look of dazzled recognition that he knew so well. "My goodness! You're—what's his name, aren't you? The football player?"

"Jim Fleming," he said briefly. Then, as the woman hesitated, flushing with embarrassment, he added cheerfully, "Are you a football fan, too?"

The plump woman chuckled warmly. "Hardly. In fact, I personally think it's just about the most senseless game ever invented. The reason I know you," she added, reaching down to pull up one of her heavy woolen socks, "is because my two grandsons have that poster of you...you know, the one where you're standing with your helmet under your arm, smiling just like that...?"

Jim nodded. "I know the poster," he said without enthusiasm.

"Well, they've had that picture hanging between their beds for ages. In fact, you've watched me read a lot of bedtime stories over the years. How could I not recognize you?"

He laughed, beginning to enjoy his conversation with this pleasant matron. "You know my name and everything, and I don't know anything about you."

"Maude Willett," she said, smiling and extending a damp, mittened hand.

"Hello, Maude," Jim said, shaking her hand and smiling back at her. "How do you happen to be on the Timberwolf Trail all by yourself?"

"It's a long story," she said mournfully, and extended one plump turquoise leg. "You see these terrific skis, all shiny new?"

Jim nodded again, trying to keep his face sober.

"Well, my son and his wife bought these for me last year for Christmas. Everyone else in my family is just a fiend on skis, and they wanted me to learn, too."

"But you didn't."

"I went out once last year, during the holidays, tripped and rolled down the hill the little kids were practicing on, wound up at the bottom looking like the world's largest snowball and decided this wasn't my thing. My favorite athletic event is double canasta, actually."

"You bet," Jim said solemnly. "It takes a lot of conditioning to play a whole game of double canasta. The deck is so heavy with all those extra cards."

She giggled and continued. "So I decided that my Christmas gift to *them* this year would be that I'd surprise them by learning how to ski. We're all going on a winter family holiday to British Columbia after Christmas, and I was going to dazzle them all by being able to swoop down hills like a bird and fly across the countryside like a speeding bullet."

Jim found himself growing more and more fond of this plump lady.

Apparently this opinion was mutual, because she examined him thoughtfully for a moment and then said, "You know, for a world-famous football pinup, you're not such a bad type, actually."

"I'm not just another pretty face," Jim told her solemnly. "I'm really a very sensitive guy."

She guffawed loudly and shifted awkwardly on her expensive skis. "So," she went on, continuing her story, "my granddaughters brought me out here today, and the idea was that they were going to teach me everything I needed to know to become a world-class athlete in one easy lesson. At least that's the way they made it sound."

A light began to dawn in Jim's mind. "But after you got here..."

"After we got here, they ran into a couple of boys they know from school, and they all wanted to ski together, so the girls took me to the beginning of the Chipmunk Trail and told me to practice, that the only way to learn is just to do it...."

Jim was careful to hide his sudden, quick surge of irritation with this nice woman's selfish and thoughtless grandchildren. Instead, he smiled at her pleasantly and said, "Well, I guess you took a wrong turning. Several trails converge up there by the warming hut, and you got onto a much more advanced one."

"Oh, good," she said with relief. "So it's not just me, right? I've been so scared by some of these hills that I wanted to lie down and slither along on my tummy." She was silent for a moment. "Several times that's what I *have* done, actually," she confessed. "But not voluntarily."

Jim grinned again. "Well, all you need is to master a little basic snowplow and you can handle any downhill. Just watch and I'll teach you."

Her plump face brightened and then fell again. "Look, you shouldn't be spending all this time with me. Don't you have...you know...people waiting for you, or anything?"

"Not a soul," Jim said cheerfully. "I'm all alone up here."

"You're retired, right?" she asked curiously. "You don't play football anymore?"

"Not anymore. Knee surgery," Jim explained laconically. "The same thing that ends most professional football careers eventually."

"Oh, I see," she said. "You know, when my husband was alive, he was a great admirer of your father, the senator. Me, too, as a matter of fact, but then he's so handsome, isn't he? Just like you, actually. I just finished reading your father's book," she added with a warm, ingenuous smile, "and I thought it was just wonderful."

Jim's pleasant mouth tightened a little. To forestall further conversation he launched immediately into a demonstration of downhill technique. "Now what you do, Mrs. Willett," he explained, "is slide your skis out like this, so the edges catch..."

He suited actions to words while Maude Willett watched gloomily.

"Then you drop your bottom like this..."

As he spoke, Jim tucked in that muscular and extremely attractive portion of his own anatomy, lowering himself into an easy, relaxed crouch, and turned to look over his shoulder at the matronly woman behind him.

"What you want to do," he explained, "is pretend you're riding a horse and keep your hands low on the reins like this..."

He began to slip down the hill, his long, narrow skis skillfully held in their inverted V, riding the incline with perfect control. At the curve he paused and smiled encouragement up at the plump, lonely figure on the top.

"Your turn," he called cheerfully. "Give it a try."

The woman in turquoise gripped her poles, spread her skis, brought the tips together, dropped into a crouch and then, dismayingly, just kept on dropping, sinking onto the snow and rolling frantically over into the soft powder at the edge of the trail.

Maude swore quietly and fervently, got up, dusted herself off grimly and tried again. This time she got halfway down the hill before her ski tips crossed and she once again became, in her own words, "the world's largest human snowball."

Jim continued to give instruction and encouragement, helping her to brush the snow from her clothing and position her skis correctly. On her fourth attempt she snowplowed slowly and awkwardly all the way down the incline, arriving upright beside him, her round pink face blazing with triumph.

"I did it!" she shouted to Jim, overcome with joy. "I did it. Just wait till I show the kids! They'll never believe it, never. Oh, thank you so much!"

Jim grinned, delighted by her pleasure with herself.

"Look," Maude said finally, puffing and bending to examine her skis with enormous satisfaction, "I'm going to stay here and go up and down this hill till I can do it perfectly. You just carry on, all right? I feel guilty already about taking up so much of your time."

"It was a pleasure," Jim said sincerely. "Are you sure you'll be all right on your own?"

"Absolutely," his new friend said. "After all," she added smugly, "I know how to snowplow, don't I?"

"Yes," Jim agreed solemnly, "you certainly do."

She chuckled and then watched with affection as he prepared to depart down the winding trail. "Mr. Fleming . . . Jim!" she called suddenly.

"Yes?" He paused and looked back over his shoulder, his burnished hair shining warmly in the afternoon sunlight.

"Would you...would you like to come to dinner with us tonight? I'm feeding all the grandkids at my apartment. It's not much...just meat loaf, but my meat loaf is pretty fantastic, you know. And the girls would be so thrilled to have you, to say nothing of their brothers.... I have two grandsons, too, just old enough to be really interested in football...."

"It's very nice of you to invite me," Jim said sincerely, "but I'm afraid I can't. I'm a creature of habit, you see, and every Monday in the winter I watch the Monday night football game with some friends of mine. Otherwise I'd really like to come."

"Well," Maude said cheerfully, "some other time then, okay? I'm in the phone book, the only M. Willett, and I'm all alone. I'd love a visit from a handsome football star."

"*Ex*-football star," Jim said with a grin.

Maude grinned back, nodded and began toiling back up the hill, setting her skis with new confidence, her plump body fired with determination.

Jim smiled and watched her for a moment longer, then turned, kicked once and surged powerfully off down the trail again, settling rapidly into his easy, rhythmic stride.

But, as he stroked and poled, he was thinking about meat loaf in Maude Willett's household, visualizing the warmth and chatter and uproar of her big, happy family. His feeling, he realized with surprise, was one that he hadn't consciously experienced for a long time—a troubling sense of oppressive loneliness and a deep, wistful yearning.

AT APPROXIMATELY the same time that Maude Willett was rejoicing in her very first successful snowplow attempt, another small victory was being celebrated about thirty miles away in the same prairie city of Calgary, Alberta, that was home to both her and Jim Fleming.

This triumph, though, was being observed under very different conditions in a botanical laboratory where the heat hovered near thirty degrees Celsius and the air was warm and humid, heavy with the earthy fragrance of green and growing things.

The laboratory was part of a huge, sprawling complex of greenhouses, atriums, clinically sterile research facilities and warrens of offices all occupied by swarms of white-coated research scientists and staff assistants. In this particular portion of the complex vast banks of plants were germinating under moisture-beaded plastic hoods, all of them carefully monitored as to soil heat, air temperature, moisture conditions and mineral balance.

Near one of the banks a woman and a man stood together, staring down at the neat rows of tiny seedlings. The woman smiled, turning aside to make a series of notations on the clipboard she carried.

She wore gray fitted slacks and a pink turtleneck of soft angora wool, but her body was concealed by a crisp white loose-fitting lab coat that fell almost to her knees. Her long hair was dark, pulled back severely into a ponytail and then neatly braided, and her appearance was further concealed by a big pair of dark, heavy-rimmed glasses that looked far too large for the delicate structure of her face.

The elderly man beside her was small and roly-poly, with a rosy face that radiated enthusiasm, and a gingery fringe of hair encircling his shiny bald head.

"Look at that, Sarah!" he exulted. "*Ninety-one percent!* That's the best germination rate we've ever had on this genetic structure."

The woman smiled, and even the heavy glasses were unable at that moment to disguise the exquisite warmth and classic beauty of her face.

"It's wonderful, Carl," she said in a voice that was gentle and musical, strangely appropriate in this room filled with fresh and flowering greenery. "Now," she added, her tone suddenly rueful, "if they can just survive drought, blight, genetic insufficiencies we don't know about, the tendency to root too shallowly, a weakness in propagation and so on, we might just have a viable new structure."

Carl shook his head. "What a pessimist. Sarah, I've been working for you...how long has it been?"

"Seven years," she said, looking at him in surprise. "Since I first came here. You were assigned to me right at the start, and you've been helping me ever since. Why?"

"Well, in all that time I've never known you to get excited over any of your accomplishments. Everybody else in the field is getting excited over them, but you're always just looking for flaws in your work. You're so hard on yourself."

She grinned and reached out to touch his chubby shoulder fondly. Her face, behind the heavy glasses, was pink with the humid warmth of the greenhouse and glowing with pleasure at the successful germination rate of her experimental plants, and she was, all at once, almost incredibly lovely. The elderly little man beside her, accustomed though he was to her appearance through all the days and seasons of their working lives, nevertheless was briefly astounded, gazing at her with word-less pleasure.

"People don't succeed by standing around patting themselves on the back, Carl," she said cheerfully. "You know that. Looking for the flaws in my work keeps me honest and humble."

He smiled back at her with undisguised affection. "Honest and humble!" he jeered gently. "If you ask me, Sarah, it wouldn't hurt you to toot your own horn a little just occasionally."

"You just wait. When I have a horn to toot, old friend, I'll make more noise than anybody. I just want—"

She was interrupted by a voice calling loudly from the doorway at the end of the corridor.

"Dr. Burnard! Hey, is there a Dr. Burnard in here?"

"Here I am," Sarah called, peering around a bank of tall, leafy oat plants, heavy with seed, to the doorway where a young man leaned in, his face pink with cold.

"Supplies," he said briefly. "Where do you want 'em?"

"Supplies?" Sarah echoed blankly. She turned to Carl, still at her elbow. "How can it be time for sup-plies? They always come on Monday."

"It *is* Monday, Sarah," he said gently.

She stared at him, her lovely face puzzled, her big gray eyes full of alarm. "But...how can it be Mon-day?" she asked again. "We didn't have a weekend."

Her assistant stifled a chuckle. "Everybody else had a weekend, Sarah. You spent both days in here doing moisture graphs. Didn't you notice there weren't a lot of people around the past couple of days?"

Sarah continued to gaze at him, wide-eyed, strug-gling with her own thoughts. "Oh, my goodness," she breathed finally. "*Monday!* You mean today is *Monday*, Carl?"

"All day, my girl. What's so special about Monday?"

"It's just...oh, my goodness," Sarah repeated helplessly with a touch of panic in her voice. "It's just that Monday is..."

She shifted on her feet, her face reflecting a growing alarm while the others watched her in surprise. Finally she turned to leave, heading off down the wide, steamy corridor at a rapid pace.

"Show him the right shelves in the storeroom, Carl," she called back over her shoulder. "And if he has the new shipment of culture dishes, leave a box of them out for me, okay? I'll be right back."

She hurried out of sight, moving swiftly on her long legs, her white coat swinging, while her lab assistant and the delivery boy stood side by side watching her.

Sarah left the greenhouse and entered the office complex, relieved by the feeling of the cooler air on her hot face and body. She almost ran through the wide, gleaming wood-paneled corridors, arriving soon at her own door and shutting herself gratefully inside the neat, austere confines of her office.

She leaned against her polished oak door for a moment, reaching up to remove her glasses, closing her eyes and rubbing her forehead. Her face, without the heavy glasses, looked vulnerable and lovely, with a delicate, fine-boned structure, alluring high cheekbones and smoky gray eyes set in a sooty fringe of eyelashes, with dark, strongly defined eyebrows. Her mouth was rich and curving, surprisingly sensual in a face so disciplined and intellectual.

After a moment, she replaced the glasses, composed her features and instantly became once more a scientist, clinical, efficient and impersonal in appearance. She drew a deep breath and crossed the room to her broad teak desk, opening a small upper drawer and taking out a chart and a thermometer.

Sarah popped the thermometer into her own mouth, glancing over the chart while she waited for her body temperature to register. After a few minutes, she removed the thermometer, examined it and made a couple of tiny, neat notations on the chart. She sat for a moment, tense and still, studying the figures while her face grew pale and her eyes darkened with emotion.

"Okay," she murmured aloud finally in a small, shaking voice. "That's it, then. I guess tonight's the night."

With trembling hands she restored the thermometer and chart to their place and drew out a file folder from a concealed compartment in the lower part of the drawer.

She placed the folder on her desk unopened, her hands hovering just above it as she stared at it with a sort of fascinated reluctance. There was a small, neat tag on the edge of the folder, labeled with Sarah's own meticulous printing. The tag read simply, "Jameson Kirkland Fleming IV."

Sarah studied the folder for a moment longer, drew a deep, shuddering breath and slowly opened the cover. The first thing exposed was a large color photograph of a smiling blond man holding a football helmet under his arm. It was, in fact, a smaller print of the same picture the plump woman on the ski hill had mentioned to Jim Fleming.

This picture, though, wasn't nearly so interesting to Sarah as it apparently was to other women. She gave it a quick, cursory glance, pausing only to observe the fine, clean lines of the man's handsome face, the breadth between his eyes and the height of his forehead, all positive genetic features. Then she moved on to items of greater interest.

There was a surprising amount of material in the manila folder: newspaper clippings about Jim Fleming's marvelous career as one of the few Canadian athletes ever to succeed in American pro ball, about his final damaging injury, the painful surgery he had undergone and his eventual decision to retire and attend to his business interests.

Sarah skimmed over these as well, barely pausing to concentrate. Jim Fleming's football career, though colorful and impressive, was hardly even of passing interest to her. But she paused and began to read with careful attention when she reached the documents at the back of the folder.

These included a variety of items. There was a clipping about Fleming's graduation from the University of Alberta, where, while launching his football career, he had also managed to earn a law degree with highest academic honors. And there were news clippings and stories about his father, Senator Jameson Kirkland Fleming III, with a couple of good pictures of the craggy old man, which Sarah studied with approval.

Jim Fleming bore a remarkable resemblance to his father—the same intelligent, alert facial expression, the same tall, erect, wide-shouldered body, the same clean, muscular lines and planes of bodily structure. This genetic dominance of positive traits was, as Sarah well knew, an extremely favorable indicator.

She set aside the pictures of Senator Fleming and picked up a neat, exquisitely documented genetic chart, drawn by Sarah herself, setting forth as much of Jim Fleming's family tree as she had been able to ascertain in the course of her meticulous research. This information was also highly favorable, showing strong, hardy bloodlines, vigorous character traits, no intrusive genetic illnesses and an inherent tendency to be healthy and long-lived.

For the family name they had, apparently, only counted back four generations to the last Fleming to live on the ancestral estate in Scotland. But, as far as Sarah could tell, there had been Flemings around—rich, vigorous, intelligent and combative—since long before records were even kept.

She grinned suddenly, thinking that she wouldn't be at all surprised to learn that when the first Romans arrived to work on Hadrian's Wall, they were met by a Jameson Kirkland Fleming, riding up in a swirl of hoofbeats and tartan to inform them arrogantly that they were trespassing on private land....

Her smile faded and her hands trembled a little as she set aside the genetic chart and picked up the final documents in the file.

These were more real and immediate, with information considerably more troubling and unnerving to her than the cool, impersonal data of the other material. They consisted of notes, neatly typed and chronologically ordered, tracking what she had been able to learn in the past year of Jim Fleming's daily activities and social habits.

And there wasn't much.

For a handsome, desirable and famous man he seemed, in fact, to lead a very quiet existence. There was a restaurant he favored on the rare occasions he dined out, a badminton club he belonged to but attended only sporadically and, surprisingly, an art class were he had studied watercolors during the previous spring session on Tuesday afternoons. But now there was only one regular appointment he kept, and Sarah had only learned of it by accident, through a friend who had worked briefly at a downtown pub until her student loan came through.

"He never fails," Wendy had said. "Jim Fleming, the ball player, you know? He comes into the pub every single Monday night, rain or shine, to watch the football game with a couple of other guys. And, Sarah, he's just the most delicious man you ever saw. Absolutely gorgeous. I mean, he's just so incredibly..."

"Alone?" Sarah had interrupted, careful not to look too interested. "Does he come alone, or does he bring a date?"

"Oh, alone," Wendy had said. "He's always alone. And women try all the time to pick him up, but he's just so good at getting away from them without being rude. It's really an art form. I know he dates sometimes, but he's terribly selective. He's got to be careful, you know, because there's *millions* of girls who'd love to get their hands on him, and believe me, I should know, because I'm one of 'em...."

Sarah remembered her effusive friend's chatter, staring moodily down at the chart of Jim Fleming's habits and activities. Her face grew pale, and her hands still shook a little as she idly traced the outline of the molding on the edge of her desk, her gray eyes dark and preoccupied.

For such a long time this had all seemed safe and distant, just a game of research she was playing, something that would never turn out to be real. But, like many scientific endeavors, Sarah's project had carried itself of its own momentum to a conclusion that she now faced with nervous reluctance.

All she knew definitely was that the moment had arrived. Monday was the day, because that was the only time when she knew for certain where Jim Fleming would be in the evening. And this was the Monday she had been waiting for, because today her body temperature indicated that her cycle was precisely at midpoint, and she was ovulating today.

And tonight, though he would never, ever know it, Jameson Kirkland Fleming IV was going to father Dr. Sarah Burnard's baby.

CHAPTER TWO

SARAH RETURNED to the research lab behind the greenhouse and went through the rest of the day wrapped in an intense preoccupation, her mind far away from the routine chores that her hands performed. While she stained and mounted slides of wheat kernel cross sections, her thoughts circled and whirled with a kind of panic-stricken excitement.

Part of the problem, of course, was that although she had chosen Jameson Kirkland Fleming IV as the ideal male to father the child she wanted so desperately, she hadn't actually laid eyes on the man for almost twelve years.

Sarah paused in her work with her hands poised above the tray of tiny glass plates, her pale face distant and withdrawn, her eyes far away.

She had been just twenty when she first saw him, already into her third year of university, academically brilliant but shy and withdrawn in her plain, drab clothes and thick, heavy glasses. And that year Jim Fleming, who was a year older and finishing his second term of pre-law, had been in her English literature class. She could still recall the fine golden splendor of him, with his sunny, handsome face, his tall, fine body and the easy grace of his movements, and the horde of adoring fans, both male and female, who seemed to follow him everywhere.

And as clearly as if it were yesterday, she could remember the warm autumn day when he sat across from her, listening intently to the lecturer, his intelligent, handsome features alert with interest, his big athletic body relaxed and confident in the wooden desk.

Sarah, concealed behind her dark-rimmed glasses, neat and studious in a gray pullover and skirt, had stolen a glance at him, and the thought had popped unbidden into her mind.

If I ever have a baby, that's the man I'd want to be its father....

At the time she had dismissed the thought as idle foolishness, even been irritated with herself for jumping on the bandwagon, ready to fall all over herself and make herself look silly over this man, just like all those other poor moonstruck girls who constantly dogged his footsteps. Afterward, she had carefully avoided even looking at him. During the course of the semester, they had never even exchanged a word of conversation.

In the years afterward, of course, Jim Fleming had faded from her mind, to be recalled only when his picture was in the paper, or his famous father did something newsworthy. But after her own father's death, when Sarah had earned her doctorate and embarked on her distinguished career, she was haunted more and more by the aching sense of something lacking, of something she didn't have and desperately wanted.

Finally she realized the truth. What she wanted more than anything else in the world was a child of her own. She was over thirty, time was flying by with alarming swiftness, and if she was to have the experience of pregnancy and motherhood, she couldn't afford to delay much longer. But now she was so deeply into her study and work in genetic research, so conscious of the crucial role that heredity played in the development of all living things, that choosing the right father for her child was a matter of paramount importance.

Alone in the big gleaming lab, Sarah shook her head and returned to her chore, meticulously staining the slides, holding them to the light to check then, labeling and filing them for future use. Her beautiful face was pale and calm under the broad banks of fluorescent lights that illuminated the worktables, but her mind still wrestled with memories and the anxious, panic-stricken doubts that had tormented her ever since she had read the thermometer and realized the significance of this particular Monday.

Her career these past ten years had allowed no time to build any kind of serious relationship, and Sarah understood that few men had any desire to compete with her beloved cereal grains. In fact, her patient, obsessive search for a drought-resistant strain of wheat had always seemed far more important to her than the need to find a man. As a result, at the age of thirty-two, Sarah didn't know any man she wanted to share much of anything with, let alone something as wondrously important as her own baby.

And artificial insemination wasn't an option, either, although the concept had initially been interesting to her trained, scientific mind. But after Sarah researched the process, she rejected it outright. The only information they were willing to give you about the prospective donor was his hair and eye color and, if you were lucky, his occupation. For someone who spent her whole life studying genetics and the importance of inherited properties, this was far too little data on which to base something so monumentally important as the birth of a human baby.

So eventually, almost against her will, Sarah had found her thoughts turning once more to Jim Fleming, who possessed all the physical and mental attributes she considered genetically critical, whose family tree was impeccable, whose gene pool complemented her own perfectly—Jim Fleming, who was now retired from his football career and back in his home city....

As she worked, frowning intently over her tray of slides and trying not to think about the evening ahead of her, the winter sky darkened beyond the laboratory windows and the lights began to flicker all over the compound. Carl popped his head in to say good-night, receiving only an absent smile and a nod from Sarah, who didn't see him leave, bundled like a dumpling in his heavy winter overcoat, his kindly round face puckered with concern.

As so often happened the building began to empty while Sarah worked, but she was hardly aware of the deepening silence, the dimmed corridors and the hushed stillness of the parking lot beyond the windows where her own car finally stood all alone, plugged in against the winter cold, covered with a ghostly dusting of fresh snow.

At last she paused and leaned back in the hard metal chair, arching her back wearily and rubbing a hand over her forehead. She glanced out at the deserted, moonlit parking lot, suddenly becoming aware of her lonely little car huddled in its blanket of white.

It's snowing, Sarah thought with a wild surge of hope. *It's probably too cold to go out tonight anyhow. Maybe I'll wait till next time....*

Then she shook her head, her gray eyes bleak and troubled.

She knew all too well she couldn't wait till next time. It might take a long, long time for her cycle to coincide again, to fall on a Monday night when she knew the man would be accessible. He might even move away, or go on an extended holiday after Christmas—anything could happen. If she wanted to get pregnant, and she wanted this particular genetic pool for her future child, then it had to be tonight.

And, Sarah thought wearily, *I'd better get busy, because it takes time to stage a seduction scene, especially if you've had as little practice at the whole business as I have.*

She shuddered with distaste, tidied up her equipment and left the laboratory, walking briskly through the darkened corridors to her office. Finally, muffled in her heavy tan duffel coat, she let herself out of the complex and waded through the fresh snow to her car.

On the way home Sarah was bemused, as frequently happened in the winter, by the intense contrast between the humid green warmth of the research facility and the wintry, moonlit bleakness of the snow-shrouded world beyond her car windows. On any other evening she would have been enchanted by the journey from one world to another, by the austere beauty of the winter moon shining on the silvered snow and the buildings etched with Christmas lights like gingerbread houses, flinging jeweled bands of light across a black velvet sky.

But tonight she found no pleasure in the magical scenes all around her. She could think of nothing but the evening ahead, and of her own extreme reluctance to do what she knew was necessary.

Because, of course, Jim Fleming must never know that he had fathered her child. She couldn't bear the idea of that kind of involvement. He had to be convinced absolutely that what happened on this night was nothing more than a casual sexual encounter, a one-night stand with a total stranger.

For Sarah, who had never in her life had a one-night stand, it wasn't going to be easy....

Still preoccupied with her thoughts and concerns, she pulled into her garage, plugged her car in and slipped through the connecting door into the house. Sarah shrugged out of her overcoat, hung it up in the entry closet and switched on the lights, walking slowly into the bright yellow kitchen.

"Amos?" she called. "Where are you?"

Amos padded into the room, a huge marmalade tomcat with an awesomely impressive air of personal dignity. He rubbed politely against Sarah's legs, allowed himself with a long-suffering sigh to be picked up and tickled beneath the chin and then commented that his dish was empty and somebody had better attend to the matter immediately.

"In a minute, okay?" Sarah said, setting him gently on the floor. "I really need a cup of hot coffee, Amos. It's freezing out there."

Amos gave her a reproving frown and marched from the room, head high, tail waving ominously.

"All right, all right," Sarah said meekly, padding along behind him. "First I'll fill your dish, *then* I'll make a cup of coffee."

Satisfied, Amos watched as his food was carefully measured out, then expressed his appreciation by allowing Sarah to pick him up again and bury her face in his warm fur, smelling deliciously as it always did of sunshine and catnip.

"Oh, Amos," Sarah murmured, "I love you, you big fat tyrant...."

He wriggled impatiently, and she set him down hastily by his dish, then went back into the kitchen to place a mug of water in the microwave. After it boiled and she stirred in a judicious amount of instant coffee, Sarah wandered down into the sunken living room, curled up in a big, padded armchair and looked around wistfully.

It's so cozy and nice, she thought with painful longing. *I wish I could just stay home tonight, forget the whole thing, not have to go out and...*

Forcibly she quelled her treacherous thoughts and sipped her coffee, still gazing absently at the room.

Sarah had inherited this house when her father died. Carlton Burnard, also a scientist, had loved his only child deeply, and had invested all his hopes and dreams in her when his lovely Spanish-born wife had died just a few years after their little girl was born.

Sarah had never lived in any other house, but familiar though her home was to her, it still looked vastly different than it had when she lived here with her father. Carlton Burnard hadn't lived to see his daughter earn her doctorate and become a distinguished scientist, nor had he been around to enjoy the fruits of Sarah's success—the research grants and fellowships and salary increases that went along with her growing importance in the world of botanical genetics.

These days Sarah could afford to make her home the way she wanted it to be, and its appearance would have surprised many of her co-workers who didn't know her well and sometimes thought of her as cold, mechanical and passionless.

The room around her glowed with color and richness, with deep, warm earth tones and vivid splashes of crimson and gold and turquoise. Sarah loved the

American Southwest, traveling there whenever she managed to drag herself away from her work, and the square sunken living room bore evidence of her wanderings—woven Navaho rugs, throws and murals, heavy, rough-hewn furnishings and small, bright paintings that sparkled like jewels on the white plastered walls.

And everywhere there were horses, Sarah's favorite animal.

Dainty china horses pranced and postured in glass-fronted display cases, rough, textured clay horses marched across the deep, plant-filled windowsills, and whimsical straw horses stood casually in the shadowed corners. The focal point of the room was a full-sized wooden carousel horse mounted on an oaken stand near the hearth on the shining hardwood floor, his sorrel mane flying, his black eyes gleaming, his pale blue saddle and bridle exquisitely detailed and outlined in gold and silver.

Sarah sipped her coffee, gazing moodily at the beautiful little horse, crafted so lovingly by some long-ago artisan. But, for once, even the carousel horse brought her no pleasure.

She finished her coffee in preoccupied silence, debated briefly whether to toss a frozen dinner into the microwave and decided she wouldn't be able to eat, anyway. Reluctantly, with dragging steps, she climbed the stairs to her loft bedroom, followed by Amos, and began the difficult and unappealing task of transforming herself into the kind of woman who would be able to entice a man like Jim Fleming into going to bed with her....

Sarah's bedroom, like the rest of her house, was surprising and delightful. The room was homey and comfortably old-fashioned, with heavy antique maple furniture, ornate picture frames holding faded sepia photographs of long-deceased family members, rich lace curtains against dark-papered walls and a hand-made patchwork quilt on the massive bed.

And, of course, more horses.

Also in the loft of her house were Sarah's bathroom, as well as a tiny alcove equipped with a personal computer system, and another little dormer just large enough to hold a crib and dresser.

The other small bedroom down on the main floor was where the nanny would have to live after the baby was born....

Sarah paused, frowning with sudden concern as she thought about the rooms in her house. This was a familiar worry, the knowledge that this house, much as she loved it, was far too small and impractical to stay in once her baby became a reality. The rooms were just too tiny, and there wasn't enough space for live-in help, and no yard to speak of—the empty lot next door that Sarah had played in as a child was now occupied by a huge fourplex that dominated the whole block.

She had been planning and saving for years, and there was enough money in the bank now, added to the proceeds from the sale of this house, to buy a bigger place after she had the baby. Probably next summer, much as she hated the idea, she'd have to start looking at real estate. She frowned again, her face reflecting the pain of this decision. Then she thought about the baby she longed for, about a bright, sunny nursery and a cosy eating nook with a yellow high chair, and a big, shady yard with a swing set....

Sarah felt a sudden surge of immediacy, of vibrant, stirring excitement. She ran across the rough braided rug in her bedroom, stripped rapidly from her working clothes and pulled on a long, heavy terry-cloth robe, navy blue with crisp white trim, and a pair of fluffy white mules.

Amos leaped onto the foot of the bed and marched up its length, sinking down on the big pillow next to a pair of whimsical white fabric horses with manes and tails of blue yarn. He slitted his eyes rudely and began to knead the patterned surface of the quilt with his paws.

"You can stay there while I get ready," Sarah told him darkly, "if you don't say a single word. *And* you'd better have your claws in while you're doing that, buster."

Unperturbed by her tone, Amos shouldered the fabric horses aside, turned around twice and subsided into a warm furry ball on the pillows, resting his chin on his paws and watching her lazily through narrowed lids.

Sarah hurried into her bathroom, leaped in and out of a quick hot shower and set her hair on hot rollers. Then, working with unusual care and trying not to feel silly, she applied her makeup in the manner she had practiced in preparation for this night, using a good deal more than her customary touch of mascara and dash of lipstick.

When she finished, she carefully inserted her seldom-used contact lenses, combed out her hair and regarded her face critically in the mirror.

"Okay," she said aloud. "So far you look all right."

In fact, she looked very good indeed. Her dark chestnut hair tumbled in soft curls around her shoulders, full of bronze highlights, and her naturally lovely features, artfully enhanced by the subtle but dramatic makeup, were both glamorous and alluring.

Sarah gave herself one more careful examination, added a touch more blush to accentuate her high, beautiful cheekbones and hurried back across her bedroom to the closet.

She had spent a long time deciding on just the right dress for the seduction of Jameson Kirkland Fleming. Her first inclination had been to buy something frankly suggestive, something bright and vulgarly loaded with sequins that would fit tightly over her hips and show a lot of cleavage.

But, after listening to Wendy's ingenuous chatter about the fascinating and famous man who came regularly to the bar on Monday nights, Sarah had changed her mind.

"You should just see all the gorgeous, sexy women who come on to him," Wendy had said, "and it's like he doesn't even notice them, you know? Like, the only time he ever shows any interest at all, it's gotta be someone kinda classy, you know? He seems to have a built-in radar, like he only responds to classy women, not sexpot types."

So, armed with this information, Sarah had gone in search of a dress that would look both seductive and "classy," and finally she had found it. The dress was deceptively simple, a soft smoky black silk with a high, demure neckline and a bodice and skirt that slid with casual suggestiveness over her breasts and thighs, clinging gently in places and swaying deliciously as she moved.

Sarah was only medium height but appeared taller because she was unusually slim, and because she held herself so proudly erect. Her figure, sculpted and firmed by miles of walking in all kinds of weather, was trim and slender, with full, high breasts, a taut, flat abdomen and long, shapely legs. When the black dress slipped over her head and fell with a soft, silky whisper around her body, she was transformed instantly into a woman so alluring that no man could fail to give her at least a second glance.

Sarah tugged on a pair of black snakeskin sandals with high spike heels and moved across the room to her dresser, opening a gleaming mahogany jewel case and taking out an exquisitely fashioned necklace and ear-ring set of heavy antique silver, one of her few legacies from her beautiful Spanish mother. She fastened the jewelry carefully in place, then stepped aside to regard herself critically in the long cheval mirror, holding the black silk skirt a little away from her body and pirou-etting slowly.

"So, Amos," she asked the big cat, who lay watch-ing her in sleepy silence, "what do you think? Will he approve?"

Amos parted his mouth in a huge, toothy yawn and twitched his whiskers with drowsy insolence.

"Well, he'd better," Sarah said. "Because we've waited a long time for our baby, haven't we, Amos? We want to buy a crib, and wallpaper with bunnies on it, and little dancing mobiles, and stacks and stacks of snowy white cotton diapers...."

Overcome with sudden joyous excitement Sarah whirled across the room in her high heels, picked up the big cat and hugged him fervently while he glared out beneath her chin in baleful silence. Then she tossed him back onto the bed, watched with affection as he rolled himself into a fuzzy orange ball of insult, and slipped into her little white fox jacket. Her beautiful face glowed vividly above the soft fur of the collar, and her gray eyes shone like stars in the shaded lamplight.

"I'll be back by midnight, Amos," she said softly from the doorway. "And when I come home, I'm going to be pregnant."

Then she was gone, slipping the shoes from her feet to run lightly down the stairs while the house closed in upon itself, warm and silent, to await her return.

SARAH HAD BEEN inside the pub briefly one fall day in the interests of research after she first formulated her plan. But she knew all too well that a rehearsal, even a dress rehearsal, was never the same as the real thing, and she was filled now with terror and a disconcerting sense of not belonging, of being in absolutely the wrong place at the wrong time.

She sat alone at the bar, nursing a weak mixed drink, trying hard not to panic. Everybody here seemed to know everybody else, to have a kind of easy kidding relationship that made her feel isolated and excluded. But when a couple of men approached her with clumsy attempts at friendliness, she felt even greater panic.

What if someone moved in on her and she wasn't able to shake him, so that when Jim Fleming arrived he would think she was already taken and lose interest?

Coldly Sarah resisted their advances and left them feeling chilled and shaken by her beauty and aloofness.

By the time she started her third watered drink, the football game was well advanced, being watched with lusty cheers and comments by a group of men on wooden chairs and stools drawn up near the big-screen television, but there was still no sign of Jim Fleming.

Tonight of all nights he chooses to be undependable, Sarah thought gloomily. *Every other Monday night he's here in his place by seven o'clock. Tonight he won't even show up.*

Just as she framed this thought the door opened and the man himself entered in a gust of chill night air, pausing to brush the snow from his wide shoulders and smiling at the roar of greeting that went up from the rowdy circle of football fans.

Turning casually on her stool at the bar, Sarah stared across the room at him, feeling her throat suddenly tighten and her palms begin to grow moist.

He was just so...so...

She floundered, trying to absorb the reality of the man without losing her resolve, all at once terribly unnerved by the fact that she hadn't seen him face-to-face since those long-ago college days. All of her information about him had been gleaned from three sources: the press, the very discreet and highly expensive services of a private investigator she had hired for a couple of weeks earlier in the year, and Wendy's idle chatter.

Now, despite all her careful research, Sarah found herself totally unprepared for his sheer physical impact, his big, graceful maleness and his overwhelming personal presence. She swallowed hard, trying not to appear obvious as she watched him brush the snow from his shining blond hair, hang his jacket on the coatrack near the door and cross the bar to his circle of noisy friends.

Jim Fleming wore blue jeans, casual suede shoes and a tan crewneck sweater over a blue plaid shirt that made his eyes look even bluer, and he still moved with the easy athletic prowl that Sarah remembered so well, his big shoulders relaxed and easy, his stride lithe and powerful.

Sarah heard the loud chorus of affection that greeted him, and his deep voice explaining cheerfully, amid much delighted male laughter, how he had driven into a snowdrift coming down from the ski hill that afternoon and been forced to wait over an hour for a tow truck.

Sarah's heart began to hammer painfully in her chest. As she gazed across the room, Fleming swiveled idly in his chair, glancing around at the occupants of the bar, calling greetings to others in the room. His eye caught hers and he fell abruptly silent, staring at her in startled admiration for a moment. Sarah returned his look, cool and unsmiling, deliberately keeping her face calm and impassive.

She was the first to turn away, returning to her drink and the polite attentions of the bartender, but she could feel the way his glance lingered on her before he turned back to the television screen.

So far so good, Sarah told herself nervously. *He's shown some interest at least. Now, if I can just keep from making any really dumb mistakes . . .*

She sipped her drink in silence, facing the long, glistening rows of glasses and colorful decanters that lined the back of the bar and listening to the bartender with an occasional absent smile as he talked about his children. He was, apparently, an ardent family man, with a growing brood who participated in a bewildering variety of sports and cultural activities, all observed and recounted with enormous pride by their doting father.

I'll probably be just as bad with my own child, Sarah thought wistfully. *Bragging to anybody who'll listen about how smart she is, how fast she learns, her rare and incredible talents . . .*

She smiled suddenly, her lovely, delicate face glowing, her huge gray eyes shining, almost incandescent with pleasure. The bartender stared at her, transfixed, then turned aside hastily to take another order, his cheerful, blunt features still awed and amazed.

Unaware of his reaction, Sarah drank her warm tomato juice and brooded on the mysteries of male and female attraction. Grimly she wondered how she could have been so foolish and presumptuous as to think *she* could capture the attention of a man like Jim Fleming just by dressing up and sitting in the same room. After all, a lot of women who were sexier and prettier had tried to attract him with little success. Why should Sarah be any different?

But then there was Wendy's theory about attracting men.

"Any woman who's reasonably presentable," Wendy had once said, "can attract any man she chooses, just by being near him and concentrating hard enough. Like, we give off…a scent or hormone or something, like insects, or moths, you know, and they feel it and can't resist? Like, a male moth will fly miles and miles to get to a female who wants him. It's, like, nature, you know?"

Sarah, whose scientific training included an encyclopedic knowledge of the processes by which smaller creatures managed to reproduce, had merely smiled with amusement, enjoying Wendy's chatter. For somebody working toward an advanced degree in economics, she often thought, Wendy had retained a great deal of childlike naiveté.

But now, in desperation, she recalled the conversation and wondered if there really was any truth to it. Could she actually draw Jim Fleming to her side just by wanting him badly enough?

She swiveled slightly on the bar stool and stole a look across the room at the back of his head with its smooth cap of golden hair, and his broad, flat shoulders beneath the soft, creamy wool of his sweater. Then she turned back to the bar, concentrating on him, narrowing her thoughts so that the only thing in her mind was this one man and the passionate depths of her need to be with him, to draw from his body the magic spark that would ignite her own waiting cells, form a new human being, bring her precious little baby to life and start its wondrous cycle of growth.

I want you, she thought fiercely, staring into her drink. *I want you and nobody else to do this thing for me, and I'm going to have you. Right now, tonight, within a couple of hours, it's going to happen, because I'm willing it to happen, with all my energies.*

"Could I buy you another drink? That one's looking pretty low," a voice said at her elbow.

Still deep in concentration, Sarah was about to make a cool, dismissive response when something in the man's tone caught her attention. She turned and stifled a gasp of astonishment.

Jim Fleming sat on the stool next to her, smiling, his big, lean body almost touching hers.

Sarah had never been this close to him before, and she was stunned by his physical magnetism, his pure masculine appeal. His face, with the fine, arrogant bone structure that she admired so much, was tanned by the sun and wind, glowing with good health, his blue eyes clear and vivid. His features were alight with friendliness and good humor, and a kind of easygoing, considerate warmth that would probably be irresistible to most women.

Sarah, however, wasn't at all concerned about this man's personality, because she was convinced that such qualities weren't genetically transmitted. She was greatly interested in his physical structure, his background and heredity, but she wasn't in the least impressed by his charm.

"Thank you," she said calmly. "One more drink would be nice. I'm leaving soon and it's a cold night."

Jim Fleming signaled the bartender and turned back to Sarah with increasing interest. "You know, you have a beautiful voice," he said. "Really beautiful."

"Thank you," Sarah said, wondering if she was going to be able to go through with this whole thing. She just felt so silly....

"Pardon me for the line, but do you come here often?" he went on with an easy grin. "I mean, I keep having the feeling we've met before, but I can't remember where."

Sarah felt a quick stirring of alarm that clutched briefly at her stomach and made her feel a little sick. Then she reminded herself sternly that those college days had been twelve years ago; he couldn't possibly remember her from then.

"That sounds like yet another line, doesn't it?" she asked lightly. "The old 'haven't we met before?' routine."

Jim Fleming chuckled. "I guess it does at that. But I'm serious, except I just can't seem to place..."

"Probably," Sarah said, accepting her new drink with a smile for the bartender, "it was just somebody who looked like me."

"I doubt it," the tall blond man said abruptly. "I don't think I've ever met anyone who looked like you."

Sarah stared at him, wide-eyed, and found him regarding her with a steady, intent look, all the laughter and teasing stilled.

She was dismayed to feel a little flush mount on her cheeks, and turned aside quickly, biting her lip, painfully aware that women accomplished in the art of seduction weren't supposed to blush at compliments.

"*Another* line," she said with a small, brittle laugh, trying to keep her voice from shaking. "You're just a walking guidebook to singles repartee, aren't you?"

"Hardly," he said. "In fact, I'm really not very good at this sort of thing at all. My problem," he added, swirling his rich amber rum in its tall glass and gazing thoughtfully into the golden depths, "is that I'm not good enough at being insincere. I tend to say what I think, and it costs me every time."

Sarah, who often did just the same thing, felt a warm surge of empathy and stifled it instantly. She had no intention of establishing any sympathetic human communication with this man. She didn't want to be friends with him, and she certainly had no wish to see him again, ever, after he served his biological purpose. In fact, she couldn't allow herself to respond to him at all. She had to remain within the character she had shaped for herself and carry it through to the end so that he could be successfully seduced and then discarded.

"Sincerity," she said lightly, sipping her drink, "is highly overrated."

"Why do you say that?" he asked with interest.

"Well, because people run around being sincere, helping each other, getting all involved in things that don't really concern them, and in the long run everybody winds up taking advantage of each other and getting hurt. A nice, comfortable hedge of insincerity is absolutely necessary for protection in the modern world, I think."

"Lord, what a cynical outlook," Jim Fleming said with awe. "I couldn't live if I felt that way about other people."

Neither could I, Sarah thought. *But I'm not about to tell you all the secrets of my soul, Jameson Kirkland Fleming IV.*

"Do you know anything about me?" he asked abruptly. "My name, for instance?"

"How would I?" Sarah asked idly. "Is it embroidered on your mittens, or something?"

He grinned. "No, I just wondered. Most people seem..."

He fell silent again while Sarah struggled to keep her expression light and casual, with the cool, mocking tone she had adopted to suit the character she was portraying.

"All I know about you," she said, "is that you appear to be a fairly presentable physical specimen, maybe a little too given to honesty and sincerity, but with definite possibilities."

"Possibilities for what?"

"For the capacity to be highly entertaining."

"I see," her companion said lightly. "And what exactly do you find entertaining, my pretty lady?"

Sarah turned and met his eyes steadily, gazing fully at him, desperately aware of the crucial importance of this one moment—probably the most vital and pivotal moment of her life.

"I'm entertained," she said in her low, beautiful voice, "by the music of the universe, the conjunctions of celestial bodies, the fact that when two entities coincide with perfect precision, the earth moves...."

A small, amused Sarah somewhere inside her head, who was watching this whole scene with detached merriment, chuckled and hooted at the trite, hackneyed words.

Corny, she thought in despair. *Just so ridiculously corny. What's wrong with me? Why can't I do this a little better?*

But Jim Fleming stared back at her, mesmerized by her words and the stunning, hypnotic beauty of her face and form.

"I think," he said slowly, "that you might be bad news, pretty lady."

Sarah's heart began to pound, and she bit her lip, hoping frantically that it wasn't audible, knowing with her rational, scientific mind that, of course, it couldn't be, but still afraid of betrayal by her body.

"I just might be really good news, too, you know," she whispered. "And there's only one way to find out, isn't there?"

Jim Fleming leaned toward her, so close that she could smell the soft fabric of his sweater mingled with a faintly spicy after-shave, a clean, fresh scent of outdoor cold and warm, healthy maleness.

"What's your name?" he asked.

"Whatever you want it to be," she murmured. "Pick something that pleases you."

He settled back, studying her thoughtfully. "That's the way it is? No names exchanged?"

Sarah nodded. "That's the way it is," she said quietly.

"And where do we go? Your place or mine?"

Sarah made a conscious effort to hide the overwhelming surge of relief that suddenly flooded through her.

It's going to work, she exulted. *Oh, my God, it's actually going to work!*

"Neither," she said aloud. "You don't want me in your life after tonight, and I certainly don't want you in mine. So we just go somewhere neutral, like the hotel down the street."

"The Kingston Arms, you mean?"

Sarah nodded, sipping her drink calmly.

"Maybe you're overestimating me," Jim said with a sudden grin. "Maybe I can't afford the Kingston Arms, you know."

Sarah slid from the stool, reached for her fur jacket and gave him a calm, level glance. "That doesn't really matter," she said quietly. "I can."

CHAPTER THREE

JIM FLEMING STOOD in the small white-and-gold bathroom adjoining the luxurious room at the Kingston
Arms, which despite his companion's quiet objections,
he had insisted on putting on his own charge card.

He splashed cold water on his tanned face, buried
himself in the depths of a big soft yellow towel and then
examined his reflection thoughtfully in the mirror,
thinking about the woman waiting in the other room.

There was something about her...something so
strange.

Jim frowned and shook his head, still disturbed by his
own behavior. This particular episode was completely
out of character for him, something he hadn't done for
as long as he could remember. For one thing, sex with
strangers was distasteful to his naturally fastidious nature. And then men in his position had to be so careful,
pursued as they were by publicity seekers, neurotics,
cunning manipulators and others who just wanted to
ride their coattails to a bit of the limelight.

That was the problem, he thought, running a hand
moodily over his shining blond hair. Life for men like
Jim Fleming could be surprisingly lonely. Come to think
of it, his sex life hadn't been exactly terrific lately. In
fact, if the truth were told, it had been an uncomfortably long time, which had probably helped to make him
vulnerable to this particular encounter.

But there were other influences, too: the sad brittle gaiety of the big city all dressed up for Christmas, the glowing warmth of lighted windows that sheltered families in their little houses all cozy with togetherness, even the thought of the plump woman he had met skiing that afternoon who was now having meat loaf with her grandchildren.

Jim shook his head, fighting off the gray sadness that sometimes crept into his soul these days and threatened to upset the careful structure of his life.

Besides, he thought briskly, hanging the towel away on the rack and stripping off his shirt and sweater, it wasn't just the holiday surroundings, or even his uncharacteristic blue mood that caused him to be here. The main reason for this liaison was the woman herself.

He tugged off his socks, stepped out of his jeans and folded his clothes carefully on a shelf opposite the basin. Then he stood for a moment, naked except for his shorts, his tall, splendid body filling the little bathroom with golden hard-muscled male beauty.

But he wasn't even looking at his reflection in the long, gilt-edged mirror. He was still musing about the woman who waited for him in the other room.

She was such a woman of contradictions, a fascinating, quicksilver kind of person. In the bar her incredibly alluring beauty had attracted him at first, given him the urge to hear what her voice would sound like and see how her face looked when she smiled, just the way anyone would want to get a closer look at a lovely work of art. Then, after he began to talk with her, he had been powerfully aroused by her smoldering, evident sensuality, her subtle suggestiveness, the obvious indicators that she was passionately interested in him as a sexual partner.

All of this, though, was no new experience to Jim Fleming. He had met many, many beautiful women and heard all kinds of sexy come-ons. What he found most enchanting about this particular woman were the mysterious nuances of her personality, the things that didn't quite mesh. For instance, she had seduced him with quiet authority and raw sex appeal, and yet on the brief walk to the hotel she had seemed to relax, as if at a task accomplished, and had pretty much ignored him altogether. Instead, he had noticed that she gazed about with childlike pleasure at the Christmas lights and decorations on the snowy downtown streets.

And at the hotel desk she had smiled shyly at the desk clerk and then withdrawn hastily and stood muffled in her soft fur, looking around at the elegant lobby and seeming, all at once, like a little girl embarking on some scary adventure.

Either she was playing some kind of really weird game, or else she was an actress so accomplished that she could create the impression of a deep, multilayered personality.

Probably it was *all* playacting, Jim thought. Most likely she was just another adventuress, out for a thrill, living her own complex fantasy.

But she was undeniably classy, and she was so incredibly beautiful.

He switched off the bathroom light, opened the door and walked out into the other room, pausing in the semidarkness to give the woman in the bed a level, challenging look as he faced her and slowly, deliberately, stripped off his undershorts.

He stood naked before her, all taut, flat muscles and hard, arrogant maleness, looking carefully into her face. She rested against the crisp, soft pillows, her wings of dark hair flowing behind her, the sheets drawn up to her creamy, bare shoulders, and returned his gaze with apparent calm. But again there was something about her, a flicker of alarm when he stripped in front of her, a brief unreadable expression, that made him suspect, implausible though it seemed, that she wasn't really as used to this sort of thing as she pretended.

Anyway, who the hell cares? Jim thought with sudden weariness. *A one-night stand is a one-night stand, and nothing more.*

He reached down with an abrupt gesture and drew the sheet away from her body, surprised by her quick reflex move to cover her nakedness. Then, as if making a conscious effort, she relaxed and stretched languidly in the bed, displaying herself to him.

Jim stared down at her in silent, stunned amazement, feeling the first urgent stirring of strong physical desire and the resulting thrust of maleness.

She was so absolutely exquisite—the most beautiful woman he'd ever seen. Her breasts were full and high, pink-tipped and virginal-looking, although he calculated that she had to be close to his own age. Her pale skin was silken smooth, and her figure was both slender and lush, with firm, shapely curving lines connecting breast to abdomen to hip and thigh in a symphony of richly delicate womanly beauty that enraptured him.

"Lord, you're beautiful," he whispered in spite of himself. "You're just so unbelievably beautiful..."

"You're not so bad yourself," she said in a low, husky voice, gazing up at him as he stood over her. "Come here," she whispered.

And yet as he climbed into bed beside her, shuddering with desire, his sense of puzzled surprise mounted. There was something really strange going on here... something that was so hard to figure out....

The way she moved against him, and the warmth of her lips as she kissed him, were provocative and enticing, arousing him to a fever pitch of need that was painful in its intensity. But her hands didn't seem to match. They were awkward, hesitant, almost as if she were inexperienced in the art of touching a man. Far from being a turnoff, Jim found this the most exciting thing of all, the sense that she was somehow innocent and new to the arts of love, needing his guidance and instruction.

God, she's good, he thought in some part of his mind that was able, even in the throes of passion, to remain detached and objective. Not many women would be able to create an impression of innocence in the midst of all this heat.

Deliberately he slowed and paused, lost in pleasure, caressing the length of her body with slow-sensual hands. He wanted to go on forever, just touching her and holding himself in check to prolong the experience, to spend the rest of his life in this warm bed with this woman's lovely, rich curving body, fondling her sweetness....

But the urgent rush of his desire was too strong. At last he surrendered to his pounding need and moved to enter her, groaning with passion, his body arching and plunging as he lost himself in the silken depths of her, breathing hard, moaning out loud with joy.

And she responded to him like no other woman he had ever known. It was as if she wanted all of him, every ounce of maleness he could give her, as if she wanted to draw the very essence of himself into her body and make it her own.

The intensity and excitement of her passionate, silent response was more than he could bear. He reached his climax and felt her slender body shudder beneath him in her own private release. Then, abruptly, he relaxed, drawing gently apart from her and taking her tenderly in his arms, so overcome with sleepy satisfaction that he could hardly think.

They lay for a long time in drowsy silence while the warm-air register hummed softly near the bed and passing traffic in the streets below threw ghostly fingers of light over the walls and ceiling. Finally Jim leaned up on one elbow and looked at the woman beside him.

She lay with her eyes closed and an intent, wondering look on her face, curled up in a little ball as if she were protecting something precious within the curve of her body. In the dim light and the aftermath of passion her delicate face looked vulnerable and childlike, not at all the seductive, sophisticated woman she had been in the bar.

Jim remembered the marvelous, fiery passion of her body's response and the strangely inexperienced, almost shy movements of her hands, and wondered again....

"Hey," he whispered huskily. "Hey, pretty lady. You're really something, you know that? You're just incredible. That was awesome."

She made no response, her body still curled carefully in upon itself, her face quiet. Jim watched her for a moment in silence, then eased himself carefully out of the bed and padded into the bathroom to collect his clothes. He carried them back into the bedroom, along with one of the big yellow towels, which he placed gently over her shapely body.

"Here," he murmured, "Your bathrobe, my lady. You can use the bathroom, and I'll get dressed out here. Unless," he added hopefully, struck by a sudden thought as he looked down at her, "you were perhaps interested in seconds?"

She shuddered delicately and sat up, avoiding his eyes, wrapping the towel securely around her. Then, still silent, she gathered her clothes and vanished into the bathroom.

Jim switched on the bedside lamp and dressed rapidly, savoring the rich warm glow of sexual contentment that still flooded him, but realizing with a small tug of alarm that it wasn't going to be very long before he wanted her again.

She was bad news, after all, just as he had suspected. She was one of those alluring, bewitching women who somehow possessed the ability to ensnare a man, to captivate him and make him drunk on her charms, hopelessly, insatiably addicted to the sweetness of her rich womanly body.

Well, whatever she wants, he thought helplessly, *I'm willing to go along with it. I'm hooked. I just have to see her again, be with her.*

As he framed this thought, the bathroom door opened and she emerged, fully dressed even to her shoes, looking quiet and self-contained. She was as lovely as ever in the simple black dress, but there was no longer anything provocative or alluring about her movements at all, no flirtation or suggestiveness. Her step was brisk and businesslike as she crossed the room, still not looking at him, picked up her handbag and fur jacket and started toward the door.

"Hey!" Jim said abruptly. "Not so fast, all right? Can't we . . . just relax a bit, and talk?"

"What about?" she asked, pausing with her fur coat over her arm.

"I don't know," he began helplessly. "Just about . . . the kind of things people talk about." He paused, his eyes widening in surprise as she hesitated nervously near the door.

She looked back at him, obviously waiting for him to finish speaking so that she could leave.

"You mean," he began slowly, "this is it? Nothing to say to each other, no names exchanged, no plans to meet again?"

"That was our understanding right at the beginning," she said.

"And what if I've changed my mind? What if I've decided I'd like very much to see you again? What then, pretty lady?"

He caught the brief flicker of panic in her eyes and his heart sank.

She's married, he thought. *Probably to some rich guy that she hates, but she doesn't want to lose him because of the money, so she sneaks around looking for adventures just to make life bearable.*

But Jim Fleming wasn't a man to be dismayed by obstacles. He had held this woman in his arms once, and he fully intended to have her again, regardless of the consequences.

"In that case," he heard her say quietly, "I suppose you would have to find me."

"And you think that's going to be really difficult?"

"Very difficult," she said.

He nodded, reached for his jacket and stepped up beside her. "Then I guess I'll just have to give up," he said cheerfully. "Won't I?"

She looked up at him suspiciously and then nodded, clearly relieved. "That would be best," she agreed with quiet seriousness.

"Can I at least see you into your car, or put you into a taxi or something? It's late for a pretty lady to be on the street alone."

"Thank you," she said, "but I'm fully able to look after myself."

"You know something?" Jim said, staring down at her intently. "An hour ago I would have agreed with that. Now I'm not so sure."

SARAH WALKED down the frosty midnight sidewalk beside her tall blond companion, still brooding over his last words. He seemed to have suspicions about her, and some kind of insight into her personality that was surprising and unsettling.

In fact, Sarah thought, the whole experience had been surprising and unsettling. She had expected the man beside her to be arrogant and self-absorbed, narcissistic and dull, and he had turned out to be quite the opposite. He was funny, witty and tender, deeply intelligent and gently considerate, with an endearing boyish side to his nature that made him extremely appealing.

And, Sarah mused, striding along with her hands thrust deep into her pockets and her breath gusting in the chill blackness, the sex act itself had been amazing, too.

Completely absorbed in her work, reserved and distant as she always was, Sarah's relationships were few and far between. She could hardly remember the last time she'd made love, and she could never recall an experience so exciting, so erotic and fulfilling and deeply, richly satisfying.

She smiled grimly. All the books said there was a better chance of conceiving if the woman had an orgasm, and considering the shattering intensity of the one Jim Fleming had given her, it had to be practically a sure thing.

"Would you like me to go back to the hotel and call a cab? There should be one coming along here soon, but I can..."

His voice interrupted her thoughts, and she forced herself to concentrate. She had been reluctant to have him call a cab from the hotel, thinking that it would make her too easy to remember and trace if he should actually set out later to find her. Her own car, of course, was parked just a couple of blocks away, but she had no intention of letting him get a look at the make, model and license plate.

If she could get into a cab, have the driver take her a few blocks and drop her off, then she could just circle back to her car on foot, drive home, have a hot bath and relax.

Oh, God, she thought plaintively, *I hope I'm pregnant, because I can't go through all this again.*

Jim hunched his broad shoulders against the chill night air, peered around the deserted streets and looked down at the woman beside him. "Look," he began with concern, "I think we should..."

Sarah glanced up at him, trying to keep her tired mind clear, desperately anxious to get away from him. By now, all that she wanted was to be safely home with the precious burden she carried so that she could concentrate on nurturing and protecting it. If she had really conceived, or was about to, then the wondrous new cells within her body were like a tiny, pale flame that needed to be guarded, shielded, coaxed gently to life.

Suddenly, as she stood gazing up into his tanned, sculpted face, a great many things seemed to happen all at once, leaving her shuddering and limp with terror.

She felt something pressing harshly into her ribs beneath the soft leather of her little jacket, saw Jim's jaw muscles tense with startled alarm, heard a rough, deep voice in her ear.

"Anybody makes a move," the voice said behind her, "and I cut the lady to pieces. And I ain't kidding."

The words sounded like a line from some low-grade movie. Sarah almost laughed hysterically, but the look on Jim's cold, set face told her that this was no joke.

This was the real thing.

Sarah felt hollow and sick, nearly on the verge of fainting, and struggled frantically to maintain control, to think clearly, to keep herself upright and rational.

"Get that thing away from her," Jim said harshly to the unseen presence just behind her.

"Shut up. I'm the one giving the orders here. Now, first, you take off your watch, nice and slow, and give it to me. And then I want what you got in your wallet, and no tricks, okay, 'cause I'd hate to hurt this nice lady."

Sarah couldn't see him, but she could hear the rough voice grating on her ear, the breath hot and ragged, and judged that their assailant wasn't a tall man, perhaps not even her own height. She could feel his nearness, smell the musty, unwashed human scent of him, sense the terrible dank coldness of his fear.

He's more scared than I am, Sarah thought, but the idea wasn't at all comforting. She knew enough of human psychology to understand that with a knife in his hands, their attacker was even more volatile and dangerous because of his fear.

Jim seemed to realize the same thing, because he quietly did as he was told, removing his slim, expensive gold watch and handing it over, carefully emptying his wallet of bills. His brown hands trembled with fury, his big shoulders were tense and his handsome face was so grim that Sarah grew even more terrified.

Something was going to happen, something dreadful and inevitable, and she was powerless to do anything about it, caught as she was between two violent, angry men, with a knife jammed against her ribs....

"Now, you," the voice grated. "Give me your money and your jewelry."

Sarah swayed on her feet, and Jim looked down at her with grim concern. He reached toward her, but the knife point jabbed painfully, making her wince. Then there was a quick, threatening gesture, and Jim drew back, his blue eyes smoldering dangerously.

"You heard me, lady," her attacker repeated. "Get a move on."

"I don't have...all I have in my bag is a twenty-dollar bill. Just for cab fare."

"Give it to me."

Sarah fumbled in her bag, her hands shaking, and took out the bill, handing it blindly behind her, feeling it grabbed from her fingers.

"Now the jewelry."

"But..." Sarah's voice rose in panic. "But...this was my mother's! It's all I have of hers. It's not valuable.

It's just silver. Please don't make me give you my mother's—''

"Shut up!" the voice said again, low and furious. "Don't give me all that crap. Just take it off and hand it over."

Tears trickled down her cheeks, warm and salty in the cold night air. With a great, aching sense of sorrow and loss Sarah unfastened her necklace and earrings and handed them back to be snatched greedily.

"Okay," the voice said. "Now I'm gonna leave. But I'm taking the lady with me for a ways, just so *you* don't get any ideas, mister. C'mon, broad. Nice and easy. Just walk along in front of me here."

Suddenly, as he spoke these last words, the mugger's voice rose a couple of registers, ending on a high, fluting note that contrasted oddly with his earlier course, grating tone. After a brief instant of stunned silence, Jim launched himself forward, his athletic body moving with incredible swiftness, and threw himself onto the other man.

Sarah turned, shaking in terror, her eyes wide, her hand covering her mouth, and watched as the big knife clattered to the pavement and Jim wrestled with their assailant. For the first time she could see the man—a small skinny figure in ragged jeans and a tattered, dirty ski jacket with a black stocking mask over his face.

Though he was wiry and agile, he was no match for Jim Fleming. Silent and frantic, he struggled vainly in the bigger man's grasp, as slippery as a fish. While Sarah stood looking on Jim held him firmly in the crook of his arm, ripped off the stocking mask and then gasped in astonishment.

The face that stared out at them defiantly was that of a boy, barely into his adolescence, with smooth, childlike cheeks and a liberal dusting of freckles across his nose.

The boy glared at them furiously, blinking back tears of angry frustration. Jim shifted his position to get a better grip, and quick as a cat the child seized the opportunity. He ducked under the big man's arm, wrenched himself free and was gone, flying off down the street in his dirty sneakers with Jim pounding along behind him.

Sarah watched them vanish around a corner, still stunned by everything that had happened to her within the space of a couple of hours.

"Hey!" she suddenly shouted out loud to the deserted street. "He's got my mother's jewelry!"

She bent, slipped off her high heels and jammed them into her pocket, then began to sprint along the sidewalk in the direction the other two had disappeared, barely conscious of the rough, frozen pavement that burned harshly against the soles of her feet.

As she ran along narrow streets and through garbage-filled alleys, trying frantically to keep Jim's distant running figure in her sight, Sarah was only dimly aware of the neighborhood she passed through. They were in one of those dismal downtown slums situated so incongruously near the tall, gleaming office complexes and elegant little boutiques—pockets of sad squalor and poverty side by side with areas of great wealth. In these smoke-blackened, crumbling old brick buildings people actually lived out their lives in cramped, airless rooms that sometimes lacked even the most basic amenities.

But she didn't have the time to ponder the social contradictions all around her. Her breath was coming in huge, ragged gasps, her side ached and there were sharp pains in her feet. Worst of all, Jim, far ahead of her, seemed to be on the verge of disappearing forever.

But just as she was about to abandon her pursuit, she saw him pause at a narrow doorway and then plunge inside, and she forced herself to run faster. Sarah entered the dim, musty building soon after he did and peered up the sagging, dirty stairs to see him hesitating by a scarred wooden door on the rickety landing.

Sarah shuddered. The whole building was so dank and depressing, full of smells that she didn't even dare to analyze.

And who knew what was behind that door.

But before she could call a warning to him, or even let him know she was in the building, he had set his big shoulder against the door and begun to push. The flimsy lock gave way immediately under his strength, and the door swung inward on a square of sickly light. Cautious and catlike, he peered into the room and then stepped slowly through the open door, disappearing from her sight.

Sarah watched in horror, her eyes wide, her chest heaving, expecting at any moment to see him stagger and reel back out into the hallway under a rain of gunfire.

Nothing happened. It was silent in the smelly foyer, silent on the grimy wooden stairs, silent out in the littered, moonlit alley. Sarah cast a frantic glance outside, looked up the stairs again and gathered all her courage. Then she climbed slowly upward, pushed the door aside, slipped into the room and stopped in astonishment.

Jim stood in the center of a tiny, dingy space that contained almost nothing except a narrow metal cot, a heap of blankets in another corner and a shabby little crib half concealed behind a tattered old curtain hanging in front of a doorless closet. Besides these basic furnishings, there were just a few scraps of household equipment, an old hot plate sitting on a battered cupboard and a couple of cardboard boxes apparently used for storage. The boy who had stolen Sarah's necklace stood defiantly in front of the cot, trying to shield it from their view. Behind him another child peered up at them from the nest of rumpled, musty blankets, its wide eyes and pinched face giving it the look of a sleepy, frightened owl.

The boy's eyes flicked over Sarah as she came in, and Jim turned in brief alarm. "You shouldn't be here," he muttered.

"He has my necklace," Sarah said doggedly.

The boy tensed and appeared to be on the verge of flight. Jim leaped suddenly across the room and grabbed their small attacker once again in a firm bear hug. Skilfully, without relinquishing his hold, Jim reached into the boy's dirty jacket and took out their money and belongings, slipped them safely into his own pocket while the boy struggled in furious silence and the child on the cot began to whimper with terror.

Sarah hurried across the room, pushed past Jim and the boy and knelt by the cot, gazing down at the contorted, pale face. It was, she judged, a girl about ten, with fine, straight blond hair cut raggedly around her ears and big blue eyes swimming with tears. Sarah stroked the matted, silky hair back from the child's forehead, almost unbearably moved by the little girl's fragile thinness, her wide, imploring eyes and her painful fear.

"It's all right, dear," Sarah whispered. "Nobody's going to hurt you. What's your name?"

"It's..." the child gulped and swallowed, then began again in a low, husky voice. "My name's Ellie."

"And is he your brother?" Sarah asked, indicating the wiry figure that still struggled frantically in Jim's iron grasp.

"Yes," the little girl whispered. "His name is..."

"Shut up, Ellie!" the boy said, stopping his futile wriggling long enough to glare furiously at the little girl on the cot. "Don't tell them anything!"

The thin blond girl bit her lip, and her eyes filled with tears once more.

"Look, kid," Jim said to the boy, "I don't think you have this whole situation completely figured out, do you? Now stay still for a minute and listen to me, okay?"

He emphasized his words with a gentle pressure of his restraining arms that made the boy wince a little with discomfort, then stand meekly silent.

"Now we know where you live, and we know what you did, you understand? And if we decide to press charges, you could be in big trouble. So you're not really in a position to be giving orders, are you?"

The boy stood glaring at the scarred wooden floor and didn't answer.

"*Are* you?" Jim repeated softly with another gentle pressure of his muscular arms.

"No," the boy muttered sullenly. "I guess I ain't."

"Good. Now what's your name?"

"Billy."

"Fine. Now, Billy, who looks after you kids? Who's the adult in this household?"

"I am," the boy said proudly, lifting his freckled face to glare up at the big man who held him.

Jim stared back at him silently and began to tighten his grip once more. "Tell me the truth, Billy," he warned. "I don't want to hear any lies."

"It *is* the truth," Billy said. "Let me go, okay? I won't run away."

"How can I be sure of that?"

"Because," the skinny boy said, as if amazed at his captor's stupidity, "I ain't likely to run off and leave you alone here to take the kids away, am I, now?"

"Kids?" Jim said blankly. "Is there another one besides the little girl there?"

As if in response to his words, a small furor suddenly erupted from behind the dirty, ragged curtain. The crib began to creak and rock, and a tiny figure heaved itself erect, grasping at the curtain with chubby hands and beginning to roar in a surprisingly lusty voice. All four people stared at the little indignant person balanced precariously on dimpled pink legs, the round red face screwed up with indignation.

"I think he's getting another tooth," Ellie explained, as concerned and apologetic as any young mother. "He has five already," she added proudly while Sarah smiled at her.

Ellie slid from the cot, exposing a pathetically thin little figure in a limp yellow T-shirt and ragged jogging pants, and lifted the plump baby from the crib, sagging under his weight. He continued to howl, squirming in her grasp.

"Here," Sarah murmured, "let me take him."

After a moment's hesitation, Ellie handed the baby over, and Sarah took him, cuddling him on her shoulder, resting her cheek against his downy fair head. He was about ten months old, healthy and sweet-smelling in his little cotton shirt and diapers, the only clean and beautiful thing in this whole squalid place.

Ellie and Billy were both silent, watching anxiously. Sarah smiled reassurance at them, patting the baby's small back tenderly while he hiccuped, quieted and nestled warmly against her.

"What's his name?" she asked Ellie, who came bustling toward her with a soft blue blanket to cover the little bare pink legs.

"Arthur."

"That's a nice name. And he's a lovely baby," Sarah said gently to the two older children. "You're taking very good care of him."

"That's why...that's why I tried to rip you off," Billy said. His voice was low and abashed, all the toughness gone, and he sounded for the first time like the child he really was. "Like Ellie says, Arthur's getting more teeth, and there's all this flu going round, and he needs lots of milk and orange juice and expensive stuff, and he's almost walking already, so he needs shoes, 'cause the floor is cold and there's slivers..."

Sarah shuddered a little and held the baby's soft, warm body closer to her.

Jim was staring at the two children, his open, handsome face drawn with concern, his blue eyes full of disbelieving horror. "You mean..." he began slowly, and hesitated. "You mean, you weren't kidding? There's no one looking after you kids? You're all alone here with this baby?"

"Yeah," Billy said.

"I don't believe it," Jim said flatly. "It's not possible."

"Why not?" Billy asked. "I'm thirteen, and Ellie's almost eleven. I guess we're old enough to look after one little kid. Matter of fact, Arthur gets looked after better than most kids around here."

"For how long?" Jim asked, still stunned by the boy's words. "How long have you three been alone here?"

"Since summer. Our Mom died in the summer. She drank," Billy added by way of explanation.

"She was nice sometimes when she wasn't drinking," Ellie said loyally. "For a long time before Arthur was born she didn't drink at all, and she even had a job working nights cleaning buildings and stuff, and she brought us apples and chocolate bars and things sometimes."

Ellie sighed in bliss, her wide blue eyes reflecting the joy of those long-ago remembered treats.

"But after Arthur came she started drinking again," Billy said. "She was too drunk most of the time to look after him, and she wanted to give us all to the Welfare, but she said they'd split us up and send us to different places."

"What then?" Jim asked.

"I told her I'd run away and take the kids if she tried to give us to the Welfare," Billy said calmly. "And I told her I'd look after us all, so she didn't need to worry about it. And I have."

"By stealing from people," Jim said.

"Hey, man, I *never* did that before. This was the very first time. Usually I find papers and sell them downtown, run errands for people, lots of things. It's just that, like I said, we were scared Arthur was gonna get sick, and he needs so much stuff...."

Sarah still clung to the warm, yielding softness of the baby's little body, feeling faint and sick hearing this story.

"When your mother died," she said softly to Billy, "how did you manage to stay on your own? Didn't the authorities realize then that you were alone and . . ."

Billy shook his head. "Nobody knew. She died . . ." He glanced at Ellie, who stood pale and tense beside the crib, clutching a baby bottle in her small, thin hands, and then continued. "She died in an alley quite a ways from here, and nobody there knew anything about her. I was watching," he added without emotion, "when they took her away in the ambulance. They called her Jane Doe."

"But . . . the other people in the building," Sarah began, "don't they . . . ?"

"The other people don't even know she's gone. They think somebody's looking after us, and they ain't the kind who care much what happens to anybody else. I just cash the Family Allowance and give the man the rent money every month, and nobody ever bothers us here, not a bit. They're all busy looking out for themselves. That's just the way it is," he said, concluding his little speech with a touch of defiance, glancing up at the two well-dressed adults.

"We have to . . . we have to call somebody," Jim began helplessly. "You can't go on living like—"

"If you do," Billy interrupted calmly, "I'll just take the kids and run away, and then they probably won't even be in as good a place as they are now."

"But why?" Jim asked. "Why would you resist getting help for all of you, and food and decent clothing and school— Do either of you go to school?" he asked suddenly, glancing from Ellie to Billy.

The boy shook his head. "Not this year. Not since Mom died. Schools are too nosy," he said briefly. "I got some books, and I teach Ellie lots of stuff, and we have some book about how to take care of Arthur, too. You see," he went on, "we can't go to Welfare. Right away somebody will adopt Arthur and take him away, 'cause he's a real nice baby and everybody wants babies. But they don't want me and Ellie."

The little girl's eyes filled with anguished tears that welled up suddenly and flowed unchecked down her wan, pale cheeks.

Sarah looked at her with concern, then turned to Jim. "Don't," she said softly. "Don't do anything just now. Let's give them some money for the things they need, and tomorrow we can come back and make sure they're—"

As if suddenly remembering her existence, he shot her a quick, keen glance, his face registering a strange mixture of emotions at the sight of her standing flushed and lovely in her stockinged feet, her elegant fur jacket and black silk dress, tenderly cradling the sleepy baby against her breast.

"Tomorrow, pretty lady?" he asked softly. "That sounds great. Should I pick you up at your place or meet you somewhere or what?"

Sarah suddenly came crashing back to reality, remembering the purpose of the evening, the precious seed she guarded within her body, the absolute necessity to maintain this charade of hers and keep Jim Fleming from ever finding out who she was or what she had done.

"On second thought," she murmured coolly, "I'm sure you can handle it on your own. You'll have to fix their lock before you leave, of course, and make sure they're safe, so don't think about leaving them alone and trying to follow me. Could I just have my necklace, please? And then I'll be on my way."

I'll come back, she told herself. *As soon as I can be certain he's not around, I'll come back and bring them a whole lot of things—food and clothes and some warm things for the baby and books and toys....*

With a painful surge of regret, carefully concealed, she handed the drowsy, sweet warmth of Arthur back to his anxious sister and moved over beside Jim. Silently gazing into her eyes, he handed her the silver necklace and earrings along with her crumpled twenty-dollar bill.

Sarah pocketed the jewelry, gave the money to Billy, and bent to slip her shoes on, moving gracefully toward the door.

In the dank, musty hallway she hesitated, ignoring Jim altogether and smiling at the two older children, who stood watching her in silence.

"He really is a beautiful baby," she told them softly, and then ran swiftly down the creaking stairs and out into the silent, moon-washed night.

CHAPTER FOUR

JIM GLANCED HELPLESSLY at the three children, looked around the shabby little room and then clattered down the stairs to peer frantically out at the receding figure of his beautiful mystery woman. He watched as she neared the corner, walking swiftly, her dark head high, her slender, elegant legs flashing beneath the swinging silky fabric of her skirt.

"Damn!" Jim muttered aloud, pausing in the doorway, torn by powerful and conflicting emotions. Part of him wanted to run after her, seize her in his arms, demand that she tell him her name and where she was going. He was haunted by a desperate certainty that if he let her vanish tonight, he would never, ever be able to find her again.

And yet the three children were upstairs, alone and unprotected in this dreadful neighborhood, and he had broken the lock on their door.

As he continued to hesitate, the woman rounded the corner and disappeared from sight, swallowed up in the rumbling late-night stillness of the big city. Jim stood for a few moments longer, gazing at the emptiness of the frosty streets. Finally he shrugged his shoulders in despair, turned back into the dingy building and trudged up the stairs.

He stepped through the sagging door and into a scene of considerable noise and activity. Arthur sat in the middle of his crib, howling lustily and gnawing on his fist, his little red face screwed up alarmingly. Ellie and Billy were moving quickly around the room, gathering things up and throwing them into the cardboard boxes. They appeared to be having an argument in furious whispers, and it was obvious by the dispirited set of Ellie's shoulders and the tears on her thin cheeks that Billy was winning the dispute.

Both of them looked up guiltily when Jim came into the room. Ellie dropped the pile of tattered baby clothes in her arms as if they had burned her, while Billy gazed defiantly at the tall man, his freckled face pale and set.

Jim looked from one young face to the other, wincing as Arthur's howls increased in volume and the crib began to rock violently. One of the corners, Jim noticed, was heavily reinforced with masking tape, and the whole structure looked dangerously unstable.

"Is he all right?" he asked Ellie. "Shouldn't you pick him up or something?"

She opened her mouth to answer, but Billy silenced her with an abrupt gesture and turned to face Jim. "Look, mister," he said wearily, "just give it a rest, okay? Go home and leave us alone. I'm real sorry I tried to rip you off, and now you got your stuff back, so there's no problem, okay? Just leave us alone."

"Sure," Jim said, returning the boy's gaze steadily. "Leave you alone, and two minutes after I'm gone you'll have these poor kids out on the street in the cold, running away."

"We've done it before," Billy said flatly. "I've always looked after them before. I guess I can do it now."

"Look..." Jim began helplessly, and then broke off to look over at Ellie, who had lifted Arthur from his crib and was attempting to silence his roars of misery.

She glanced at her older brother, her little white face pinched with worry. "He's hungry, Billy, I think. He needs a bottle."

"So give him one."

"But…we don't have anything. We used the last milk at bedtime, and you said you'd get some money to-night and bring some home, but you—"

"Shut up!" Billy hissed at her, casting a quick, warning glance in Jim's direction. "Look, Ellie," he went on in a gentler tone, "the lady gave me that twenty. I'll go out right now and buy some milk at the store. Give him a bread crust or something to chew on. Maybe that'll hold him till I can—"

The boy paused, looking up at Jim as if just remembering his presence. "Please," he said wearily, "can you just go away and let us be, mister? I'll look after the kids. You don't have to worry about us."

Something in the boy's voice caught Jim's attention, not the tough-guy bravado or the raw defiance, but a tired undertone that spoke of a weariness almost too great to be borne.

The poor kid, Jim thought suddenly, forgetting all his earlier anger. *Thirteen years old, and he's got all the responsibility of the world on his shoulders.*

"Listen," he said with sudden decision. "This has gone on long enough. I'm taking you kids home with me, okay? And I don't want any arguments. I'll give you a place to sleep, and we'll feed the baby, and to-morrow we'll think about what to do with you. Now come on. Get some coats on and dress the baby."

Ellie's face turned even whiter. Her wide blue eyes filled with panic as she clutched her tiny brother in her thin arms.

Billy glanced at her, then turned back to Jim. "No way," he said grimly. "As soon as we get there, you'll be on the phone to Social Services, and within a week they'll have me and Ellie in two different foster homes and Arthur put up for adoption. No way! I'll kill you first."

Jim looked at the boy, chilled and dismayed by the cold anger in Billy's voice and the furious glint in those young eyes. But he faced him steadily with a calm, level glance until Billy finally dropped his eyes and kicked at the rotten floorboards, his thin cheeks flushed.

"Maybe you can push your little sister around and scare her with threats like that, kid," Jim said quietly, "but you can't scare me. I have no intention of calling Social Services, and I give you my word that I won't allow you three to be split up. I just want to see these two little kids warm and fed and safe, and I intend to take them home and make sure they are, with or without your cooperation. Now, are you coming with us or not?"

Billy glanced up sullenly, his eyes dark and cold with suspicion. But he said nothing, just gave a weary shrug and another of his harsh gestures to Ellie. She handed the baby to Jim, giving him one sad and desperate glance of appeal, and then returned to her task, stuffing baby clothes into the cardboard box.

Jim held the baby awkwardly, surprised by Arthur's wriggling strength and the startling volume of his screams at close range. Automatically he shifted the baby's firm little body to the crook of his left arm and began to rock him. Arthur, who had never been held in a grasp so large and muscular, paused in midbellow, looked up at Jim with startled blue eyes swimming in tears and then suddenly smiled.

Jim gazed down, enchanted by the smile and by Arthur's little pearly teeth. "Hi," he murmured, smiling back foolishly. "Hi, there, big fella. Are you hungry? Should we take you home and give you some milk? Yes, we should. Oh, yes, we should."

Ellie looked over at them, the ghost of a smile on her anxious face, and lifted the big cardboard box, staggering a little under its weight. Billy, still grim and silent, carried another box, and the two of them paused in the doorway.

"Okay," Billy said sullenly. "We're ready. Let's go if we have to go."

Jim held the baby while Ellie wrapped him in a big torn blanket. Then he looked with dismay at the ragged cardboard boxes and the thin jackets of the two older children. "What about the rest of your stuff?" he asked. "There's no lock on the door. Won't somebody steal it?"

"This is all our stuff," Billy said. "Everything we own, except the furniture, and that ain't worth nothing."

"What about your coats? Doesn't Ellie have something warmer? It's really cold out, and my car's a few blocks away...."

"Ellie's used to cold," Billy said grimly. "Come on, let's get going before Arthur starts yelling again."

Hesitantly, still holding the bundled weight of the baby in his arms, Jim guided the two children out of the building and through the wintry streets to his car. They trudged silently beside him, each carrying a cardboard box. Ellie cast an occasional anxious look at the silent, wriggling cocoon in Jim's arms. Billy, though, stared straight ahead, his expression cold and unreadable.

Jim glanced sidelong at him, realizing the boy was planning to take the two smaller children and make a break for freedom just as soon as he found an opportunity.

Oh, God, Jim thought wearily, *I'm going to have to watch them every minute. How can I go to work in the morning? How can I take care of them? What in hell am I getting myself into?*

They reached his car and dumped the two cardboard boxes into the back seat with Billy. Ellie sat beside Jim in the front, clutching Arthur in her arms, gazing in wondering silence at the Christmas lights decorating the rows of houses.

"Oh, my, but they're pretty," she said so softly that Jim could hardly hear her.

"What's pretty, Ellie?"

"The lights. I never seen anything so pretty."

Jim glanced at her in surprise. "Haven't you seen Christmas lights before, Ellie?"

She shook her head, setting her fine blond hair swinging. "I don't think so. Just on the stores and stuff. We never had a car, you see. And Mom, she was always out at night, so Billy looked after me, and he never took me anywhere after dark. We were always just at home." She gazed out at the multicolored display that spangled the winter darkness and gave a little sigh of bliss. "This is just so pretty," she repeated, holding Arthur's body tightly. "It's like fairyland, or something all magic. I love it."

Jim swallowed hard and pulled up into his own parking spot beneath his massive high-rise apartment building.

"Will the lady be here?" Ellie asked suddenly as they were walking through the parkade.

"The lady? Who do you mean?" Jim asked.

"The beautiful lady who was at our place. Will she be here?"

"No," Jim said, glancing down at the little girl's anxious features. "She won't be here."

Ellie's face fell, but she persisted despite her shyness. Obviously this was important to her. "Will she be here tomorrow?"

"Why do you ask, Ellie?"

"She was so beautiful. Just like a princess," the little girl breathed. "And she was so nice to me. I'd just ... I'd like to see her again."

"So would I," Jim said softly, while Ellie gazed up at him in surprise. "So would I, Ellie."

Awed by the size of the building and the splendor of the lobby with its uniformed doorman, both children stood silent and nervous in the elevator, clutching their cardboard boxes while Jim once more held Arthur, who seemed, mercifully, to have fallen asleep during the car ride.

Jim shifted the sleeping baby gently into the crook of his arm and unlocked his apartment, standing aside to let the two thin, shabby children precede him into the living room.

Ellie stood gazing around with shining eyes and parted lips, as if she had been suddenly ushered into paradise. "Oh, Billy," she whispered in rapture as amazement overcame her fear. "Look how beautiful it is! Look at them pretty pictures and stuff, and that big rug. That's real fur, isn't it, Billy? And look at them big couches and all the plants, just like on TV!"

Startled by the little girl's reaction, Jim examined his warm, comfortable apartment, trying to see it through her eyes. The rooms were well-proportioned and tastefully finished with the earth tones and rough, natural fabrics he favored. The rug that had enchanted Ellie was a huge white goatskin spread in front of the fireplace, and the plants that Jim loved were everywhere, some of them the size of small trees.

But the apartment was really quite modest, particularly by the standards of many of Jim's friends. Knowing his background and the vast wealth of his family, they often wondered, sometimes aloud, why Jim refused to move into something "a little more appropriate." What none of them knew was that Jim had sunk all of his own money into his business and hadn't taken a penny from his father since his school days. Many of those same friends, Jim thought grimly, would have been amazed if they knew what a struggle he had sometimes just to pay the rent on this place, let alone something larger and more lavish.

"Don't get all excited, Ellie," Billy said coldly. "This ain't the place for people like us, and we sure won't be here long."

Once again Jim hesitated in dismay, wondering just what he thought he was doing.

Billy was right, he realized. It was cruelty, not kindness, to give these poor children a taste of comfort and security if it was just going to be snatched away again immediately. But how could he look after these three waifs in a one-bedroom apartment? What would they do all day? How could he look after their needs, get them to school, get medical attention for the baby...and a baby-sitter for Arthur, too, he realized suddenly, if Ellie were to attend school.

Suddenly he became uncomfortably aware of Billy's eyes resting on him with a knowing and sardonic expression as if the boy were reading his mind, seeing all his fears and panic.

Jim's tanned cheeks flushed a little and he squared his shoulders, turning to Ellie with forced heartiness. "It's okay, Ellie," he said with considerably more confidence than he felt. "You're going to be here for a while, and if you do leave, it'll be to go somewhere just as nice. And both your brothers will be with you. I promise. Now let's find places for everybody to sleep, okay? This couch here makes out into a bed, and there's a corner back here that I think would be safe for Arthur."

While Jim and Ellie bustled around, making up beds and barricading off a comfortable space to deposit the sleeping baby, Billy slouched in a corner and followed their movements with his eyes. The boy said nothing, but his face was cold, his expression grim and watchful.

"THE LENGTH of the shot blade stem on the sample group has increased an average of 2.6 millimeters," Sarah dictated into her small microphone, "while the ancillary leaves are now—"

She broke off suddenly and whirled around in her chair, gazing absently out the window at the snowy landscape as she toyed with the cord on the little tape recorder. Her face softened, and she lifted her big glasses off, rubbing her temples and smiling faintly.

"It is now three days..." She paused to check her watch and then continued speaking into the microphone, her voice gentle, almost dreamy. "Approximately sixty-two hours since conception. The zygote has advanced through orderly mitotic process to the blastocyst stage and is now preparing for implantation in the wall of the uterus."

As she spoke the words, she felt a strange flutter inside her, a mysterious little thrill deep in her core, and smiled once more at her own foolishness. Even if she had conceived on Monday night, Sarah was fully aware that it was far too soon for her to feel anything resulting from the pregnancy. And the chances that she had conceived were really not good, considering all the ensuing trauma...the shock of the "mugging" immediately afterward, her breathless sprint through icy streets and her upset and alarm over the plight of the three children. The odds for a successful conception under such adverse conditions were, scientifically speaking, almost nil.

And yet there was this mysterious little tug within her, this awesome, mysterious sense of something wonderful happening.

"Soon," she murmured ruefully into the little tape recorder, "I'll be having morning sickness and food cravings, and some poor doctor will be forced to tell me that it's all in my mind."

She switched off the microphone, ran the machine backward to erase the tape and then gazed out the window once more, her lovely face withdrawn and troubled.

Once again the image of the three children invaded her thoughts, urgent and distressing. In the few days since her encounter with them Sarah had quelled all impulses to go back and see how they were, determined to leave that entire evening behind her.

She was haunted by the irrational fear that Jim Fleming would somehow use the children as bait, that he would be in hiding somewhere, waiting for her to go back to their dreadful little room so he could pounce on her.

Her fears weren't based on the fact that she considered herself particularly desirable or unforgettable, but simply because she might be pregnant. Now that the possibility of pregnancy actually existed, Sarah was constantly tormented with the possibility that Jim Fleming might somehow find her, learn who she was and lay claim to her child.

After all, she reasoned, the Flemings were a wealthy and powerful family. Jim was the only child of Senator Jameson Kirkland Fleming III, and Jim had never married. And they kept giving the boys in the family these numbers. What if Sarah had a little boy and they found out about him and wanted to make him Jameson Kirkland Fleming V?

The thought of the powerful Fleming family making a claim to her child, possibly going to court to argue their rights to him, interfering with Sarah's careful plans for his upbringing, was almost more than she could bear. More than anything, what Sarah wanted now was to forget about Jim Fleming and his part in her life, put it all behind her and carry on.

At this point she refused to consider what she would do if she hadn't conceived, whether she would seduce Jim Fleming another time or look for some other man to father her child.

Wearily Sarah shook her head, put her glasses back on and turned back to the pile of computer sheets and folders on her desk. But she couldn't erase the image of Billy's stubborn freckled face, of the sweet, drowsy weight of the baby in her arms, of Ellie's pinched and terrified little features.

Abruptly Sarah flipped the lid on her tape recorder and stored it away in her desk. As she did so, there was a brief knock and the door popped open to admit Carl, her assistant, who was brimming with holiday spirits.

Literally as well as figuratively, Sarah thought, grinning privately. There had been a small but lively staff Christmas party in full swing down the corridor over the lunch hour.

"Well, I'm off, Sarah," Carl said. "Merry Christmas. See you next week."

"Next week?" she asked in alarm. "But this is only Thursday, isn't it?"

"Sarah," he said patiently, "Christmas is on Sunday. Most of the staff is taking tomorrow off, as well. The facility is going to be closed down for four days except for maintenance. Remember?"

She gazed at him blankly for a moment, her lovely, delicate face clearing as she absorbed this information. "Right," she said briskly, getting to her feet and shrugging out of her lab coat. "Christmas is on Sunday. I'd better get going."

Carl watched as she folded the big glasses away, crossed her office and took her long tan duffel coat from the closet.

"Sarah . . ." he began hesitantly, "where are you going?"

"Christmas shopping," she said cheerfully. "I have to buy some Christmas presents."

Carl continued to watch her in troubled silence. "But I thought you said you weren't going to bother with Christmas this year," he began cautiously. "You said you didn't know anyone to celebrate the holiday with, and you were just going to use the long weekend to get a lot of extra work done."

"I am," Sarah said. "But there are some children I know, you see, and I want to buy presents for them."

"Sarah... Sarah, dear, you know that Melanie and I would love to have you at our place. You know we've always said you're absolutely welcome, and the kids would love to have you with us."

"I know you have, Carl." Sarah smiled at him as she wound her heavy plaid scarf over her shoulders. "I know you have. But Christmas is no big deal, especially if you have no family, and I don't want to be part of another family's holiday. I really do intend to get a lot of work done while I have the place to myself. I just happen to know these children who could use a little touch of Christmas, that's all."

She patted his shoulder, smiled and gathered up her big leather shoulder bag. Carl stood watching in silence, bemused as always by the classic, exquisite lines of her face without the heavy glasses, and the sudden glow that lit her huge gray eyes when she smiled.

"GREEN WOOLLY WORMS," Sarah said to the clerk in the department store. "I want a couple of green woolly worms. They're the best thing for lake trout."

"If you say so, ma'am," the harried young clerk said. "It's just that, you see, fishing items aren't really seasonal right now, and I don't know if..."

"Please," Sarah said, smiling shyly at the tired young man. "I know it's an inconvenience, and I'm so sorry. But I'm buying a fishing outfit for a boy who's probably never gone fishing in his life, and I'd really like him to have a couple of green woolly worms in his tackle box."

At the sight of her glowing, incandescent smile the clerk was as enchanted as Carl had been a few hours earlier. He swallowed hard, forgetting all his tiredness and irritation with the floods of last-minute Christmas shoppers. "Sure thing ," he murmured, his face warm with admiration. "I'll just...I'll just check the back and see what we've got."

Sarah watched him vanish, still smiling to herself as she recalled long-ago summer days with her father, idling on the cool, shaded banks of the creek while they trailed their fishing lines in the water and he lectured her serenely about the botanical properties of the plant life growing all around them.

Had Billy ever known an afternoon like that?

Suddenly she frowned, her eyes almost brimming with tears at the thought of the dingy, horrible little room where the three children lived and the pinched, undernourished look of their faces.

I'll take him this summer, she told herself, forgetting for the moment how completely irrational this plan was. *The first nice day of spring I'll bundle them all up and we'll take a picnic lunch and spend the whole day fishing.*

The clerk returned with some gaudy lime-green bits of fluff and plastic in his hand. "Just two left," he said apologetically, "and they're four dollars each, I'm afraid. We had a real heavy run on green woolly worms over the summer."

"Oh, I'm glad you found some! They're the only thing for lake trout," Sarah said gratefully. "Thank you so much for your trouble. I'll pay for them at the front, because I have a lot more things to pick up yet."

With another shy, luminous smile she took the lures and the other equipment she'd selected, put them into her shopping cart along with a leather baseball glove and a yellow plastic radio, then vanished into the depths of the store, leaving the young clerk grinning after her foolishly and smiling to himself as he turned to serve his next customer.

Shopping for Arthur wasn't difficult. Recalling the cold, bare room with its splintery, wooden floor, Sarah picked out a pile of warm blanket sleepers, sweaters, fuzzy little socks and overalls, as well as several pairs of sturdy shoes and slippers. She agonized briefly over the sizes and then, remembering Arthur's weight and substance, opted for generously large shoes and garments.

After selecting the clothes, she gave some careful thought to toys, picking things designed to emit interesting squeals and impressive bursts of music when the proper buttons and levers were manipulated.

The older children seemed to be taking good care of Arthur's physical needs, but Sarah wasn't as confident that his intellectual development was being guided properly.

At last, with the boys taken care of, Sarah turned her attention to gifts for Ellie. She had deliberately saved Ellie for last, because shopping for the little girl was going to be so much fun. Sarah had the scientist's gift for full recall of detail, and she vividly remembered what it was like to be ten. She had a pretty good idea what would appeal to the child.

Not dolls, of course, since Ellie had Arthur and any facsimile would seem pretty pale in comparison with the real thing.

But clothes... Sarah frowned, thinking about Ellie's torn jogging pants. She browsed through the girls' clothing section, selecting warm sweaters, skirts, slacks and tights in the pale pastel colors that would suit the little girl's delicate complexion and her prim, endearing old-fashioned manner.

At last Sarah turned her attention to the really fun things—a complete set of ''Anne books'' by L. M. Montgomery, a beautiful little leather-bound diary with gold lock and key and a shellcraft set. Sarah beamed with delight when she discovered the hobby kit, remembering the one she'd owned and what fun it had been to construct delicate little pieces of jewelry and ornaments from the array of dainty seashells. Still smiling to herself, she bought extra packets of shells and adhesive just to be sure Ellie would have all the materials she'd need.

Finally she wheeled her loaded shopping cart through a front checkout, not even blinking at the staggering total of all her purchases. Sarah was usually so preoccupied with her work that she had very few opportunities to spend money. Buying gifts for these unfortunate children wasn't a sacrifice at all, just a pleasure to her.

Humming along with the canned Christmas music that echoed through the downtown streets, Sarah stashed her mountains of gaily wrapped boxes into her car and drove through the crowded afternoon traffic to where the children lived. As she neared the familiar area and passed the pub where she had seduced Jim Fleming, Sarah felt a brief stab of alarm and a cold little shiver of fear. She glanced around nervously, almost as if people in other cars were watching her and remarking her presence, and then shook her head, distressed by her own foolishness.

Still, she felt frightened and conspicuous when she parked in front of the shabby tenement that was home to Billy, Ellie and their baby brother. Casting a quick anxious glance over her shoulder, she locked her car securely, kicked aside a couple of bulging black plastic garbage bags that crowded the doorway and hurried up the rickety flight of steps, holding her breath in the fetid dampness of the old building.

Sarah hesitated on the landing, staring at the broken lock on the door. Tentatively she swung the door open and peered into the room. It was empty except for a few scraps of paper, the sagging old crib, the dirty cot and the pile of blankets in the corner. The room already had a musty, unused smell, and it was obvious that nobody had been there for several days.

Sarah gazed around, her gray eyes wide and strained, her mind racing.

They've run away again, she decided. *After we left, Billy must have taken the little ones and run away so we couldn't come back for them.*

She thought of the snowy, bitter streets, of Arthur's soft, sweet-scented pink skin and Ellie's pinched and frightened little face, and felt tears stinging behind her eyelids once again.

"Oh, no," she murmured aloud. "Oh, no..."

Then, suddenly, she recalled Jim Fleming as he had looked on Monday night in this room. She remembered his sunny features drawn with alarm and disbelief when he realized the three children were alone here, and the warm, confident way he had responded to all of them and their situation.

Sarah felt a sudden surge of hope. Maybe Fleming had done something for the children, found a decent place for them to live and taken them away from this dreadful room to something more suitable. He had seemed like the kind of man who would do the right thing...had seemed, in fact, like a really warm and caring person—much to Sarah's surprise.

But it wasn't enough for her to speculate. She had to know if he'd taken care of the children or if they were, even now, roaming the frozen streets in search of a place to stay. And that meant, Sarah realized with a sinking heart, that she really had no other option.

Much as she hated the idea, she was going to have to call Jim Fleming and ask him.

CHAPTER FIVE

THE BOTANICAL laboratories were almost deserted by late afternoon, with only a few stragglers in the halls exchanging cheerful greetings as they prepared to dash off for last-minute Christmas shopping or holiday preparations.

Sarah hurried to her office, tossed her coat over a chair and seated herself at the big teak desk, taking Jim Fleming's file from its place in her top drawer. She glanced through it rapidly, confirming what she had suspected.

Fleming's home phone was unlisted, and even the dogged private detective she'd hired last spring hadn't been able to get hold of the number. So she couldn't just call his home and hope to find anything out from a housekeeper or maid. She'd have to call Fleming at his office.

Sarah frowned, her face drawn with anxious reluctance. Jim Fleming was executive director for a company that managed a small chain of sporting goods shops, and also marketed an independent line of athletic clothing and footwear. And he was no figurehead boss, chosen for the position just on the strength of his colorful and successful football career. According to all indications Jim Fleming took his job seriously, spending long days at the office and only taking occasional breaks for his regular hobbies and activities, like the badminton club and the watercolor classes.

Today, on a Thursday afternoon, it was likely that Jim Fleming would be in his office. And the office number was printed clearly on a sheet of paper right in front of Sarah's eyes. She stared at the number gloomily, fighting a growing sense of reluctance. Then, thinking about the fishing tackle, and the little fuzzy socks for Arthur, and Ellie's shellcraft set, she drew a deep breath and dialed the number.

"Could I speak with Mr. Fleming, please?" Sarah asked the receptionist, hoping crazily that he wouldn't be in, that he'd already left for his Christmas holiday, that she could just hang up...

"May I say who's calling?"

Sarah hesitated in panic.

"Just say...say it's a friend of Billy and Ellie's, please. Tell him it's...it's the lady in black," she added, feeling hot and foolish.

Jim's receptionist, who had to be superbly trained, gave no reaction to this apart from a polite, murmured response, and a moment later Jim's voice came on the line.

"Hello?" he said. "Is it really you? Is it you, pretty lady?"

At the sound of his warm, masculine voice memories washed over Sarah with a sudden and astonishing flood of feeling. She remembered with vivid clarity the feel of his hands and his lips, the strength and gentleness of his big, lean body, the incredible, fulfilling sweetness of his lovemaking....

"Hello? Are you there?" he asked, a note of anxiety in his voice.

"I'm ... I'm here," Sarah whispered. "I just ... I wanted to ask you about ... about the children."

"What about them? And how did you know how to get hold of me, by the way? I thought you said you didn't know my name."

"I never said I didn't know it," Sarah told him calmly, beginning to regain a little of her poise. "I just allowed you to assume I didn't, that's all."

"I think," he said cheerfully, "that you allowed me to assume quite a few things, didn't you, my lady? I wonder why."

"Well," Sarah said firmly, "I didn't call you to argue or to discuss our evening together. I just wanted to ask about the children."

"Go ahead," he said. "Ask about them."

"They're not in that room anymore," Sarah said. "I wondered if you knew where they'd gone."

"How do you know they're not in the room? Did you actually go to see them?"

"I bought them some Christmas presents," Sarah said, her voice deliberately cool, "and when I went to deliver the gifts this afternoon, I realized that nobody's lived in the room for several days. I was afraid ..."

"That Billy took them and made a run for it," he finished cheerfully.

"Yes," Sarah said. "The thought crossed my mind. Billy seemed pretty defensive."

"No kidding," Jim said, his voice suddenly gloomy. "That was really nice," he added, "buying gifts for them, I mean. Ellie's going to be so happy."

"So you *do* know where they are," Sarah said, surprised by her sudden flood of relief and happiness.

"Oh, yes, I know where they are," Jim said. "Ellie talks about you all the time," he added. "She calls you the 'Princess Lady,' like somebody from a fairy tale, and she keeps asking when you're coming back. She just refuses to accept the fact that I don't know."

"Oh." Sarah smiled helplessly, her cheeks suddenly warm. "That's . . . that's nice."

"So," Jim went on, "what can I tell her? When are you coming back?"

Sarah hesitated, feeling edgy and frightened. "Are they . . . do you mean the children are with *you?*"

"Yes," he said briefly. "They are. Four of us in a one-bedroom apartment. Five, counting Maude, but she goes back to her own place at night."

"Maude?" Sarah asked, feeling a sudden, inexplicable stab of pain.

"Maude Willett," Jim explained. "She's a terrific grandmotherly type that I met on the ski hill. Just on Monday, in fact, the day you and I—"

"Yes," Sarah said hastily, her face pink with embarrassment. "I understand. Go on, please."

"Anyhow, I made friends with her when we were skiing, taught her to snowplow, actually, and she gave me her name and invited me over for meat loaf. I didn't go, but next day when I found myself with these three kids on my hands, I called Maude and she came right over and made order out of chaos. She's a marvel, Maude is. One of the seven wonders of the modern world."

Sarah grinned, tempted to ask him about the other six and then pulled her thoughts firmly back into line. There was something so diverting and entertaining about Jim Fleming, something that made him so enjoyable and easy to talk to.

"So," she asked briskly, "what are your plans? Are you going to keep them with you now, or what?"

"Oh, Lord," Jim said, his voice suddenly strained and weary. "It's not so simple, pretty lady. You see..."

A woman, probably the secretary, interrupted him in the background, and he paused to say, "Not for a while, Shelley, thanks. And hold my calls, okay? This is important. Whoever it is, tell them I'll get back to them later."

Sarah waited, and then heard his voice come back on the line, strong and warm. "Hello? Still there?"

"Of course," Sarah said. "You were telling me about the children?"

"Right. I don't know *what* to do. I'm in a real mess. Have you ever noticed," he added surprisingly, "that when you set out to help people, even with the best intentions in the world, how often you just wind up making a big mess?"

Sarah heard the note of pain and bewilderment in his voice and felt a powerful surge of sympathy, which she repressed firmly. "What's the problem?" she asked. "Aren't they adjusting to life in the lap of luxury?"

"Oh, they're adjusting, all right. It's amazing how fast kids can adjust. They already know how to program the VCR and run the remote control, and how the microwave works, and how to adjust the room temperature and all kinds of exotic technical stuff."

Sarah began to understand. "And the problem," she said softly, "is that they're adjusting *too* well, right? After just a few days of warmth and comfort, they're not going to be able to go back to their old life."

"Billy knew it," Jim said helplessly. "He understood better than I did, that first night when I took them home with me. He just looked at me as if to say, 'Okay, mister. Here we are. *Now* what?' And he was right.''

"You can't..." Sarah began cautiously, and then continued. "You can't just... keep them with you? I mean, is it impossible for..." Her voice trailed off.

"Not impossible," Jim said grimly, "but damn difficult. Billy's mad at me all the time for what I've done to the kids by giving them a taste of comfort and luxury. He's a cold, cynical, streetwise kid, and he just doesn't trust me to keep on providing for them. He'd grab them and run in a minute if somebody wasn't watching him all the time. And there's no room at my place for all these people, and besides, other tenants already know they're there, and the super's warned me, ever so tactfully, that they have to be gone as soon as possible."

"It's an adults-only building?"

"Yes. It is."

"Oh, my." Sarah was silent for a moment, thinking. "What about Social Services? Have you checked with them?"

"Yes, I have. And Billy was absolutely right. They're overburdened, understaffed and underfunded. There's no way they can guarantee a foster home that would keep the kids together. The caseworker I talked to told me frankly that in all probability Arthur would be put up for adoption while the other two went into some kind of interim-care facility."

Sarah shuddered, picturing shy and gentle little Ellie in an "interim-care" facility.

"I suppose," she began cautiously, "that government care would still be better than... than where they were when you found them. Wouldn't it?"

"Not for those kids," Jim said. "You just can't believe how much they both love that baby. It's heart-rending. Ellie's just ten years old, but if she lost Arthur, I truly believe she'd never recover from the anguish of it."

Sarah hesitated, looking around her office at the piles of folders, the neat rows of books and technical abstracts, the framed prints on the walls along with complex charts of cereal grains.

"So," she said finally, "what can you do?"

"I don't know. Maude's going to help as much as she can, but she's leaving soon for a winter holiday with her family, and I'll be on my own. I guess I'll have to take time off work to stay with them. And I'll have to look for somewhere else to live, maybe buy a house, though God knows how I'll come up with that much money on short notice."

He sounded weary and overburdened, and Sarah's heart ached for him. She was tempted to offer her own house, but resisted firmly, knowing how many complications *that* would create. She would become involved with Jim Fleming's life, he would know where she lived and how to get to her, and if it should happen that she was really pregnant, she would soon have a baby of her own to provide for. Besides, her house was so small that she probably didn't have much more room for the three children than he did.

"Anyhow," he said, his voice cheerful again, "this is my problem, right? I'm the one who took them home with me, and I'm the one who has to deal with the consequences. I'll figure something out. Meanwhile we have to decide what to do about you."

"Me?" Sarah asked, startled. "What about me?"

"Well, you have these presents for the kids, right? And you want to deliver them?"

"I'd...yes," Sarah said, feeling shy all at once. "Yes, I would, if that's possible."

"Of course. How about tonight? You could just stop by for a Christmas drink, and we'll put your presents under the tree. It's the first time," Jim added ruefully, "that I've ever had a Christmas tree in my apartment. Ellie wanted one so badly. We bought lights and a star and everything."

"Oh," Sarah said softly. "It must be lovely."

"When we finished decorating, we dimmed the room lights and switched on the tree. Ellie burst into tears, crawled into the pantry and cried for an hour. It was all I could do to coax her to come out and settle down."

"Why?"

"According to Ellie, it was just too beautiful. It made her hurt inside, she said, because it was just too beautiful."

"Oh," Sarah said again, feeling her own eyes stinging with hot tears of sympathy.

"You see what a position I'm in," Jim said. "After a few experiences like that, it'd be damn hard to put those kids back out onto the street or into some kind of institutional care."

"Yes," Sarah whispered. "Yes, I can see that it would."

"But," Jim added cheerfully, "the tree isn't quite as beautiful now. It's looking a little ragged these days. Between Arthur and Lancelot the lower branches are getting far too much attention."

"Lancelot?"

"Maude's puppy. He doesn't like to stay alone, so Maude brings him with her every morning. He and Arthur play their own version of 'demolition derby' in my front room.''

"Poor Jim!'' Sarah said, laughing helplessly.

"Oh, pretty lady, it's nice to hear you laugh,'' he said, his voice gentle and husky with emotion. "You just don't know how much I've wanted to see you again.''

"Please,'' Sarah whispered helplessly, shivering a little at the intimate tone of his voice. "Please don't...''

"Okay,'' Jim said briskly, all business once more. "I get the message. No pressure. Now, about those presents. Is tonight okay?''

Sarah paused, twisting the phone cord anxiously.

"I understand,'' Jim said. "You don't want to see me, right?''

"I'm...I'm sorry,'' Sarah whispered. "It's just that—''

"No problem,'' he interrupted. "How about tomorrow? After lunch, maybe? I'll be at the office all day, and I'll give you my address so you can stop by with their gifts and stay as long as you like.''

"That would be best, I think.''

"I promise I'll be out of the way, and nobody will spy on you or try to follow you. Word of honor. Not that I wouldn't like to,'' he said frankly, "but it would mean a lot to the kids if they can see you again, so I won't do anything to spoil it. Do you trust me?''

"Yes,'' Sarah said, surprising herself. "Yes, I do.''

"Okay. Here's my address. Got a pen?''

Sarah knew the address off by heart...had, in fact, driven by the building several times while planning the seduction of Jim Fleming. Actually, he lived in an elegant residential area not too many blocks from the laboratory where she was sitting right now. But she just muttered something in reply, pretending to write down the directions as he dictated them.

"Good," Jim said briskly. "I'll tell the kids you're coming sometime after lunch, okay? Little Ellie will be out of her mind with excitement. When she's excited," he added, his voice softening, "she just gets quieter and quieter and paler than ever and her eyes get as big and round as saucers."

"Thank you," Sarah murmured, smiling into the phone. "Thank you very much."

"That's okay. Just remember," he said softly, "that if you ever change your mind and want to see me, after all, *I'd* be pretty excited, too. Will you remember that?"

"Yes," Sarah whispered, feeling warm and shaky. "Yes, I'll remember."

"Goodbye, pretty lady. Thanks for calling," he said, and then hung up, leaving Sarah wide-eyed and thoughtful, gazing at the telephone receiver.

JIM, TOO, SAT for a long time after he hung up, staring at his own telephone. His mind was a confused blur of thoughts and impressions, foremost among them a kind of boyish delight that she had actually remembered him and called him.

Not that she was particularly interested in *him*. She'd made it clear that she was only concerned about the children. But still, she'd taken the trouble to learn his name and find out his office number.

Jim frowned, staring with narrowed eyes at a glass-fronted display case on the opposite wall filled with football trophies.

Something nagged at his mind, the ghost of a memory...the echo of her voice, the way she'd laughed when she said, "Poor Jim!"

Somewhere, sometime in the distant past, he'd heard that voice before. Jim's recall for voices was almost uncanny in its keenness, and he knew he wasn't mistaken this time. More and more he was growing convinced that his meeting with his lady in black hadn't been the casual encounter it had seemed. She knew him, in spite of her denials, and she'd sought him out for some reason, some motivation of her own beyond the casual gratification of a one-night stand.

I'd give anything to know what it was, he thought. *Damn! If I could only remember where I've seen her before... where I've heard that voice....*

"Jim? Are you free now?"

He looked up to see his secretary's cheerful young face in the doorway, and nodded. "Yes, Shelley, I'm free. Who've you got out there who's so important?"

"It's the senator," Shelley said with a cautious, sidelong glance at her employer.

Jim's thoughtful, bemused smile faded and his handsome features grew tense. He glanced at his watch, swiveled to gaze briefly out the window while he composed himself and then turned back to his secretary. "Okay, Shelley," he said tonelessly, "show him in, please."

He picked up a small jade paperweight and gripped it in his hands, holding it so tightly that his knuckles were white. Apart from this, he displayed no emotion as the door opened and his father entered the room.

"Hello, Jim," Senator Fleming said, seating himself casually in a leather armchair across from his son. "Merry Christmas."

"Merry Christmas, Dad," Jim said, giving the older man a cold, level gaze. Jameson Kirkland Fleming III, at sixty-three, was a powerfully handsome and attrac-

tive man. For Jim, looking at his father was like looking into a mirror that reflected the future, because he
knew that this was exactly how he himself would look
in thirty years.

Jim's father had thick iron-gray hair, bright blue eyes
in a tanned, weathered face and a tall firm body that
still retained much of the athletic strength and trimness
of his youth. He wore shining gray riding boots made
of fine, soft leather, charcoal dress slacks with a knife-
edge crease, and an expensive tweed blazer in a western
cut that sat beautifully on his wide shoulders. His dress
shirt, as always, was snowy white, his tie crisp and perfectly coordinated.

The old man took good care of himself, Jim admitted grudgingly. No matter what you thought of him,
you had to acknowledge that he created a good impression....

"How've you been, son?" Senator Fleming asked as
casually as if they spoke to each other every day instead of once a year.

"I've been fine, Dad," Jim said briefly. "Just fine."

"Business good?" the older man asked, glancing
around Jim's well-appointed office. His voice was still
easy and casual. If you didn't notice how firmly he
gripped the arms of the chair and how taut his body
was, you'd assume the old man was perfectly relaxed
and comfortable, Jim thought.

"Yes," Jim said noncommittally. "It's pretty good.
The high interest rates are costing us, just like everybody else, but we can weather it."

The senator nodded thoughtfully, cleared his throat
and looked at his son with a sudden expression of appeal in his blue eyes. "We were wondering ..." he began, and paused.

Jim watched him calmly, offering no help, and his father finally went on, his voice carefully composed once more. "Your Aunt Maureen and I...we were wondering if you'd like to come out to the ranch for Christmas. There'll just be the two of us and some of the staff members, and Mo thought it would be nice if you'd...I mean, she'd like to cook all your favorite things and give you a family Christmas for once."

Jim's blue eyes, so like those of the man opposite him, hardened with sudden anger. "Look, why do you *do* this every year?" he asked, his voice low and furious. "When will you ever get the message? You and I have nothing to say to each other. I told you long ago what I think of you, and you've done the same for me. We've got nothing to talk about, Dad. Why don't you just give it a rest?"

The senator looked steadily across the broad desk at his son. "Maybe it's not as cut-and-dried as all that, son. It's been almost seventeen years since your mother died, more than ten years since you left home. Times change. People change. Maybe I'm a different man than you thought I was back then."

"I doubt it," Jim said coldly. "You're like a force of nature. You'll never change."

"Nor will you if you don't give things a chance. Life needs tending, son, and so do relationships. They don't just happen by accident."

Jim stared at his father in disbelief. "I wonder if you have any idea how completely ironic that sounds," he said softly. "The fact that *you,* of all people, should be lecturing me about relationships. My God."

Jameson Fleming returned his son's cold gaze in silence. "Look, Jim," he said finally, "I know you don't like me, and I know why, and in some ways you're probably justified. But could you consider calling a brief truce for your aunt's sake? Mo would love to see you this Christmas."

"I see Aunt Maureen occasionally," Jim said. "I don't have to go to your house to see her. She understands that."

Senator Fleming shook his handsome gray head. "You're a bitter man, son," he said finally. "Terribly bitter. I'm sorry." The older man got slowly to his feet and started for the door, then paused.

Jim watched, his face expressionless, waiting for his father to leave.

"Someday, Jim," his father said, pausing by the door, "I hope someone will come into your life that you really care about. And when that happens I truly do hope for your sake that you'll be able to be warm and accepting. I hope you won't be so cold and uncompromising that you lose her and all your chances for happiness along with her."

Jim's blue eyes kindled dangerously, but he restrained himself, merely giving his father a curt nod, watching as the heavy oak door closed behind the older man's departing figure.

Alone in the office, he clenched his hands tightly together to stop their trembling and gazed blindly out the window. Part of him regretted his own brusqueness and cold response to the older man's plea. He genuinely wished, sometimes, that he could be more forgiving, more accepting, more able to provide what his father and his aunt wanted of him.

But another part of him, an urgent, angry part, could never forget his mother's suffering. As if it were yesterday, Jim remembered her tears, her pain, her anguished longing for the kind of love and warmth that her powerful, wealthy husband selfishly refused to give her.

He killed her, Jim thought. *As surely as if he'd taken a gun and held it to her temple, he killed her. And how am I supposed to forget that? How do they expect me to laugh and be sociable, to pretend we're just one big happy family, when I know what happened between my parents?*

With a small, grim smile he recalled his father's parting words and shook his head at the incredible gall of the old man.

If there ever was a woman in Jim Fleming's life, he thought, it was certain she would be better treated, more warmly loved and cherished than his father's wife had been.

Restlessly he got up and prowled around his office, touching objects here and there, straightening chairs and pictures, closing file drawers and rearranging the little nativity set that Shelley had set up on the gleaming wooden console along one wall.

At last he took his leather jacket from the closet, shrugged it on and opened the door, pausing in the outer office to look at his secretary.

"I'll be out for the rest of the day, Shelley, all right? If there's anything really important, you can reach me at home later on. Otherwise just hold things till tomorrow."

"Okay." Shelley hesitated, fingers poised over her computer keyboard. "About tomorrow," she began, flushing a little, "I mean, I promised my boyfriend I'd go with him tomorrow to his parents' place, and you said last week that I could have the day off, but if you'd rather I came in for the morning, well, I guess I could."

"No, no," Jim said hastily. "Take your holiday. I'd forgotten all about it. I'm going to be here all day, but I doubt that anything much will be happening. Merry Christmas, Shelley."

"Merry Christmas," she said, brightening and smiling at her employer. "Jim," she added cautiously, "is everything all right?"

"What do you mean?" Jim asked, standing in the doorway and glancing back at his secretary.

"Oh, I don't know. Lately you've just been looking kind of tired, you know?"

Jim smiled wanly. "Family troubles," he said briefly. "I've got family troubles, Shelley."

His secretary knew nothing about Jim's new responsibilities. In fact, partly due to Billy's dark warnings, Jim was so nervous about the powers of Social Services that he had told nobody about the three children he sheltered in his apartment, except for Maude, of course, who was sworn to secrecy.

Shelley obviously assumed that her boss, when he spoke of "family troubles," was referring to the visit from Senator Fleming, who arrived every year about this time in a vain attempt to coax his son into coming home for Christmas.

"It's hard," she agreed, nodding her young, curly head with great wisdom. "Family stuff, it can really eat you up. Believe me, I know."

Jim grinned at the girl's knowing tone, smiled at her again and let himself quietly out the door.

"YOU MEAN you've never seen her before? *Never?*" Jim asked the bartender in disbelief.

"Just that one night," the bartender said, polishing another glass and hanging it carefully away in the ceiling rack.

"But she seemed...I mean, I assumed she came here frequently."

"So how come *you* never saw her before, then?"

"I only come to this bar on Monday nights," Jim said. "I thought maybe she came on...weekends or something."

"Never," the bartender said emphatically. "Never been here before. Just the one night."

Jim felt a rising tide of hopelessness and quashed it firmly. "Are you absolutely sure? It isn't possible that you're mistaken?"

The bartender paused with another glass in his hand and looked directly at Jim. "Look, son," he said cheerfully, "I may be middle-aged and potbellied and married, but I'm still human, you know. Now, you saw that woman. You really think a woman who looked like that could be at my bar without me *noticing* her?"

Jim smiled. "I see what you mean. Okay, I guess I'll just have to ask around at some other bars, that's all."

He set down his empty glass, pulled his jacket on and started for the door. There were just a few other people in the place—a solitary executive, some weary Christmas shoppers and a couple incongruously attired in formal wear who seemed to be arguing bitterly in low tones. Jim glanced idly at the other drinkers, his sense of loneliness and depression growing deeper.

"Hey, mister!" the bartender called as Jim reached the door.

"Merry Christmas," the little man said. "And I hope you find her."

"Thanks," Jim said. "So do I."

But his sense of futility deepened as he tramped the snowy streets, working his way in and out of all the bars on the grimy strip of theaters and night spots. Nobody had ever seen a woman who looked like his description of the mysterious lady in black.

Maybe, Jim thought gloomily, she patronized other, classier bars in more elegant neighborhoods and just made an occasional brief visit to this part of town. If so, how was he ever supposed to find her? He could hardly go to every drinking place in the city. Besides, it was a waste of time when he didn't even have a picture to show people, just a description of an incredibly alluring woman, a beautiful dark-haired woman with shining gray eyes and a serene, ladylike manner.

He began to regret the promise he'd made to her earlier that day. The woman he was searching for, the woman he longed more than anything to see one more time, was actually coming to his own house tomorrow. She would be there in the flesh, walking up to his apartment and ringing the bell, and he had promised he wouldn't be around. He had even given his word that nobody would try to follow her or search her out in any way.

And Jim was a man of integrity, a man who took promises very seriously.

Frantically he considered his options, trying to think of some way to find out who she was and where she lived without breaking his word not to follow her.

At last he decided that his only choice was to write her a letter. He would leave it with Maude to deliver to the mystery woman when she paid her visit to the children, and in it he would tell her how much he wanted to see her again, stress that it could all be on her terms, invite her to take the initiative and arrange the meeting place.

Feeling a little more optimistic now that he had a plan, Jim circled back across the wintry streets to his car. He drove home through rushed and crowded early-evening traffic, tapping the wheel idly and whistling along with the Christmas music on the radio, composing the letter in his mind.

But, as he drove, he was haunted once more by that old nagging sense that he knew this woman, that at some time in his life he had encountered her before under different circumstances. He had seen her face and heard her voice, and if he could somehow force his mind to make the connection, then he would have it all. He would know her name, who she was, everything about her.

Jim frowned, his handsome face taut with frustration, and then forced himself to relax, diverting himself by thinking about the children who were waiting eagerly for him at home, and the superb meal Maude would have on the table.

Almost voluntarily he smiled. The dimple popped into view in one flat, tanned cheek, and he began to sing softly as the traffic rumbled and snarled around him.

CHAPTER SIX

SENATOR JAMESON FLEMING drove his white Lincoln up the curving drive to the long garage, pausing in front of one of the doors and waiting for it to flow upward. Inside the garage he heaved his tall body from the car and made his way carefully along the row of shining parked vehicles to a small lighted room at the rear of the big building.

In this room a little man of indeterminate age, wearing navy blue coveralls, crouched beside a large cardboard box lined with sacking. As the senator entered the room and pulled off his leather driving gloves, the little man looked up, his wrinkled face breaking into a vast, toothless smile of adoration.

"Hello, Manny," the senator said. "How's she doing?"

"Verr' good, sir," Manny said happily. "She's-a doin' verr' good. Six puppies, sir. All beauties."

"Well!" the senator exclaimed, pleased. "You were right after all then, Manny. I didn't think she was ready."

He squatted by the box, still smiling, and fondled the silky ears of the big golden spaniel who lay exhausted and triumphant with her new brood of puppies.

Jameson examined the puppies, touching them gently with his broad, finely shaped hands while their mother watched in loving pride.

At last he stood erect, shaking out the creases in his crisp trousers, and turned to leave. "Thanks, Manny," he said in the doorway. "Anything else?"

Manny frowned. "The new fence posts, they're not delivered yet, sir. Me and the boys, we can't do that job without the posts."

"Right. I'll call them as soon as I get into the house. If we don't get the posts today, we'll have to wait till after Christmas, I guess."

"And the new bull, he's-a look a little down, you know?"

"Down? What do you mean?"

Manny waved one hand in an eloquent Latin gesture. "Just...not so good, sir. Maybe a little sick, needs some vit'mins, you know?"

"I'll have a look at him and call the vet if we need him. Has my sister seen the puppies?"

Manny's grin widened, threatening to split his seamed, leathery face.

"Miss Mo, she been out here most the afternoon. She already got names for all of them."

Jameson smiled suddenly, nodded to his foreman and left the garage by the side door. Outside, he took a deep breath of the crisp afternoon air, marveling at how much fresher and cleaner it seemed out here than just a few miles away in the city. He glanced around at the rolling acres of his ranch. The house and grounds were bleak and sere in the winter chill, but they were still well groomed and impeccable, the hedges neatly trimmed, the curving fieldstone ledges and walks swept clean of snow.

The senator paused, looking with pleasure at his property. Since his career in politics had become so absorbing, he had sold off much of the holding, and the ranch was now more of a hobby than a living, just a few hundred acres where he ran a small herd of purebred Galloway cattle and a few beautiful horses. But the setting was lovely, and Jameson never came back here, even after the shortest of absences, without an overwhelming sense of peace and homecoming.

He hesitated briefly, looking over at the cattle sheds and thinking about Manny's concern about the new bull, which had cost just over forty thousand dollars at a recent auction. Finally, deciding that the bull could wait an hour or two, Jameson turned and strode along the curving flagstone path to the big house. As he walked, he remembered every word and detail of the interview with his son. His handsome, creased face was grim, his blue eyes bleak.

He entered the foyer, hung his long fur-trimmed suede coat away in the front closet and then paused, looking around. Somewhere deep in the house Handel's *Messiah* was playing loudly in stereo. The majestic chords of music flowed over the gracious curving staircase, the gleaming rich oak paneling and wainscoting, the leaded glass and fine old crystal and priceless jewel-colored Turkish carpets.

The house smelled richly of flowers, furniture polish and spicy baking, and Jameson took a deep, appreciative sniff before he went in search of his sister.

He paused in the archway leading to the dining room, grinning. A pair of sneakered feet protruded from beneath the big oak table while a muffled thumping noise emanated from the same general area.

"Mo!" Jameson said, bending to peer under the table. "What on *earth* are you doing?"

The sneakers slid along the carpet, followed by slim, denim-clad legs and a small, active body in a pink sweatshirt. Maureen Fleming ducked her head out from beneath the table and stood erect, clutching a battered red oil can with a long spout.

"The damn thing sticks," she said with dignity. "I was just giving it a drop of oil, that's all."

Jameson smiled at his sister, whom he still thought of as "the kid," although she was now fifty-three years old.

Maureen Fleming was indeed a pleasure to behold, even in the casual clothes she wore for her active daytime life at the ranch. She was small and brisk, with the trim, athletic figure of a young girl. Her face, too, was youthful despite the creases and laugh lines around her eyes and mouth, and always warmly tanned from hours spent outside on the cross-country ski trails behind the ranch house. Maureen had the dark flower-blue eyes so common in the Fleming family, and a bright mass of red-gold curls that were fading now and lightly streaked with gray.

When Jameson's wife died, leaving him alone with a big house and a fifteen-year-old son, Maureen had come to the ranch for a few weeks to help out. At that time Maureen was thirty-five, and she had already lost one husband to divorce and a second, a few years later, to cancer. She faced a bleak and lonely future, and she was happy to be absorbed into her brother's household, where she soon became indispensable. Her visit stretched into months, and then years, and now Jameson sometimes wondered how he would have managed without her.

He stood in the dining room and examined her gravely, troubled by the taut energy of her small body and the look of contained excitement in those beautiful blue eyes.

"Why are you fixing the table, Maureen?" he asked quietly.

"I told you, it sticks. You can't pull it open to put the leaves in, and I thought—"

"Mo, we won't be opening the table out for Christmas. We won't need to. There'll just be you and me, Manny and Tom, Clarice and Eloise. Just the six of us."

Maureen hesitated, clutching her oil can and staring down at the carpet while her brother gazed unhappily at her bent head.

"He's not coming, Mo. I tried, but he still feels exactly the same. He'll never come back here as long as he lives."

"Oh, Jamie..." Maureen gazed up at her brother, her blue eyes eloquent with sympathy and unhappiness.

"I wish I could do it all over, Mo," Jameson said abruptly, staring at the lavish Christmas centerpiece on the gleaming oak table. "If we could only get second chances in life, we'd do so much better, wouldn't we?"

"We *do* get second chances, Jamie," Maureen said firmly. "We always do. And yours will come. Jim won't be this way forever. Someday, somehow, he's going to realize there's two sides to every story, and that your side is worth listening to as well as his. Just wait and see, Jamie. He'll come back someday."

Jameson shook his head, giving her a bleak smile. "I wish I had your optimistic outlook, kid. But I'm the one who goes and talks to him every year, and he's as cold as ice. Not a flicker of warmth or forgiveness, not ever."

"Just every bit as stubborn as his old man," Maureen said, trying to smile back at her brother. "A real chip off the old block."

Jameson nodded, bending to take the oil can from his sister's hands. "And now we won't talk about it anymore, Mo. We'll enjoy our Christmas with the staff members and not mention Jim again, all right? And I'll take this back to the garage for you. I have to go out later to check on the new bull. Manny says he looks 'a leetul down,' whatever that means.''

Maureen brightened. "Did you see the puppies? Aren't they lovely?''

"Absolutely lovely. You were right. That dog of Willoughby's was the perfect sire. We'll have to use him again. By the way, did the lumber yard call about the posts? Manny says . . .''

Still talking cheerfully, Jameson took his sister's arm and escorted her firmly out into the foyer. In the archway he paused, casting a wistful glance back at the big dining table with its warm centerpiece of holly and juniper. Then, abruptly, he flicked off the switch for the sparkling chandelier overhead, plunging the room into darkness.

SARAH HESITATED in the lobby of Jim Fleming's apartment building, her arms piled high with brightly wrapped Christmas gifts, and glanced around nervously. There was nobody in sight near the doorway, but she still had an irrational fear that people were hiding in every alcove and behind every marble column, ready to jump out and grab her.

She was so terrified of having Jim Fleming learn her identity that she had even come by cab this afternoon rather than use her own car. The cabdriver stood just behind her, also laden with parcels.

"Okay, ma'am?" he asked. "You look kind of funny. Is something the matter?''

"No,'' Sarah said, touched by his evident concern. She glanced once more around the lobby, quiet and deserted except for the sturdy gray-haired doorman in his little cubicle who watched them with polite detachment.

"So, do you need help to get this stuff upstairs? You want I should hang around?" the driver asked.

"No, thank you," Sarah murmured again, glancing nervously over her shoulder at the street beyond the plate glass windows. "No, that's fine. Thank you so much for all your help."

She set her pile of gifts down on a velvet love seat near the entry doors, rummaged in her handbag and handed the cabby a bill, smiling shyly. He gazed at her, dazzled both by the smile and by the size of the bill. Then he set his mountain of packages down next to hers, tipped his hat respectfully and backed out the door, still gazing at her with warm admiration. Sarah returned his smile gratefully and crossed the lobby to speak to the doorman.

"Excuse me," she began tentatively, "but I have some parcels to deliver...to Mr. Fleming's suite. I wonder if I could...?"

"Certainly, miss," the older man said politely. "Mr. Fleming told me to expect you. I'll help you carry the things up."

"That would be nice of you," Sarah said. "There's quite a pile here."

She followed the doorman into the elevator, her heart pounding thunderously in her chest as the door slid shut and enclosed them.

"Still cold," he observed politely as the elevator glided soundlessly upward. "But then it's nice to have snow for Christmas, isn't it?"

"Yes," Sarah murmured. "Yes, it is."

She was gripped by sudden panic, by a shattering, breathless certainty that Jim Fleming had deceived her, and that even now he was waiting in his apartment, ready to seize her as soon as she rang the doorbell, to force her inside and make her reveal her identity, to tell him her deep, precious secret about the baby she longed for, and then he would—

"Here we are, ma'am. Are you sure you can manage all those parcels? You look a little pale."

"I'm fine, thanks," Sarah said, taking a deep breath and stepping out into the carpeted hallway. Suddenly, with overwhelming stunning clarity, she remembered the way Jim Fleming had looked when he stood naked and arrogant in front of her, and how his hands and lips had felt on her skin, and the wild, sweet magic he had wrought in her own body.

She shivered, bit her lip and tried to smile at the anxious man beside her. Then, with a carefully neutral expression, she followed him to a door marked J. K. Fleming on a discreet brass plate.

The door was answered by a plump, smiling woman in an orange velour jogging suit, whose gray curls framed a soft pink face of great sweetness.

"You must...you must be Maude," Sarah whispered. "I have some things for the children."

"Yes, of course. Jim hoped you'd be coming," Maude said cheerfully, beaming at the doorman who gazed back at her with silent adoration. "He's at the office, but the kids are here. Even Billy's here."

The doorman retreated back along the corridor, with obvious reluctance and one last abject look at Maude, who took charge of the packages, deposited them on a table in the foyer and drew Sarah inside, taking her coat and scarf while she continued to talk. Finally Maude directed Sarah toward the living room and then disappeared tactfully into the depths of the kitchen, murmuring something about coffee.

Trembling and feeling breathless, Sarah stepped into the big, plant-filled living room. Despite its size the room seemed crowded and cluttered, jammed full of children's clothes, toys, and a big white crib and changing table that dominated the long wall by the windows. A huge, bushy Christmas tree filled one corner, sparkling with shiny new ornaments of all kinds. Near the tree Arthur sat on the soft white goatskin, banging a wooden spoon against an aluminum cake pan with noisy satisfaction. A fat black puppy crouched beside him, worrying one edge of the rug, gripping it between his sharp little teeth and flinging himself about in a fury of flapping ears and puppy growls.

Ellie and Billy sat side by side on a creamy leather couch near their baby brother, silent and tense. They both seemed warmer, cleaner and less pinched and hungry than they had been on the memorable night of that first meeting, but their expressions were still the same. Billy looked guarded and watchful, almost sullen, as he examined Sarah. Ellie was wide-eyed and breathless, her features pale and taut, her thin hands gripped tightly on a small cushion in her lap.

All thoughts of Jim Fleming left Sarah's mind as she smiled at the three children. She crossed the room hesitantly and crouched near Arthur, who looked up at her with a sparkling, damp grin and pounded lustily on his cake tin in greeting.

Sarah laughed and picked him up. He felt even heavier than she remembered and comfortably cozy in a pair of warm denim overalls and a tiny hockey sweater.

"Hello, Arthur," Sarah murmured. "How are you? How's our great big baby?" She nuzzled against his sweet, fat neck, and Arthur chuckled deep in his throat, making Sarah laugh with him.

She held the merry baby in one arm and moved over to stroke Ellie's hair softly while the little girl gazed up at her, blue eyes round with adoring wonder.

"Hello, Ellie," Sarah said softly. "You look so pretty in that blouse. The color suits you perfectly."

Ellie blushed as pink as the ruffled shirt that she wore. "Maude brought it," she whispered. "It used to belong to one of her granddaughters."

"Well, it looks like it was made just for you."

Ellie clutched her pillow more tightly and moved over to let Sarah sit between her and Billy, giving Arthur a reproving frown as he clutched at Sarah's dark plait and tugged it.

Sarah gently disentangled her hair from Arthur's damp pink fist and gave him back his wooden spoon, which he examined with deep satisfaction. He began to wriggle and whimper, looking around for the cake tin, and Sarah set him back on the white rug. Immediately he crawled briskly back to the center and set up his noisy drum chorus once more.

"How are you, Billy?" Sarah asked, holding Ellie's small hand and looking at the tense, silent boy on her other side.

"Fine," he said briefly, avoiding her gaze.

Sarah studied him thoughtfully. Unlike the other children, Billy still wore his ragged jeans and sneakers, and Sarah suspected he had resisted attempts to attire him in anything better.

"Is something the matter, Billy?" she asked gently. "What is it that's bothering you?"

His face turned so pale that the freckles stood out on his strong young cheekbones in stark relief. "This!" he burst out, waving his hand at the warm, luxurious room, the big Christmas tree, the chuckling, well-dressed baby. "This is bothering me, if you want to know."

Ellie gripped her hand convulsively, and Sarah winced at the strength of the little girl's grasp. But she went on holding Ellie's hand tenderly and looked at Billy again.

"What about it, Billy? Why does it bother you?"

"Well, it can't last, can it? And then what happens to us?"

"What do you mean?"

"Oh, come on," Billy said roughly. "I'm not stupid. I mean, he brought us home like a sackful of kittens or something. But he can't keep us. They're already mad at him for having us here. And if he turns us over to Social Services, they'll split us up and give Arthur away. And after this—" Billy waved his hand in fury at the luxury all around them "—after all *this*, how can I take them back where they were before? Huh? How can I?"

Sarah regarded him in silence and then put an arm around Ellie, who had begun, in utter silence, to cry. Big shining tears rolled down the little girl's thin cheeks and dripped onto the pink ruffled collar of her new blouse.

"Billy..." Sarah began. "Billy, don't you trust anybody? Can't you believe that Mr. Fleming means what he says, and that we're all going to look after you and see that the three of you are kept together?"

"How?" the boy asked bluntly. "Maude can't help. She lives in a tiny little apartment even smaller than this one, and anyway, she's going away next week for a holiday. We can't stay here because they don't allow kids in the building. And how can you help? Jim doesn't even know your name. He told me so."

"That may be true," Sarah said, "but it doesn't mean I can't help you. I wish you'd trust us a bit, Billy."

"I don't trust anybody," the boy said darkly. "Trust anybody and they'll wind up messing you around. That's what I believe."

Sarah was saved from answering by Maude, who came bustling into the room with a purposeful gleam in her eye. "Well, mister," she said to Billy, "that may be what you believe, but *I* believe that our guest is probably cold and hungry, and she'd like a cup of coffee and some of those Christmas cookies Ellie and I baked this morning. Am I right?"

Sarah smiled up at her gratefully. "You're right, Maude," she said. "That sounds wonderful."

"Good," Maude said briskly. "Ellie, you come and help me get a tray ready. Billy, you get the lady's presents from the hall and put them under the tree, and give Lancelot a good swat if he tries to rip them open. And *you,*" she said, lifting Arthur and tucking him under her arm like a loaf of bread, "you need a new diaper, my little man. And not a moment too soon."

She carried Arthur, still beaming and wriggling, over to the changing table. Ellie slipped from the couch, reluctantly letting go of Sarah's hand, but Sarah got up and followed her. "I'll come with you, Ellie," she said, "and help get the coffee things ready."

As they went toward the kitchen, Arthur cooed and gurgled, waving his bare pink legs on the changing table while Maude tickled him. Billy knelt to arrange Sarah's pile of gifts under the tree and gently cuffed

Lancelot, who crowded close enough to seize one of the trailing ribbon ends in his tiny teeth.

Lancelot howled and retreated, glaring balefully. Maude laughed, Arthur crowed, and Sarah and Ellie giggled together in the doorway. All at once Sarah forgot her fear and nervousness. She felt wonderful, contented, warm and at home, and happier than she could remember being in a long time.

JIM HESITATED outside his door, his heart beating fast. He knew he was being irrational, that there was no chance his mystery woman might still be in the apartment. In fact, it was most likely that she hadn't come at all. But still his mouth felt dry, and his heart hammered as wildly as if he were a boy ringing the doorbell for his first date.

He walked through the foyer, shrugging out of his jacket, and glanced into the living room. A new pile of colorful gifts glowed beneath the tree, but there was no other sign of company. Ellie was curled quietly in a corner of the leather sofa, reading, while Billy was nowhere to be seen.

Arthur lay on the rug at Ellie's feet, flat on his back, squinting thoughtfully up at his interlaced fingers and murmuring unintelligible phrases. When he saw Jim, he rolled promptly onto his stomach and began to crawl across the floor with astonishing speed, arriving at Jim's feet and grasping a handful of trousers to haul himself upright.

Jim grinned as the plump baby swarmed up his leg. Then he bent, swooped the little boy aloft and held him high in the air, hands encircling the plump midsection while Arthur beamed down at him with sparkling brown eyes, gurgling in delight.

"Hi, Ellie," Jim said, settling the baby comfortably in the crook of his arm and cuddling him. "I see you have some more presents under the tree. Did Santa come, or what?"

Ellie smiled at him, her pale, shy face translucent with pleasure. "The lady came," she said. "The Princess Lady. She was even prettier than I remembered, Jim. She's just so beautiful and *so* nice." Ellie sighed in bliss, thinking about the lady who had enchanted her right from their first meeting.

But Jim's concerns were more practical and urgent.

"What did she look like? What was she wearing?" he asked, settling himself beside Ellie and mounting Arthur on one of his outstretched legs. The baby grasped Jim's long, tanned fingers in his dimpled hands and shouted with delight as the big man jogged him gently up and down.

"Gray slacks," Ellie said eagerly. "And a white shirt, kind of plain and soft, and a little vest made of wool or something, kind of bumpy and all soft gray and blue, sort of..." Words failed her, and she trailed off into silence for a moment. "And," the little girl added dreamily, "she smelled just wonderful. Like...like flowers in the sun."

Jim was silent, absorbing this information and wistfully recalling the scent of that particular sunny floral perfume. Ellie snuggled close to him, and he rested one arm around her thin little body.

"I don't suppose you happened to look out the window when she left and see what she was driving?" he asked casually, feeling traitorous.

Ellie shook her head, setting her pale blond hair swinging. "She went away in a taxi."

"I see," Jim said, swallowing his disappointment. "And I guess she didn't tell you her name, either?"

Again Ellie shook her head. "She said she couldn't. But she said she'll come back again and visit us sometime really soon."

Jim felt a surge of optimism and jogged Arthur higher until the plump baby was red-faced and gasping with excitement.

Maude bustled in, wearing her coat and carrying a box under one arm. Lancelot's blunt nose protruded from a hole at the front of the box, whiskers quivering. Clearly Lancelot could tell that Arthur was having a lot of fun, which he strongly desired to join.

But Maude clutched the box firmly and smiled at Jim. "I heard you come in," she said. "And I'd better be off. I still have Christmas shopping to do."

"Thanks for everything, Maude," Jim said fervently. "I mean it. I never could have managed without you."

"Oh, pooh," Maude said with a dismissive wave of her free hand. "It's been a pleasure." She paused and gave Jim a keen glance. "You're sure you'll be okay here, Jim? It's not easy, you know. And," she added hesitantly, "I could always beg off from this holiday. I don't really need to go out there and spend a couple of weeks falling down all those ski hills."

"Don't be ridiculous," Jim said firmly, setting the breathless, chuckling baby down carefully on the white rug and getting to his feet. "You've been planning this holiday for ages. And I won't have any problems here. I've got my office all organized so that they can get along without me for a while, and I've got Ellie here to help me look after Arthur. If anyone knows how to look after Arthur," he added, smiling down at the little girl, "it's Ellie."

Maude, too, smiled fondly at Ellie. "That's certainly true," she said, reaching out to stroke the child's smooth blond hair. "She's ten going on thirty-two, this one is. What a marvelous kid."

Ellie turned pink and smiled shyly.

"And there's Billy," Jim began. He paused, looking around. "Speaking of Billy, where is he, by the way?"

Maude's mouth tightened. "Who knows? *I* certainly don't know where that child goes all day. He managed to be here for the lady's visit, though. I will say that for him."

Jim hesitated, looking cautiously at the plump, grandmotherly woman who had in such a short time become one of his best friends.

"She really is lovely, Jim," Maude said softly, reading his expression. "Absolutely lovely. What a sweet woman. And so shy and nice."

"Shy?" Jim asked, remembering the elegant creature who had seduced him so skillfully. "Did you get the impression she was *shy*, Maude?"

"Oh, absolutely," Maude said, nodding with confident wisdom. "And terrified, too. Scared to death that you might pop in and catch her, I think. And yet when we settled in the kitchen with our cookies and coffee, she relaxed and had as much fun as the kids, didn't she, Ellie?"

Ellie nodded vigorously while the two adults smiled down at her.

Maude looked at Jim again, her eyes questioning. "Where did you meet her, Jim? How did you happen to be together the night you found the kids if you don't even know her name? I wish you'd tell me the whole story. She's such a darling."

Jim shook his head. "That part of it is kind of private. Just between the lady and me." He paused, struck by a sudden thought. "Maude, did you give her my letter?"

Maude nodded sadly. "But she wouldn't take it with her, Jim. She said she didn't want to have it or answer it or anything."

His heart sank. "Didn't she even read it?"

"Oh, she read it all right." Maude grinned suddenly, remembering. "It was so cute, Jim. I gave her the letter just before she left, and she said what I told you, you know, that she didn't want to take it, but she did agree to read it. So then she took these big, heavy-rimmed glasses out of her purse and put them on, and just kind of disappeared behind them. It was so cute, seeing her in those big glasses. And after she finished she smiled, handed the letter back to me and said to tell Mr. Fleming thank you."

"That's all?" he asked, aching with disappointment. "Just 'Tell Mr. Fleming thank you'? Nothing else?"

"Sorry, Jim." Maude patted his arm. "If it's any comfort," she added briskly, "I'm sure she'll be back. She seems to be crazy about these kids."

Jim smiled absently, helping Maude to gather her belongings and watching as she bade a loving, lingering farewell to Ellie and the baby.

"Well," she said finally in the doorway, still gripping Lancelot's box, "goodbye, all. Merry Christmas, and I'll see you in a couple of weeks. Jim, are you *sure* you can manage?"

Jim grinned at her with considerably more confidence than he felt, wondering uneasily where Billy was and if Arthur might be planning to cut any more molars in the near future and what could possibly be said to divert the building supervisor the next time he asked about the children....

"I'm sure," he said firmly. "You have a good holiday, and don't you dare disgrace me by forgetting how to snowplow, you hear?"

Maude beamed, her pink face dimpling, and suddenly looked about sixteen. She waved, gave them a last loving smile and departed for the lobby where her new conquest, the doorman, was waiting patiently at the end of his shift to give her a ride home.

When she was gone, Jim settled back on the couch and opened the evening paper. Ellie snuggled close to him, picking her book up again, while Arthur crawled busily across the rug, dumped a big plastic rabbit in Jim's lap and then climbed up after it in a businesslike fashion. Jim cuddled him awkwardly with one arm, turning the pages of the paper with the other.

"Ellie," he asked presently, "did you remember to slip that envelope into Maude's purse like I told you?"

Ellie nodded. "I was really careful," she reported. "I tucked it way down so she won't find it till she gets out her keys to open her apartment."

"Good girl." Jim grinned. "She'll be mad at us, Ellie. She keeps saying she doesn't want to be paid for this, but she certainly deserves something for all she's done, don't you think?"

Ellie nodded gravely and turned a page in her book.

"Did she leave anything for supper?" Jim asked hopefully.

"Baked ham and something else with a funny name. I think Maude called it scalped potatoes," Ellie said. "They're in the oven."

Jim grinned at the idea of "scalped potatoes," and then sighed blissfully as he visualized the meal that awaited them. Beside him Ellie echoed the sigh, her thin little face alight with pleasure.

"How about Billy?" Jim asked. "Will he be home, do you think?"

Ellie shook her head. "Not for a while. But he'll come later. Don't worry. Billy says he doesn't like it here," she added with one of her surprising flashes of shrewdness. "But I think he likes it a lot better than out there on the street. He just doesn't want us to know."

Jim nodded, his face briefly troubled. He returned to his paper, wincing a little as Arthur gnawed with sudden, startling intensity on his index finger.

But the printed letters swam in front of his eyes to be replaced by a puzzling, persistent image.

He pictured the mystery woman reading his letter, saw her in his mind's eye as Maude had described her, and it jogged something deep in his memory. Somehow, somewhere, he was certain he had seen this woman *wearing big, heavy-rimmed glasses*.

The image hovered at the edge of his consciousness, maddening and tantalizing, just out of reach. He was sitting somewhere in a room where he could smell a scent of warm pine and freshly mown grass through an open window, and this woman was somewhere nearby, wearing heavy glasses.

But where? And when? *When* had he seen her before?

He moaned softly in frustration. Ellie glanced up at him in concern and snuggled closer to him while Arthur, surprised by the moan, registered an expression of gratified satisfaction before biting down harder on the big man's finger.

CHRISTMAS CAME AND WENT, filled with laughter and fun, and Jim's apartment echoed with sounds never heard before within those quiet, luxurious walls. The three abandoned children adapted with astonishing ease and swiftness to a life of pleasure and plenty, especially Arthur, who crawled through Jim's life with the cheerful, buoyant confidence of a baby born to luxury.

"This is Arthur's first Christmas," Ellie said shyly to Jim, "and it's so wonderful. Maybe he'll never, ever have a Christmas like—"

She broke off abruptly. Jim looked down at her pale face, his heart aching. "Like what, Ellie?" he asked softly. "What did Christmas used to be like for you?"

Ellie shuddered and looked away, her shining golden hair falling forward to hide her face. "I don't want to talk about it," she whispered. "Usually," she added reluctantly, "Mom used to drink a lot more at Christmas time. Sometimes she didn't come home for days, and if Billy couldn't find anything for us to eat, we'd get so hungry. When I think of Christmas," she concluded simply, "I just think of being so awful hungry that I felt like crying all the time."

"Oh, God," Jim muttered, pausing by her chair to stroke her shining head. "Oh, Ellie, I'm so sorry."

"It's okay," she said, looking up at him with a smile. "We're happy now, and you're looking after us, and Maude, and the Princess Lady, and I'm not hungry anymore. Actually, I'm so full of chocolates and stuff I can hardly move," she added with a grin. "And look at Arthur."

They both examined the cheerful baby, who was sitting on the furry white rug, busy with his favorite toy. Arthur adored the big activity board that Sarah had given him, and had already shown considerable intelligence by mastering the intricacies of making bells toot, whistles shriek, balls fall through transparent tubes, and small shiny windows click open and shut. Every time he succeeded at a specific task he whooped aloud and drummed his little boots on the floor, adding to the general din.

Ellie smiled at the fat baby and then turned back to her careful work on her shellcraft set. She was ensconced at the dining room table, which had been liberally padded with newspaper, and she would sit there for hours gluing the dainty multicolored shells into position, arranging intricate designs on small glass squares and discs.

Jim watched her, smiling at the look of concentrated intensity on her delicate face. The "Princess Lady," he mused, had certainly known what to buy for these children. Even Billy had been obviously pleased by the fishing rod and tackle and frequently sorted through it, wistfully fingering the shining spoons and lures, studying his instruction book to learn the techniques of threading line onto the reel and how to attach hooks and leaders.

"Ellie," Jim asked absently, "do you think you could look after Arthur by yourself some afternoon?"

Ellie looked up at him in surprise. "I used to look after Arthur all by myself all day long," she said quietly. "Even when he was a lot smaller than this."

Jim smiled, a little abashed. "I guess you did, didn't you, sweetie? I just keep forgetting how capable you are."

"Are you going away somewhere?" Ellie asked, absorbed once more in her work.

"No, but I wondered if Billy might want to go ice-fishing with me some afternoon and try out his new equipment."

Ellie's face shone with happiness. "Oh, Jim," she breathed, "that'd be so nice. Billy would love it."

"I don't know," Jim said gloomily. "Billy doesn't seem to like me very much, you know. He might not want to go with me."

"Of course he likes you," Ellie said calmly. "You're the nicest man in the whole world, and Billy knows it. He's just worried, that's all."

"About what's going to happen to all of you?"

Ellie nodded. "Billy says we have to leave here in a month. The man told him so one day when he took the garbage down. We have to be gone by the end of January, he said."

"Well, that's not entirely true," Jim said. "I'm sure Mr. Clement would give me an extra month if I really needed it before he'd turn us out in the street."

"But we can't stay here," Ellie said. "And we can't go to Maude's, and we don't even know the Princess Lady's name. That's why Billy's worried. He doesn't know where he can take us, that's all."

Jim looked at her curiously as she selected a tiny pink shell no bigger than one of Arthur's fingernails and fitted it with a group of others that were forming a delicate rosebud.

"What about you, Ellie?" he asked. "Aren't you worried? You know about all these problems, but they don't seem to bother you."

Ellie shook her head and then lay down her tweezers to give Jim a long, thoughtful glance. "I'd be worried," she said finally, "if I thought we were going to Social Services and they were going to take Arthur away. I'd be out of my mind with worry. But I know Billy won't let that happen. If that happens, we'll just run away like before, and Billy will look after us."

She returned to her work while Jim studied her, appalled by her words. "But, Ellie," he began finally, "how could you stand that? Living in a room like you had before, and being cold and hungry all the time. Could you live that way again, Ellie?"

"If I had to," the child said calmly. "See," she added, "it would be different now. Whenever it was hard or awful, I could think about all the nice things here, and then it would be easier. Like," she went on earnestly, "one day I'd think about Maude and Lancelot, and one day I'd think about how you took us out to that fancy restaurant for Christmas dinner, and how wonderful it was, and sometimes I'd think about when the Princess Lady came and brought our presents. There'd be so many nice things to remember," she concluded. "It'd be lots easier now."

Jim swallowed hard and dashed a hand across his eyes, turning aside to busy himself with Arthur for a moment while he regained his composure. Then he looked up at the older child.

"Well, Ellie," he said calmly, "that's not going to happen. You're not going to go back to some hole and live on memories. You'll be looked after, and you won't lose Arthur, and you can tell Billy that, too. If I have to," he added, "I'll find some way to sublet this apartment and buy a house, so nobody can tell us you can't live with me."

Ellie looked up at him. "Or maybe," she said wistfully, "the Princess Lady will come back and take us to her castle. I bet she lives in a castle, don't you think, Jim? Like in the book you gave me, with a moat and a tower, and her bed would be all made of gold, with silk curtains hanging around it. Don't you think so?"

Jim grinned at this picture. "Maybe," he said cheerfully. "And maybe not."

They were both silent, watching Arthur who had suddenly discovered a knob that made a jack-in-the-box pop up with an insane grin. Arthur was holding his breath, a fist in his mouth, eyes wide with amazement. Puffing, he touched the jack-in-the-box, then stared in wonder and distress as it disappeared slowly into the box again. He screwed his face up and prepared to howl until Jim hastily lowered himself to the carpet and showed the baby how to find the magic knob again.

When Arthur was contentedly making the puppet figure appear and disappear, Jim returned to his conversation with Ellie. "Did you see the lady when she put the glasses on?" he asked idly.

Ellie nodded, searching through a pile of tinted shells for some flat ones to use as leaves.

"What did she look like, Ellie? With the glasses on, I mean," Jim asked.

After all this time he still had the feeling that if he could just picture the woman in those glasses, get a clear mental image of how she had looked, he could somehow capture the elusive memory of where he'd seen her before.

Ellie bit her lip thoughtfully, setting a green shell into position on a tiny drop of glue.

"Like a doctor," Ellie said. "That's what she looked like. Or a scientist or something. You know how they look on TV, those really smart ladies who...?"

CHAPTER SEVEN

SARAH SAT WAITING for the doctor to return. Her face was pale and tense, and she stared fixedly at a big chart on the opposite wall. The chart was arranged like a giant wheel covered with calendar dates and was designed to tell a pregnant woman precisely when her baby was due.

Sarah bit her lip and fought back a sudden flood of emotion. Lately she kept having these erratic, weepy moods for no reason at all, it seemed. Her rational, scientific mind was alarmed by the sudden bouts of depression and anxiety, of sadness and intermittent euphoria.

She knew, of course, what was wrong. By now, even though she hadn't menstruated on schedule after her encounter with Jim Fleming, she was convinced she wasn't pregnant. She felt nothing happening inside her, no sense that a fetus was developing, and she was certain that if a baby were there, she'd feel *something*. She had failed to conceive, and as a result she either had to forget the whole thing or go through it all again.

Sarah sighed and fingered the soft straps of her leather handbag. The disappointment was crushing. She had been so sure the timing was right, that she'd chosen the absolutely optimum time to have intercourse. But how could she control all the variables? There was nothing she could have done about the terrible, unexpected shock of Billy's attack on her and Jim Fleming, her frantic run through icy streets, the trauma of seeing those poor abandoned children.

Sarah shifted in the chair, gazing unseeingly at her own reflection in the steel-framed mirror across the room.

She felt weary and hopeless, crushed with doubts and uncertainties. Should she go through it all again, call Jim Fleming up at the right time of the month and pretend she'd just experienced an uncontrollable urge for another night of sex? Would he believe that?

Sarah frowned at her reflection. Jim Fleming, she realized, was much more than just a handsome, empty-headed athlete. He was a clever, perceptive man, and any time she spent with him was dangerous. There was a real possibility that he might figure out what she was doing, even find some way of discovering her identity.

And yet the thought of choosing another man upset her immensely.

Her gloomy thoughts were interrupted by a swift knock on the door. The doctor popped his curly gray head into the room, beamed at Sarah and said, "Okay? All dressed and decent?"

Sarah smiled wanly. "If I weren't, we'd both be embarrassed by now, wouldn't we?"

He grinned. "No, dear, likely just you. Now let's see what we've got."

He flipped out the tails of his lab coat, seated himself at the desk and moved aside a large framed photo of his grandchildren, one of many which filled the little office.

"Great kids," he said, smiling at the bright faces with absentminded fondness. "The joy of my life. Now,

Sarah, I'm not sure I know exactly what you want to hear from me.''

"Yes, you do, Dr. McLellan," Sarah said. "I just told you. I want to know if I'm pregnant or not."

The doctor glanced up quickly at her lovely, withdrawn features, then looked down at the file again, sorting through the papers in the folder.

"I know that, Sarah. What I mean is that I'm not sure which of those two answers is the one you really want to hear."

"I just want to know," Sarah repeated, her eyes remote, her face expressionless.

"All right, my dear. According to my manual examination, coupled with the test results, I would estimate that you're approximately four weeks pregnant. If you're confident of the accuracy of the dates you've given me, you can probably expect to give birth on or about September 10."

Sarah stared at him. Her hands trembled, and her face went white with shock.

The doctor looked back at her gravely, guarding his expression as he waited for her to speak.

All at once Sarah's huge gray eyes lighted with wondering happiness, and her delicate features flushed pink. Tears shimmered in her eyes as she gazed at him, smiling mistily, still searching for words.

"Well," the doctor said dryly, looking at her joyous, shining face, "I guess that answers *that* question, doesn't it?"

"I...I beg your pardon?" Sarah asked, her voice hesitant and faltering.

"I take it you want this baby, Sarah," the doctor said gently.

"Oh, yes," she whispered. "Oh, yes, I do, Dr. McLellan. Very much."

"Right. That's what I assumed from your reaction. Well, there shouldn't be any problem. You're a very healthy girl, and you've always taken intelligent care of yourself. I'll just give you some reading material to look over."

Sarah sat in a daze of happiness, hardly able to concentrate on the things the doctor was telling her, the pamphlets he handed over, the diet sheets and other information.

She wanted only to be out of this place, alone in a quiet room where she could think about the miracle that had happened. She wanted to brood over the wonder of her own baby, alive and sheltered within her, her very own, growing and developing this very moment within the nurturing, enclosing safety of her body.

"Four weeks," Sarah said aloud, interrupting Dr. McLellan who was lecturing her earnestly on the dangers of excessive sodium consumption. "At four weeks she already has a full three-part brain starting to form, and eyes and ears have begun to develop, and arms and legs . . ."

The doctor smiled. "It's a girl, is it, Sarah?"

"Oh, yes," Sarah said, blushing again. "I think so."

The doctor nodded. "Well, be that as it may, you're absolutely right about the development, my dear. It's a vitally important time to watch what you eat and drink, what kind of medication you ingest, all that sort of thing."

"I would never, never do anything to hurt my baby," Sarah said simply.

The doctor nodded. "Good. Your baby will never be as vulnerable in her whole life as she is right now. What you do in these next few months can have lifelong effects for her.''

''Nothing in the world matters as much as her,'' Sarah said. ''Don't worry, Dr. McLellan. I'll take good care of her.''

He grinned cheerfully, gave Sarah a few more instructions and handed over a sheaf of information, telling her to stop at the desk on her way out to make her next monthly appointment.

At last Sarah was alone in her car, driving through the snow-covered streets wrapped in January cold. She could still hardly believe the wonder of what she had just been told. Sarah had always been so certain, despite what the doctors and scientists said, that she would be able to *feel* the early process of cell divisions and fetal development, that such a momentous thing couldn't possibly be happening in her own body without her knowledge.

And right after her night with Jim Fleming she had actually felt little stirrings, whispers of something, but she had dismissed them as wishful thinking. When she finally kept her appointment with her doctor on this bitter January afternoon, she had been absolutely convinced she wasn't pregnant, and that the delay in her cycle this month was due to nothing more than stress and overwrought nerves.

''I'm *pregnant,*'' she whispered aloud. ''I'm going to have a baby. On or about September 10 I'm going to have a *baby.*''

Even hearing the words spoken aloud in her own voice didn't make them seem real. It was too wonderful...just too wonderful.

Sarah parked in the lot at the laboratory, plugged her car in and entered the building, pausing at the reception desk to check for messages.

Joelle, the receptionist, glanced up at her with a smile and Sarah wondered if her marvelous news was somehow visible on her face, if it was even remotely possible that people could look at her and not read the truth blazing from her eyes.

But Joelle merely nodded cheerfully and reached for the message pad at her elbow. "Hi, Sarah. Still cold out there?"

"Freezing," Sarah said, gripping her handbag in trembling fingers and unwinding her big plaid scarf. "Joelle, did Apex Industries call about the microscope? I've been expecting all this week to hear something from them."

Joelle shook a pencil at her and consulted her message list. "They said yes, the lens is still under warranty," she reported. "They said you can either get it fixed here and bill them, or pack it up and send it to them and they'll look after it."

"Oh, good. Anything else?"

"Let's see. Your accountant called about half an hour ago," Joelle went on. "He wants you to get your receipts and stuff into his office so he can start on last year's income tax."

Sarah made a face. "Right. I guess I can't keep putting that off forever, can I?"

"None of us can," Joelle said sadly. "Oh, by the way," she added, "there's a man in your office."

Sarah, who had been on her way down the hall, paused and cast an inquiring glance over her shoulder. "A man? Who? What does he want?"

"I didn't get his name. Carl came out and talked to him. But he's a *very* acceptable item. I can tell you that much. Absolutely gorgeous, actually."

Sarah looked alarmed. "What do you mean?"

"Never mind, Sarah," Joelle said fondly. "The man will be completely wasted on you, anyway. I swear, I never met a woman with more potential and less interest in the finer things."

Sarah grinned at her friend's teasing, tossed her dark plait of hair back over her shoulder and rummaged in her handbag for her heavy glasses, which she fitted onto the bridge of her nose.

"There," she said cheerfully. "That's about as glamorous as I can manage on such short notice. Now what did you say this man wants?"

"I don't know," Joelle said patiently. "Like I told you, it was Carl who talked to him. I think he was asking Carl something about your college days and your early training, stuff like that."

"Oh," Sarah said, her face clearing. "He'll be from the committee for the new fellowship, then. They've been exploring my educational history all the way back to kindergarten, it seems. I hope he doesn't take too long," she added half to herself. "There are so many things I need to—"

She paused abruptly, stared into space for a minute and then flashed a warm, distracted smile at Joelle and hurried off down the hallway.

Outside the closed door of her own office Sarah hesitated, then knocked briskly and entered, shrugging out of her heavy camel hair coat as she closed the door behind her.

A tall, golden-haired man stood near her bookshelves, examining the titles, and he turned as she entered to smile at her. Sarah stared back at him, thunderstruck, the color draining from her face.

The man in her office was Jim Fleming.

"Well, hi, there, pretty lady," he said softly, smiling at the look of speechless shock on her face. "Wearing those big glasses again, I see."

Sarah struggled for words while Jim stepped forward calmly, took her coat and hung it away in the closet, still smiling.

She felt terribly vulnerable and exposed under his gaze, as if those vivid blue eyes could see into the very core of her and read her precious secret. Sarah felt an urgent terror, a need to protect her baby from him, to keep him from ever, ever finding out about the treasure she now carried in her body. She snatched her long white lab coat from its hanger and pulled it on over her slacks and sweater, wrapped it around her with trembling hands.

"Too late, I'm afraid," Jim said, still grinning. "I've already noticed how terrific you look in that sweater, Dr. Burnard."

His handsome face was warm with amusement, the dimple very evident in one flat, tanned cheek. Sarah avoided his eyes, moving nervously over behind her desk and pretended to busy herself with a sheaf of papers on a clipboard. "How did you find me?" she murmured.

"Not easily, that's for sure. May I?" Jim asked, giving her another brilliant blue glance and walking casually across to one of the leather chairs opposite Sarah's desk.

"Yes . . . yes, of course," she murmured distractedly. "Have a seat."

Jim Fleming seated himself and extended his long legs comfortably. He wore casual gray slacks and a black cashmere pullover with his shirt and tie, and looked heartbreakingly handsome even to Sarah, who didn't usually notice such things.

He smiled at her cheerfully and rested his firm, tanned hands on the arms of the chair. "Now," he went on, "you were asking about how I found you?"

"Yes," Sarah murmured, settling her glasses more firmly on the bridge of her nose and pretending to be absorbed in the papers in front of her. "I'm really quite curious about that."

"Well, as I said, it wasn't easy. I went back and made the rounds of all the bars and pubs in that neighborhood quite a few times, but nobody could remember seeing you. And I kept having the feeling," he added, "that I'd met you before, but it didn't register until Maude told me how you put those big, heavy-rimmed glasses on to read my letter—remember?"

He paused and gave Sarah an inquiring glance. She nodded without looking up. "I remember," she murmured. "Please go on."

"Well, a few days ago I happened to ask Ellie how you looked in the glasses, and she said you looked 'really smart, like a scientist or something,' and then it hit me like a ton of bricks."

Sarah flushed and stirred uneasily in her chair while he watched her.

"A science major," Jim went on, regarding her carefully. "That's what you were, Sarah Burnard. You were in one of my English classes in college, an absolute knockout of a girl hiding behind those big glasses, and you never said a single word to me. It was quite a blow to my youthful ego, as I recall, the way you studiously ignored me all through term."

Sarah was so startled by his words that she looked up in spite of herself, meeting his amused gaze. "You're kidding," she said flatly. "You were such a big man on campus, and I was just a drab little bookworm. You never even knew I was alive."

"You might be surprised," Jim said quietly. "It's possible that you don't know as much about me as you think you do, Miss Burnard."

Sarah remembered the hours she had spent studying this man, and the masses of meticulous research that were still filed away in a desk drawer right under her hands. She dropped her eyes quickly, hoping none of those thoughts were evident on her face.

"So, anyway," Jim went on, "as soon as I remembered that English class, it was easy. I went through my old yearbooks, found your picture and your name and then called Howie Meyer to ask if he knew where you were working these days."

"You know Howie?" Sarah asked in surprise.

"Sure. We play racquetball together sometimes. Howie still plays a pretty mean game of racquetball," Jim added with a grin. "And since he was always a shining light in the chemistry lab, I figured he might have some idea what happened to all the other science types from our college days. He told me you were working over here, so here I am."

"Here you are," Sarah echoed uneasily.

"Howie also said," Jim added casually, "that you were still single. Never been married, he said, except to your work."

Sarah flushed and bit her lip nervously. "What does that have to do with anything? Whether I've ever been married?"

"Well, I was certain you must be married and that was why you were being so elusive. You know, a married woman just out for a little night of fun and games, not wanting to get caught."

Sarah made an expression of distaste. "If I were married," she said finally with quiet conviction, "I wouldn't be out for 'a night of fun and games,' believe me. Cheating is definitely not my style."

Jim nodded. "I know. Even though that was my first impression, it never seemed to ring true." He smiled at her. "And *that*," he added, "made me even more determined to find you, no matter what it took."

Sarah looked up at Jim directly for the first time, forcing herself to meet his warm, intent gaze. "But why, Jim? Why did you go to all this trouble to find me?"

"Isn't that funny?" he asked, raising his dark brows. "You know, I was just going to ask you the same thing."

"What do you mean?"

"Come on, Sarah," he said impatiently. "That night in the bar was no random encounter, was it? Nobody could ever remember seeing you there before. Why did you happen to be out cruising the downtown bars just on that particular night?"

Sarah felt a chill of fear and fought it down, forcing herself to think rapidly enough to come up with some kind of convincing story. "Do you remember..." she began, faltering a little, and then her voice steadied as she gained confidence. "Do you remember Wendy? She worked in that bar for a while as a bartender's helper last fall."

"Small girl?" Jim asked, frowning as he searched his memory. "Frizzy reddish hair and big freckles, talks all the time without saying much?"

Sarah nodded, trying not to smile at this unflattering but accurate description of Wendy. "That's her. Well, I've known Wendy for years, and she always told me what a fun place the bar was, and that night I was feeling so lonely with Christmas coming and all that, and I decided to go down there just to have a couple of drinks. And when I saw you, I remembered you right away from college, even though I could tell you didn't know who I was. And I was so lonely," Sarah went on, her words tumbling over one another in her haste, "and I *did* know you. You weren't a complete stranger, so when it looked like...like something might be going to happen between us, I thought, why not?"

Jim sat across the desk, watching her thoughtfully. "It's a plausible story, Sarah," he said finally, "but I'm not sure I believe you."

"Why would I lie?" Sarah asked, taking a deep breath and forcing herself to meet his eyes with a calm, level gaze. "Do you think there's something sinister going on here, Jim? Do you really think I sought you out specifically for some dark, evil purpose of my own?"

Jim sat quietly in the padded chair, his big body relaxed and still as he regarded the beautiful woman across the desk. Finally he shook his head. "I guess not. It all just seems a little strange. Something kind of... doesn't quite mesh, you know?"

"People get lonely," Sarah said briskly. "Even scientists," she added with a small smile. "And when people are lonely, they quite often do some really strange things. Now forgive me for changing the subject, but how are the children?''

The austere lines of his face softened, and his blue eyes sparkled. ''As if you have to ask,'' he teased. ''You've been there what—three times since Maude got back from her ski trip? Sneaking in when I'm away at work to see them?''

Sarah blushed and avoided his eyes. ''I know, but it's been...I've been busy the past few days,'' she confessed, ''and I haven't been there to see them since early this week. I just wondered how they are,'' she added wistfully.

''Okay, you asked for it. Well, first of all, Ellie still loves that shellcraft set you gave her. Oh, I almost forgot. She made you a present.'' Jim went over to his jacket, which hung on a brass coatrack near the door. He took a small wrapped package from one pocket, crossed the room with his lithe, easy prowl and smiled as he handed the gift to Sarah.

She looked down at it and laughed. ''To the Princess Lady from Ellie with lots of love,'' the tag read in careful, tiny lettering.

''You haven't told them my name?'' Sarah murmured, feeling absurdly warm and pleased.

Jim shook his head. ''That's your business, Sarah. You can tell them if you choose. They're all just crazy about you,'' he added. ''Including Maude. You've really made some conquests in that group.''

Sarah unwraped the tiny package to reveal a square little box lined with cotton. She lifted away the top layer of cotton and caught her breath. Nestled in the soft cloud of white was a dainty pair of earrings constructed of tiny, delicate shells glued with painstaking care onto little plastic disks.

"Why, they're *beautiful*," Sarah murmured, examining them in awe. "Just beautiful. I had no idea she'd be so talented. This work looks almost professional."

"She's really good with her hands," Jim said, sounding as indulgent and proud as any young parent. "And she spends hours sitting there working at that stuff, not saying a word. I was amazed," he added, "that you managed to pick such a perfect gift. She loves it."

Sarah took off her glasses and looked up at him, her cheeks pink, her big gray eyes shining. All at once she was so lovely that he caught his breath and stared back at her in silent awe.

"I had a shellcraft set at her age," Sarah said softly, "and I've never forgotten how much I loved it. But," she added, laughing a little, "I'm sure I was never as talented as Ellie."

Jim recovered his equilibrium and laughed with her, then went on to report Billy's appreciation of the fishing tackle and Arthur's lusty absorption in his activity board.

Sarah forgot her reserve, even forgot briefly her fear of Jim Fleming's presence and what it could mean to the future of herself and her child. She pictured the scenes in his apartment as he described them and laughed merrily while Jim joined in, his blue eyes sparkling with fun.

Finally she sobered and looked at the little earrings on her desk. "Jim," she asked softly, "what are you going to do with them? These kids, I mean. Can you really keep them with you, all three of them?"

"Oh, God, Sarah," he muttered, shifting in his chair and gazing out the window with a bleak expression. "I don't know. There's just so much to consider."

"Ellie told me you can't keep them much longer in that building," Sarah ventured. "They're going to enforce the adults-only policy, aren't they?"

Jim nodded. "I'm supposed to have them out by the end of the month, with maybe a couple of weeks' grace if I really beg."

Sarah looked at him, appalled. "That's not enough time to make other plans, is it?"

"It sure isn't. Worst of all, I've just signed a three-year lease. I can't get released from it, so if I can't find someone to sublet, I'll have to pay rent on that place as well as mortgage payments on a house. I doubt if I could even qualify for a mortgage under those conditions."

Sarah gazed at him across the desk, her face soft with sympathy and concern. "Jim...what are you going to do?"

"I don't know," he said grimly. "I definitely can't keep them where I am. I've looked at houses, but just now, with the amount of money I've sunk into my business, I can hardly qualify for enough mortgage money even if I do get out of the lease. Up until now," he added, trying to smile, "a house wasn't really way up there on my priority list."

"And Maude can't..."

Jim shook his head. "Maude's whole apartment isn't much bigger than your office here. She likes it that way, says it's easy to clean and leaves her time for all the activities she's involved in. Maude's a busy girl," he added with a distant grin.

Sarah nodded, still gazing at him in concern.

"One of Maude's kids might take them for a while...in a pinch," Jim went on. "But they all have kids of their own, so it'd just have to be temporary, and I hate that idea."

Sarah nodded, understanding exactly what he meant. "They've had so much disruption and instability in their lives already. They should be able to move into a place that's going to be a permanent home, somewhere they can settle in and not have to leave again."

"Exactly," Jim said, giving Sarah a gratified look. "That's just how I feel about it."

Sarah thought for a moment, her delicate black brows drawn in concentration. "Jim," she said finally, "do you really want to keep them with you? I mean, is it important for you to have them living with you?"

He met her eyes honestly. "Not in that sense," he said finally. "I mean, I've never thought of myself as much of a family man, you know? Adopting a ready-made family was another thing that wasn't really high on my priority list. It's just that I feel so damn responsible."

"Because of what Billy says? That after giving them a taste of warmth and comfort, it's cruel to snatch it away again?"

Jim nodded, his blue eyes troubled. "Yes. He's right, you know. I brought them home with me on an impulse, without giving a thought to the consequences. And it's one of those things that takes a second to do but changes your whole life from then on."

Sarah looked with quiet sympathy at his tense features. "But," she persisted, "what you're saying is that you wouldn't mind parting with them as long as you knew they'd be kept together and properly cared for?"

"That's right. I don't need to have them in my house every single day to make me happy. Actually, I'm a man who likes my own privacy, and a quiet, uneventful kind of life. But you're right. I'd need to know they were happy and well before I could let them go. I love those kids," he added with a sudden burst of emotion. "It's amazing how quickly they can get close to your heart, little kids like that. I could get along without having them in my house, but I'd still want to see them all the time, visit them whenever I could."

Sarah twirled a pencil thoughtfully in her fingers, her brows still drawn in concentration.

"Why, Sarah?" Jim asked, looking up at her hopefully. "Can you think of somewhere they could live?" he paused, struck by a sudden thought. "Do *you* have room for them? Where do you live, anyhow?"

"I inherited a house from my father. It's on the west side near the university," Sarah said automatically, and then instantly regretted her words. Jim was sitting bolt upright, gripping the arms of his chair and staring at her intently, his eyes alight.

"You live in a *house?* And you're not married? You're all alone there?"

Sarah looked back at him, caught his meaning at once and felt a deep chill of unease. "Jim," she began hastily, "I don't really have room for—"

"But you do live in a house," he interrupted. "Isn't that right? With a yard, and a fence, and all that stuff? More than one bedroom?"

"No yard," Sarah said. "None at all. And only two bedrooms. Actually, my place isn't much bigger than yours. I wish I could—"

"Look, Sarah, I know I started this. I know I'm responsible. I wouldn't expect you to take over my burden for me. I'd pay whatever it cost for you to keep the kids, and also pay Maude or another baby-sitter to look after Arthur so you wouldn't have any interruptions in your work. Please, Sarah," Jim went on passionately, "just consider it. All these kids need is some space and a place to live where they won't be split up or turned out on the street. They're really good kids, Sarah. Please, just think it over for a minute."

Sarah gazed into his brilliant blue eyes, her soul shrinking away from his words. She pictured her house, so small and self-contained, thinking of how completely inadequate it was as a home for three active children. There would barely be room in her house for her own baby when it arrived, let alone three others.

But she wanted to desperately to help, to see the children safely and permanently settled somewhere. Maybe she could move her plans up by a year or so and start shopping right away for the new house. Still, she couldn't afford another house until she got hers sold, and the housing market was slow now, caught in the usual midwinter slump. By the time she found a buyer, it might already be too late for Jim and the three children....

She drew in a deep, ragged breath, struggling to compose herself and think clearly. "Look," she began, "I don't really have room for them, Jim. I'd like to take them, believe me. I love those kids, too, and I feel just as responsible as you do. But I have ... I have other obligations, things in my life you don't know about. And I honestly don't have any more room for them than you do. If I took them, they'd just have to move again soon, anyhow. I'm sorry, Jim, truly I am. I would if I could, in a minute. But I can't."

He nodded and settled back in the chair, still giving her a quiet, level gaze, his disappointment showing clearly in his eyes.

Suddenly she had a thought and hastened to blurt it out before she could think it over and change her mind. "There *is* one thing we could consider," she said.

"And what's that, Sarah?"

"Well," Sarah began awkwardly, studying a pile of folders stacked on the corner of her desk, "from what you're telling me, I gather the main problem is money, right? I mean, you've got everything tied up in your business, and not enough ready cash right now to make a big purchase like a house. Isn't that right?"

"Pretty much," Jim said grimly. "Don't get me wrong. Things are going well and I'm a competent manager. I expect my business to be really profitable in the future. But right now things are tight. I don't have a lot of cash reserves, and even my credit at the bank is stretched to the limit these days so that I can retain an adequate inventory."

Sarah hesitated, gripping her letter knife tightly in her hands to control their trembling. "Maybe I could help, then," she said slowly. "I've been saving for a long time to buy a bigger house, Jim. I could postpone my own plans and loan you what I've got, and I'm sure it would be enough for a down payment. And you could pay me back over the years as your business improves."

Even as she spoke the words Sarah felt a deep stab of pain and sadness, thinking miserably about all her visions of a big, sunny nursery for her baby, a yard to play in and a spacious, comfortable suite for the live-in nanny. It was so hard to see those cherished dreams evaporate before her eyes. Still, she had to think about the three children she had come to love, whose needs were so much more immediate.

But when she looked up at Jim Fleming he was shaking his head, his blue eyes dark with emotion. "It's great of you to make an offer like that, Sarah, but you must know I could never accept it. I'd sell my business and work at three jobs before I'd clean out your nest egg.''

Sarah nodded, realizing from the taut expression on his face that argument was useless. Suddenly she had another thought, and she glanced up again hopefully. ''Jim . . . how about your family? Your father, the senator?'' she asked shyly. ''I mean, everybody knows how wealthy he is. It would be a big struggle and sacrifice for either of us to buy a house right now on our own, but surely your father could advance you enough to—''

''Forget it,'' Jim said curtly.

Sarah gazed at him, startled by the sudden chill in his voice and the tense set of his jaw.

''I wouldn't take a cent from him if I was starving to death,'' Jim went on in that same tight, emotionless voice. ''I never have, and I won't start now. Not even for three kids that I love.''

Sarah stared at the handsome blond man across from her. ''Why? I mean, all the papers always describe him as being such a warm, wonderful person. The media seems to adore him.''

''Sure,'' Jim said bitterly. ''The media adores him, all right. They never had to live with him.''

''I'm just dumbfounded,'' Sarah said finally, shaking her head. ''I had no idea there was such a deep rift in the Fleming family. How long have you been angry with him?''

''All my life, Sarah. Leave it alone. It has nothing to do with any of this.''

''But do you see him?'' Sarah persisted. ''Do you talk with him?''

"Not if I can help it. I haven't talked to him of my own accord since I was seventeen years old."

Sarah gazed at him, her face drawn with concern. "When did you last see him, Jim?"

"Just before Christmas. He came to my office, like he does every year, trying to pressure me into coming out to the ranch for Christmas."

"And you refused him?" Sarah asked. "He came to make peace and you turned him away? Is that what happened, Jim?"

Jim's blue eyes glinted dangerously. "Look, Sarah, I told you. This is none of your business, and it has nothing to do with anything. How I feel about my father is my own concern. Leave it alone."

"I loved my father so much," Sarah murmured, gazing past Jim without really seeing him. "I just adored him. I'd give anything to see him one more time, just talk to him for an hour. But I never will. And *you*—" she turned to Jim, her gray eyes stormy with emotion "—you have a father who comes to seek you out, begs you to make things right between you, and you turn him away."

"There are a lot of things you don't know about my situation and my life."

"Oh, certainly. Everybody's life is like that. But there are things I *do* know about, too, like compromise and forgiveness and compassion."

They stared at each other for a long moment, eyes locked in charged intensity. Finally Jim forced himself to smile.

"Okay," he muttered. "I'm sorry if I upset you, Sarah. You're right, I came here partly for your help and advice, and I shouldn't be angry with you for offering it when you don't understand the whole situation. The fact is, I just can't go to my father, and I don't want any help from him. I'll work this out somehow without causing the kids any more anxiety or disruption than I can help.''

Sarah nodded, feeling awkward and uncomfortable under his frank, steady gaze.

"Actually," Jim went on, "I also came here for another reason. Maude and the kids and I are going cross-country skiing next Sunday, and we wondered if you'd like to come along."

"Me?" Sarah asked blankly.

"Sure. Why not? Do you have a pair of skis? You can rent some if you don't, and it's really easy to learn."

"I know. Actually," Sarah confessed, "I was a competitive skier when I was a teenager."

Jim stared at her. "No kidding? Cross-country?"

"Silver medalist in the Alberta Winter Games about fifteen years ago," Sarah told him with a shy smile.

"Wow! What a lady this is!" Jim looked at her with warm approval, as if their recent emotional exchange had never happened, and Sarah felt herself relaxing a little.

"So," he said, "how about it? Want to come with us? Come on, Sarah, it'll do you good. Howie says you work about twenty-eight hours a day over here."

"I have a project I'm working on," Sarah murmured. "We're trying to develop a drought-resistant strain of wheat. It's very time-consuming."

"Sure, but you can give yourself the occasional weekend off, can't you?"

Sarah's mind whirled. She felt an urgent panic at the thought of developing a relationship with Jim Fleming, knowing that before too long her body would begin to betray her secret. And if he counted back the

AN IMPORTANT MESSAGE FROM THE EDITORS OF HARLEQUIN®

Dear Reader,

Because you've chosen to read one of our fine romance novels, we'd like to say "thank you"! And, as a **special** way to thank you, we've selected <u>four more</u> of the <u>books</u> you love so well, a Victorian Picture Frame **and** a <u>surprise bonus</u> to send you absolutely **_FREE!_**

Please enjoy them with our compliments...

Senior Editor,
Superromance

P.S. And because we value our customers, we've attached something extra inside ...

EDITOR'S
FREE
GIFT
SEAL
THANK YOU

PEEL OFF SEAL AND PLACE INSIDE

HOW TO VALIDATE YOUR
EDITOR'S FREE GIFT
"THANK YOU"

1. Peel off gift seal from front cover. Place it in space provided at right. This automatically entitles you to receive four free books, a lovely pewter-finish Victorian picture frame and a surprise bonus gift.

2. You'll receive brand-new Harlequin Superromance® novels. When you return this card, we'll rush you our "thank you" books and gifts ABSOLUTELY FREE!

3. If we don't hear from you, every month we'll send you 4 additional novels to read and enjoy. You can return them and owe nothing but if you decide to keep them, you'll pay only $2.96* per book, a savings of 33¢ each off the cover price. There is **no** extra charge for postage and handling. There are **no** hidden extras.

4. When you join the Harlequin Reader Service®, you'll get our subscribers-only newsletter, as well as additional free gifts from time to time just for being a subscriber!

5. You must be completely satisfied. You may cancel at any time simply by sending us a note or a shipping statement marked "cancel" or returning any shipment to us at our cost.

6. Don't forget to detach your FREE BOOKMARK. And remember... just for validating your Editor's Free Gift Offer, we'll send you SIX MORE gifts, *ABSOLUTELY FREE!*

YOURS FREE!
*This lovely Victorian pewter-finish miniature is perfect for displaying a treasured photograph — and it's yours **absolutely free** — when you accept our no-risk offer!*

months, he could easily put two and two together and realize that the child she carried was his own.

Sarah shuddered, thinking about how instantly and firmly this man had bonded with three children the first time he ever saw then. What might he be like where his own flesh and blood was involved? And what would be the legal ramifications of some kind of custody battle with him over the care and upbringing of the child nestled in her womb? At that thought Sarah's throat tightened and she felt herself curl protectively around her child, ready to do battle for her absolute right to her own baby.

"Sarah?" Jim asked, watching her face with a touch of anxiety. "Are you all right?"

Sarah gazed at him blankly, her mind still surging with thoughts and emotions. Sternly she forced herself to deal with all this logically.

First, Jim Fleming knew her name and where she worked. He could find her anytime he wanted, and he probably would, so there was no real way to avoid him. Second, he had no knowledge of her real reason for going to the bar that night. He probably still thought she was an attractive but lonely woman who picked men up occasionally when she felt the urge. If she did nothing to correct this impression, then when her pregnancy started to show, she could argue that the father might be any number of men, and he would have no way to disprove it, certainly no right to lay claim to the child.

In fact, avoiding his company, especially when they all knew how much she cared about the three children, would actually look more suspicious than a casual acceptance of his invitation, wouldn't it?

"All right," she said at last. "Did you say everybody's going? Doesn't Maude have to stay home and look after Arthur?"

"Arthur's going, too. My secretary at the office has a baby ski sled, and I'm going to pull it."

"Oh, my goodness," Sarah said. "We'll have to make sure he's bundled up."

"You should see his snowsuit," Jim said cheerfully. "He looks like an astronaut. Arthur could crawl around on the moon in complete safety in that snowsuit."

Sarah laughed. Suddenly, in spite of all her misgivings, she felt a surge of pleasurable anticipation. "It's been so long since I've been up to the ski hill," she said wistfully. "Years, I guess. I used to love it so much."

"Well," Jim said, his eyes sparkling, "I have to warn you that we won't be functioning at silver medalist level, my girl. It'll be the first time on skis for Ellie and Billy, and Maude's improving, but she's still no ball of fire, she says."

"How about you?" Sarah asked, giving him a teasing glance. "As a skier, are you a pretty good football player, Jim Fleming?"

Jim drew himself up with mock outrage. "I'm a pretty good skier, you arrogant woman. Although," he added with a grin, "I've never pulled a baby sled before. That could slow me down a little."

He got to his feet and moved toward the door, reaching for his jacket while Sarah pushed her chair back and followed him. "We'll be leaving about noon," Jim said, smiling down at her. "Do you want me to pick you up?"

"No, I'll come to your place. You'll be loaded down with skis and poles, to say nothing of the baby sled. We should go out to the ski hill in two cars, anyhow, just to have room enough for everybody."

"Okay," Jim said. He gave her an intent, meaningful gaze. "It's going to be so good having you with us, Sarah. I can hardly wait."

Sarah gazed up at him, shivering all at once in the grip of another distressing flood of emotion. She was standing casually beside him in her office, but her mind was reliving the night of their passionate lovemaking, the warmth and silken fire of their naked bodies together, the glorious, sweet abandon of her own response.

Horrified at her lack of control, she stared into his blue eyes, helpless in the grip of this flood of feeling, remembering the sweetness of those sculpted lips on hers, the feel of his hands caressing her body, the rich sensation of him moving and surging within her.

Sarah turned aside hastily, murmuring something incoherent. Jim regarded her thoughtfully for a moment, smiled, patted her cheek gently, then turned to leave.

Long after he was gone the room seemed to retain the golden aura of his tall, handsome body and his sunny, vibrant personality. Sarah wandered back to sit behind her desk, her mind still whirling as she stared in bemused silence at the door through which he had vanished.

CHAPTER EIGHT

ARTHUR RODE SMOOTHLY along the snow-covered track in his padded sled, warmly bundled in a silvery gray snowsuit with fur trim and a voluminous red woolen scarf. Only his eyes were visible, round and bright with astonishment as he surveyed the unfamiliar and wondrous things that skimmed past him.

By the side of the trail, fir trees stood draped and bowed in soft white snow, glittering shapes against the deep blue of the sky. Shrubbery etched with lacy shawls of frost lined the edge of the path, and rock faces shone with frozen waterfalls.

Other skiers passed them on the trail, smiling at the little family group and beaming on Arthur, who waved back at them solemnly with tiny red-mittened hands. One group had a dog with them that looked like a collie crossed with a shepherd. To Arthur's delight, the dog paused to snuffle at his face before racing ahead to its master.

Jim paused frequently to check the baby in the sled. Every time he did Arthur registered intense impatience with the cessation of movement and made imperious demands for Jim to get back to work at once. The big man skied easily along the trail, with the sled snugly belted to his waist harness. His powerful stroke was hardly affected by the extra weight, and he had to hold himself in check, even with his added burden, to match the pace of the rest of the group. Maude skied beside Jim, also keeping a cautious eye on Arthur who chuckled and wriggled with delight every time he caught sight of her plump, smiling face.

Billy, however, had shown an instant affinity for the sport and already scorned their slower pace. The boy had vanished somewhere up ahead, but dropped back every few minutes to scoff at them mercilessly for their lack of speed.

Just ahead of Jim and Maude, Ellie floundered valiantly along, falling often, laughing and shaking snow out of her hair, her face rosy with cold and happiness. Sarah was with her, patiently helping her back to her feet, teaching the child how to hold her poles and balance on her skis, how to glide and stroke and establish smooth forward momentum.

Jim idled comfortably along beside Maude, half listening to her cheerful comments while his eyes rested thoughtfully on the bright figures of the dark-haired woman and the little blond girl in front of him.

Sarah wore a one-piece fitted ski suit, bright pink trimmed with white, the dainty shell earrings that Ellie had made for her and a wide pink knitted headband that fitted smoothly under her long, dark plait of hair. The vibrant color accentuated the loveliness of her complexion, while the ski suit hugged her shapely body, showing to perfection her narrow waist, her slender, rounded hips and long legs.

She was so beautiful, Jim thought, that no man could take his eyes off her. In fact, every man who passed them on the trail turned to give Sarah a second and even a third glance, although she was so absorbed in Ellie that she didn't even notice.

And her body was so graceful and elegant on skis—it wasn't surprising that she had at one time in her life been a championship-level athlete in this sport. Even now, after years away from it, she had relaxed instinctively into the rhythm and strength of a smooth, easy diagonal stride, and her slow pace and preoccupation with Ellie couldn't hide her skill.

Jim fretted suddenly at all the conventions and responsibilities that bound them. He wished passionately that he and Sarah could just be alone, skimming shoulder to shoulder down the trail and through the woods, free to fly and soar, to talk together and laugh and learn about each other, to kiss in the sunshine and fall in love.

Suddenly he caught himself and forced his wandering mind back into check, distressed by the turn his thoughts were taking. For one thing, all the responsibilities that now burdened him had been his own choice, and he certainly wouldn't be much of a man if he decided to back away from them as soon as they became a little oppressive. And besides, Sarah had never given him the slightest indication, apart from that one passionate night of lovemaking, that she had any kind of romantic interest in him at all. They had the children in common and nothing else, that was her clear message.

But she was so beautiful, and so completely, adorably desirable, and Jim knew he was venturing more and more onto dangerous ground here, especially since he had discovered her identity and learned she wasn't just another bored, rich housewife who sometimes went out pub-crawling in search of adventure. This was a fascinating, brilliant, complex and highly intellectual woman, with strong opinions accompanied by a puzzling and inexplicable shyness that made her even lovelier and more mysterious.

And the night he had held her naked body in his arms she had filled his whole world with sweet, shimmering wonder that shook him to the core every time he thought of it....

"Jim," she called suddenly, pulling him abruptly back to reality, "can you come up here a minute?"

"What's the problem?" he asked, a little abashed by what he had just been recalling. He skied up beside Sarah and Ellie and paused, causing Arthur to hammer on the arms of the baby sled and begin to make muffled noises of outrage beneath his red scarf.

"Arthur!" Sarah said, glancing down at the small, squirming bundle on the sled. "What's the matter?"

"He hates it when I stop," Jim explained. "Lucky for me the kid doesn't have a whip. He'd just lay it on without mercy. Arthur likes speed."

Sarah giggled and Jim smiled at her, delighting in the glow on her beautiful face, the way her eyes shone, the vibrant happiness of her whole shapely body in the bright ski suit.

"You look like you're having a good time," he observed solemnly.

"Oh, Jim," Sarah murmured, closing her eyes in bliss, "this is just heaven. I'd forgotten how much I loved it out here, you know. It's been so long since I've done anything like this."

"Far too long, I'll bet," he said critically. "From now on, Dr. Sarah Burnard, we're going to supervise your social life and see that you get out more for your own good. Right, Ellie?"

Ellie bobbed her head vigorously, but Sarah's smile faded and she looked away in sudden alarm. Jim watched her for a moment, troubled by her expression. Every time he mentioned the future, or made any kind of plans, she got this cautious, guarded look that worried him, as if she was afraid of him for some reason and searching for a way to escape.

Maybe she was just afraid of commitment, Jim thought, although she was certainly deeply committed to her work. Actually, it seemed more as if she was specifically nervous about *him,* for some reason, but he couldn't imagine why. He'd never done anything to threaten her.

"What's the problem, Sarah?" he asked aloud. "Didn't you call me up here for something?"

"I think the binding is loose on Ellie's left ski," Sarah said. "Her boot keeps slipping, and the man at the rental shop showed you how to tighten them, didn't he?"

Jim nodded, bending to examine Ellie's boot while the little girl stood patiently, looking down with interest as he fiddled with the metal bindings. Sarah, meanwhile, knelt by the sled and began to tickle and distract Arthur, who was still complaining bitterly about the delay.

Maude was just down the trail, resting on her poles and chatting with a paunchy man in a sweater and black tights who had approached her from the opposite direction.

"Who was that?" Ellie asked over Jim's shoulder as Maude detached herself from her admirer and rejoined the group.

"Oh, just somebody I know from swimming lessons," Maude said airily.

"Clarence will be jealous," Ellie said with a teasing smile, referring to the smitten doorman in their apartment building.

"Oh, pooh," Maude said, dismissing Clarence's agony with a cheerful wave of her hand. "Arthur, what on earth is all this fuss about? Give poor Jim a minute to rest, you awful baby."

Billy reappeared, skiing back to them on the opposite trail, his thin face alight with excitement. Jim glanced up at him, thinking that he couldn't recall seeing Billy look so relaxed and involved in the family, so much like a normal thirteen-year-old boy. Billy had scorned any type of formal ski wear for this outing, and was still clad in his tattered jeans and jacket. But then, Jim thought with a private grin, most of the other teenagers on the trail were dressed exactly the same, so Billy certainly wasn't conspicuous in his shabbiness.

"Hey, hurry *up,* you guys!" the boy shouted. "There's a totally awesome hill just ahead! I was going about fifty miles an hour by the time I hit the bottom."

"Oh, *great,*" Maude muttered. "Just what I need."

"Now, Maude," Jim said sternly, "you know how much you love to snowplow." Setting Ellie's binding firmly in place, he stood up on his skis, paused to smile down at the little girl and ruffled her hair gently before he pulled his gloves back on. He felt Sarah's eyes resting anxiously on his face and raised an inquiring eyebrow at her.

"The hill, Jim," she said. "Aren't you concerned, with Arthur on the sled? What if you fall or something?"

He smiled. "It's not a bad hill, Sarah. I won't fall. As a matter of fact," he added with a rueful glance over his shoulder, "Arthur will love it. We'll finally be going fast enough for him. Come on, gang!" he added. "Lunch at the warming shed in half an hour."

Jim bent to set his poles, kicked off and watched with satisfaction as his little group spread out beside him, moving off down the trail in the bright winter sunlight.

When you came right down to it, Jim thought with considerable contentment, life wasn't really such a bad deal for a family man. Not such a bad deal at all.

LATER THAT EVENING, when the children were asleep and Maude and Sarah had gone home after a merry take-out dinner of pizza and milk shakes, Jim sat alone in his living room, sipping a glass of white wine and gazing thoughtfully at the dying fire.

He got up to dim the lights, set another log on the glowing embers and moved over to his stereo to select a soft tape of Chopin waltzes, adjusting the rippling strains of music low enough that they wouldn't disturb Arthur in his crib. Glass in hand, Jim paused by the crib to look down at the sleeping baby.

The tall man smiled, his fine, sculpted features softening with affection, his hair glowing dull bronze in the muted light. Asleep, he mused, Arthur was a joy to behold. The baby's plump cheeks were pink, and his thumb, as usual, was firmly tucked into his mouth. He held a soft, woolly rabbit close to his face, its long ears lying softly against his cheek. The baby lay on his stomach, his little rounded posterior raised high into the air, his tiny feet braced to hold him in position.

Jim bent to kiss Arthur's fat neck, sniffing the delightful scent of powder and warm, milky sweetness, then tucked the soft blanket gently up around the little sleeping face and tiptoed back to his chair by the fire.

Still thoughtful, he gazed around the room at the chaos of his apartment. Ellie had been moved into Jim's room and was the only one of them to have complete privacy. Arthur slept in his crib in the corner of the living room while Jim opened out the sofa bed each night. Billy bunked in the kitchen, cramped but uncomplaining in a sleeping bag tossed onto an air mattress on the floor near the sink.

They were managing well enough, but Jim was growing more and more uncomfortable. Particularly on quiet nights like this he found himself longing wistfully for his old life, for the peace and serenity of his solitary tidy home. The crowded apartment always seemed so full of people, of noise and clutter and uproar, and Jim sometimes could hardly remember a time when he'd had his home all to himself.

At least he could get away in the daytime, go to his office where life proceeded in a quiet, orderly fashion just as it always had. Thank God for Maude Willett, Jim thought fervently. Without Maude he'd probably be a nervous wreck by now.

Jim sipped his drink and listened to the music, thinking about the ten days Maude had been away on her skiing holiday, when he was forced to stay all day long in the apartment with the three children. He shuddered, staring gloomily at the fire.

No woman's face, as long as he could remember, had ever looked as beautiful to him as Maude's plump features the morning she had finally reappeared in his doorway with Lancelot in the box under her arm, full of cheerful stories about her vacation.

It wasn't that they were bad kids, Jim thought. And it wouldn't have been necessary to stay with them all that time, either, if he hadn't chosen to. After all, the two older children were both mature and self-sufficient beyond their years and certainly able to care for their baby brother.

But Jim had an uneasy feeling whenever he caught a certain expression on Billy's face that the boy was still poised to escape. Billy didn't trust any of the adults he met, and Jim was certain that at the first opportunity he would pack up the two little ones and flee to a hiding place where he could be sure of keeping them together.

By this time the thought of Ellie and Arthur returning to the kind of setting where he'd first seen them was more than Jim could bear. And yet, in moments of deep honesty, he was able to understand Billy's point of view.

Jim felt himself growing more and more trapped in a desperate and hopeless situation, and he knew Billy was aware of his feelings. Sometimes he sensed the boy staring at him, sizing up Jim's state of mind, trying to judge how much longer it would be before the big man gave in, admitted defeat and turned to the authorities for help.

Jim shifted restlessly in the chair, drained his glass and set it down on the coffee table. Then he leaned back, still frowning, thinking wearily about the problems of providing housing and care for three children, wondering for the thousandth time just what he'd gotten himself into, and what he was going to do about it, and most of all, how he was ever going to find the money he needed to buy a house so the children would be safe and secure.

Despite himself Jim's thoughts turned to Sarah. He remembered her saying that she lived in a house, and that she was alone, and firmly quelled the little glow of speculation that flamed in his mind every time he thought about this. After all, she'd made it very clear that she didn't want the three children living in her house with her, even if Jim shouldered most of the expense.

He was still a little puzzled by her reaction, because she seemed truly fond of the children, and Howie Meyer, who knew her quite well, stated unequivocally that she had few involvements in her life. In fact, Sarah Burnard apparently had no social life at all that anyone knew about.

Maybe, Jim thought, looking ruefully around at the shambles of his living room, she just liked peace and tidiness and wasn't willing to sacrifice her own privacy for a mess like this. And who could blame her? After all, she was a scientist, involved in complex and time-consuming research. No wonder she didn't want to add a lot of complication to her life.

And yet, no matter how often he ran through this line of reasoning, it didn't quite ring true. After all, she had chosen to seek him out after their first encounter, just out of concern for the children. She had bought them gifts, come to see them, expressed a genuine interest in their welfare. In fact, she had even offered her own carefully saved nest egg to help him with his financial problems and give him enough money for a down payment on a house to shelter the three children. That certainly wasn't the act of a self-absorbed and uncaring person.

And when she was with the children, she was loving, warm, tender and deeply involved, especially with Ellie, who adored her.

Jim frowned, his blue eyes narrowing thoughtfully, the firelight glinting on his fine cheekbones.

She was such an enigma, this strange woman called Sarah Burnard.

His thoughts roamed on, wandering through all his mental pictures of her, recalling how appealing she'd looked earlier that day in her bright ski suit, and how elegant she'd been the night they met in her black silk and fur. Jim contrasted those images with the way she'd been when he went to her office, reserved and businesslike in her white lab coat and her heavy glasses. And over all, like a haunting stain of remembered music, was the incredible loveliness of her in his arms, the passion and fire and warmth that still melted his heart and turned his body to jelly even after all this time.

He was assailed by an abrupt longing to hear her voice and looked thoughtfully at the telephone. He had her home number now, extracted from her so that he could call her if he had a problem with the children and needed emergency help when Maude wasn't available. Sarah had been clearly reluctant to give it, but once again her concern for the children had overcome her obvious desire to keep Jim at arm's length.

Jim reached for the phone, wondering what she was doing, picturing her in a dainty lace nightgown, maybe reading in bed with her dark hair in a loose cloud over her bare shoulders the way it had been that night in the hotel bed.

He swallowed hard, feeling weak and shaky with desire, and set down the telephone receiver again. It wasn't fair to take advantage of her by calling the very first night after she gave him the number, especially when he had no problem with the children, no real excuse to bother her.

He'd give it a while.

But, as he stared at the fire and listened to the soft, cascading strains of piano music, he wondered how long he would be able to keep himself away from her.

SARAH SAT CROSS-LEGGED on the braided rug near her hearth, leaning back against the painted carousel horse with Amos in her lap. She wore old gray jogging pants with a heavy pink sweatshirt and socks, and she was brushing the big cat, working delicately on the snarls and tangles that always developed in his long, silky fur, murmuring softly to him to keep him from marching off in a fury of indignation.

"Just relax, you big baby. Look at the mess you're in. If I didn't comb out these tangles, you'd look like a mop. Besides, it doesn't hurt that much. You're just such a..."

She stopped abruptly, her beautiful face pale and drawn. Then she dumped Amos in a heap on the rug, scrambled to her feet and ran for the bathroom. Amos slitted his eyes in outrage and watched when she returned, halting and shaky, pausing in the kitchen to run herself a glass of water and take a couple of soda crackers from a box on the counter.

"I don't know why they call it morning sickness, Amos," she muttered, picking the big cat up again and smiling as he settled himself on her lap with a long-suffering sigh. "I seem to get it worse in the evening, actually. But it's the funniest thing, Amos, you know? I mean, I feel so sick I could die, and then I throw up, and then a few minutes later I'm just fine. Totally spry and chipper again, like nothing ever happened. I've never experienced anything like it."

Amos stretched and luxuriated in her lap, eyes half-closed, kneading his paws against her leg.

Sarah looked down at him and felt a sudden desolate wave of loneliness. She had such a longing these days to talk to somebody about all the wondrous things that were happening to her. She wanted to share the miracle and mystery of birth, but there was nobody in her life to act as confidant. In fact, nobody but her doctor even knew she was pregnant.

Two weeks had passed since the day on the ski hill with Jim and Maude and the children, and in that time Sarah had been back to the apartment twice in the daytime to visit the little ones, but had carefully avoided any further encounter with Jim Fleming.

She realized with gratitude that he was continuing to respect her privacy, and had refrained from calling her even though he'd coaxed her into giving him her phone number. Sarah told herself she was glad he was leaving her alone. After all, if he should become deeply involved in her life now, it would lead to all kinds of complications.

But still, sometimes, she felt so lonely. . . .

In spite of herself Sarah gave a wistful look at the telephone. Just as she did so, it rang, startling her so much that she jumped and dislodged Amos, who gave her a bitter look and stalked away into the kitchen.

"Hello?" she said.

"Hi, Sarah. What are you doing on this snowy night?"

"Jim!" Sarah hesitated, dismayed by the warm glow that crept through her whole body at the sound of his voice. Then she felt a flicker of alarm. "Is something the matter, Jim? Are the kids—?"

"No problem," he said. "Everybody's fine."

Sarah winced as a sudden burst of noise and merriment erupted in the background, sounding clearly along the telephone wire.

"In fact," Jim went on, "there's a bit of a party going on here. Clarence . . . that's the doorman, remember?"

"The one who has a crush on Maude?"

"Right," he said, chuckling. "Well, he organized a canasta tournament with another couple, just to get close to Maude, I think. They're having it up here at my place."

"I see," Sarah murmured, still distracted by the sweet, wild surge of excitement that tinted her cheeks and made her heart race.

"So," Jim went on casually, "I have a baby-sitter for the evening. Four of them, in fact. They're going to be here for hours."

"I . . . I see," Sarah whispered again, feeling helpless in the grip of her tumultuous emotions.

"And I wondered if I could come over to see you for a little while. There's something I'd like to talk over with you, about the kids, actually."

Sarah felt another twinge of alarm, and a sudden, panicky feeling, but suppressed it firmly. "All right," she said after a moment's hesitation. "All right, that's fine. Are you coming right away?"

"If I may? I mean, I'm not interrupting some kind of vital scientific endeavor, am I?"

"I'm combing my cat," Sarah said, and then smiled at his hearty burst of laughter.

"Well, that's interesting. I always wondered what scientists did in their free time," he said. "I'll be right over, okay, Sarah?"

"Okay," she said, and hung up slowly, letting her hand rest gently on the telephone receiver for a long time before she suddenly turned pale and raced for the bathroom again.

Sarah was so preoccupied with recovering her poise and hiding all traces of sickness that she had no time to change her clothes or tidy her hair before the doorbell rang. She hurried to open it and stood gazing mutely up at Jim Fleming, who stood tall and smiling in the porch light, his broad shoulders dusted with snow.

As always, the reality of the man was almost overwhelming, even though Sarah spent a good deal of her time thinking about him. She forced herself to smile, held the door open and murmured, "Hello, Jim. Please come in. It's so cold out, isn't it?"

He grinned and walked past her, shaking out his jacket, smiling at her sweatpants and socks and her long, casual braid. Then he paused, gazing with delight at her living room. The sunken space was cozy and inviting, dimly illuminated by the warm glow of the fire, filled with soft strains of music.

"This," Jim said with a blissful sigh, "is beautiful, Sarah. Just beautiful. I take it you like horses," he added with another warm grin, eyeing her collection.

"My favorite animal," Sarah said, hanging his jacket away. "Would you like coffee or something? Hot chocolate?" she added, trying not to think about food or drink very much and hoping fervently that he would refuse her offer.

"No thanks. This is great. And so quiet and peaceful," he added, seating himself comfortably in one of the padded leather chairs near the fire. "But you're right, after all," he added, looking around.

"About what?" Sarah asked.

"About it being too small for the kids. It's just like a little doll's house, this place. I can see the whole house right from where I'm sitting, can't I?"

"Pretty well," Sarah said, smiling. "And what you see is all there is. No yard, no basement, just this little main floor and a loft."

"What's in the loft?"

"My bedroom," Sarah said, and then flushed warmly as his bright blue eyes met hers. "You said . . . you said you wanted to talk about the kids?" she ventured, sitting down opposite him and tucking her stockinged feet under her. Amos appeared from the kitchen, gave Jim a slit-eyed look of hatred and leapt into Sarah's lap with an arrogant, proprietorial air.

"Same to you, buddy," Jim told him cheerfully.

"He's a very rude cat," Sarah said. "He's just awful to me, but then he gets jealous if anybody else is even talking to me."

"Well," Jim said, gazing at her lovely, shadowed features, "I can't say I blame him, Sarah."

She flushed and looked down at the cat, toying with his silky fur. Her eyelashes cast dark fans of shadow on her warm cheeks, and her face was delicately tinted by the glow of the fire.

Jim watched her for a moment in silence, drew himself together and said, "I'm in real trouble, Sarah. I don't know what to do."

"About the children, you mean?"

He nodded, gazing into the fire with a brooding expression. "It's the same old story. This is the end of January, Sarah. At best I can only keep them at my place for another few weeks. I can't find anyone to sublet the place, so I can't get out of my lease, and I can't get a mortgage with those payments to make. If I don't find somewhere for them to live, and find it soon, I don't know what's going to happen."

"But you don't want them to go somewhere temporary and then have to move again, do you?"

"Not if I can help it. God, I wish there was some place. . . ."

Sarah hesitated, still toying idly with Amos's velvety ears.

She wanted passionately to offer her house, but her rational mind knew it was impossible. Her pregnancy seemed much more of a reality to her now that she was suffering from morning sickness. The life within her was a real entity, a living, growing, developing human being that would soon need its own space. It was Sarah's responsibility to protect that space, to provide a comfortable, secure home for her child.

And part of protecting this child involved keeping its existence a secret from the man by the fire. No matter how genial and attractive he might be, he was a threat to her baby. He could turn on Sarah at any moment, lay claim to the baby, demand the right to be a full-time father, to interfere with Sarah's decisions about the child's upbringing, even to sue for custody.

Sarah shivered in the warmth of the small room and felt a familiar, dismaying wave of nausea.

"Ex-excuse me," she muttered in panic, dumped Amos on the floor again and raced for the bathroom.

When she returned, pale and trembling, Jim was watching her in alarm.

"Sarah! Are you all right? What's the matter?"

"Nothing," she said, trying to smile. "Just a touch of the flu that's going around. It's really awful."

"I know," he said, still concerned. "Half my staff has it, and I keep worrying that I'll take it home to the kids, but so far they're just fine."

"Jim," Sarah said after a moment's silence, "may I ask you something?"

"Sure."

"It's about your father," Sarah said, avoiding his eyes, trying to keep her voice casual. "I mean, I know you two are at odds, but I wonder if you'd mind telling me why."

Jim gazed at her, his face cold and grim in the dim light. "He killed my mother," he said abruptly.

Sarah's eyes widened.

"Not like that," Jim said. "I mean, not with a gun or something. But he still killed her, as surely as if he'd taken a weapon to her. He killed her by the way he treated her. She died of a broken heart."

"And how old were you?"

"Thirteen when she died. God," he added softly, "how I hated the old man for that. I'll never stop hating him."

Sarah nodded, chilled by the bitter depths in his blue eyes. "Did you ever talk to him about it? Tell him how you felt, or anything?"

"I have nothing to say to him, Sarah. Please don't talk about him anymore, all right? He has nothing to do with me. Let's change the subject."

Sarah nodded again, falling lightly in with his animated conversation about her collection of horses. But a tiny seed of an idea was growing in her mind, and she determined to examine it more carefully after he was gone.

They spent a long time in front of the fire, talking and laughing, discussing thoughts and dreams and ideas. Sarah, normally so private and withdrawn, was amazed at how easy it was to talk with this man, and how readily she was able to confide in him. He seemed to understand her instantly, almost without words.

But her deepest, sweetest secret she held close to her heart, determined that he would never know. Even if she had to run away for a few months, no matter what she had to do, Sarah was going to keep Jim Fleming from realizing that she carried his child. It was the only way she could guarantee safety and independence for herself and her baby. She still wasn't taken in by his pleasantness and understanding, because her primitive mother instincts kept telling her that he could rapidly become an enemy, a threat to her child, and Sarah wasn't going to allow that to happen. Not ever.

Still, when he finally got up to leave, she felt a tug of regret. She moved over to the door beside him, handed him his jacket and watched in silence as he put it on.

He paused, his hand on the doorknob, looking down at her. Then he reached out, put his hands on her shoulders and drew her close to him. Sarah shivered as his strong arms went around her, and she felt his body straining against hers, felt the warmth of his breath on her skin, felt his lips searching for hers.

She melted into his embrace, helpless and weak, loving the feeling of his nearness, the strength of his hands moving over her body, the warmth as he lifted her shirt and explored her silky naked skin. His hands moved gently around and up her sides, cupping her breasts while his lips roamed over her face, kissing her cheeks, her eyelids, her earlobes, the hollow of her neck.

Sarah felt herself burning, melting, drifting on a warm, rich sea of desire. Her body remembered their union, the sweet thrill of his lovemaking, the wonderful, satisfying fulfillment of him, and she wanted him again, more than anything.

Suddenly another wave of nausea clutched at her. She barely had time to tear herself from his arms and make it down the hall to the bathroom.

When she returned, he was standing by the door with a rueful grin. "I guess that's not so good, right? Are you saying I make you sick, Sarah Burnard?"

Sarah gave him a shaky smile. "Not really," she whispered, unable to meet his eyes.

He watched her in concerned silence for a moment, then reluctantly took his leave, striding down the snowy path under the street lamps.

Sarah stood gazing after him through a crack in the door, her heart pounding, her body gripped with a longing so sudden and intense that she had to bite her lip to keep from crying out.

CHAPTER NINE

IN MID-FEBRUARY a warm chinook wind came howling down out of the mighty Canadian Rockies and danced across the icy plains, melting the snow and warming the sky to sapphire, teasing moisture and freshness from the frozen prairie. Sparkling streams of water flowed though deep coulees into shallow, sunlit lakes, and small snowbound animals appeared miraculously from nowhere, playing and frisking through the tall, damp grass as joyously as if springtime had arrived.

Sarah's mood changed with the weather, becoming buoyant and optimistic, full of hope and delight at the new life within her. Even her morning sickness grew more tolerable. The discomfort didn't actually go away, but it settled into a regular, first-thing-in-the-morning kind of occurrence that no longer interfered much with all the activities of her busy day.

On a balmy, breezy Saturday afternoon she drove into the country outside Calgary, delighting at the space and vistas all around her, the land rolling off to the distant mountains and the blue sky soaring into infinity. She felt free and young, so light and joyous that if she were to leave her car and run across the prairie, she might just lift and glide on the warm air currents like an eagle.

But when she turned down a long, tree-lined drive toward a mansion that stood at the end partly obscured by a screen of bare, blackened poplar branches, her mood changed again. She felt tense and breathless, even frightened by what she was about to do.

"Nerves," she muttered aloud, gripping the wheel so tightly that her knuckles whitened. "Pregnant-lady nerves, that's all."

She parked in the curving front drive, trying not to feel intimidated by the looming bulk of the big stone house in front of her, standing silent and withdrawn in the winter sunlight, its glittering leaded-glass windows sheltered by discreet, expensive draperies.

Somewhere in the distance beyond the sprawl of well-kept outbuildings she heard the muffled sound of a dog barking followed by the low, outraged bellow of some large animal, probably a bull. The homely noises were somehow reassuring. Sarah took a deep breath, laced her fingers nervously through the leather strap of her handbag and rang the bell.

After what seemed like a long time, the door was answered and Sarah stood gazing at the beautiful woman on the threshold. She was small and brisk, wearing a faded denim jumpsuit with a large patch on one knee, her vivid graying hair caught up in a careless knot on top of her head. In her arms she held a fluffy golden puppy, which looked up at Sarah with the same expression of cheerful curiosity.

The woman's blue eyes were so much like Jim Fleming's that Sarah was struck speechless, her throat dry and tight. She hesitated awkwardly in the doorway, searching for words.

"Hello?" the woman said politely in a sweet, husky voice. "May I help you?"

"Yes, please," Sarah murmured. "My name is Sarah Burnard, and I'm a...a friend of Jim's. Jim Fleming,

I mean. I'd like to... to speak for a moment with Senator Fleming, if I may."

The small woman's beautiful blue eyes widened, and she stood aside, frowning at the puppy that squirmed suddenly in her arms, trying in vain to lick her ear.

"Samson, you *stop* that," she whispered furiously, and then smiled apologetically at Sarah. "He was the runt of the litter," she explained, "and I babied him a lot. I'm afraid he's completely spoiled. I'm Maureen Fleming," she added, extending a small, calloused hand from beneath the puppy. "I'm Jim's aunt."

"I know," Sarah murmured. "He talks about you a lot. He really loves you."

Maureen Fleming's fine features softened, and she smiled. "Please," she said, "come with me to the library. I'll call my brother."

Sarah followed her hostess, still feeling hot and tense, hoping desperately that she wasn't going to be sick. Maureen led her into a comfortable square room lined with books and warmed by a flickering wood fire on the hearth. Sarah sank gratefully into one of the big worn leather chairs and shook her head hastily at the other woman's offer of coffee.

"Oh, no, thank you," she murmured. "I won't be staying long. I just wanted a brief word with Senator Fleming, if he's not too busy."

"Certainly. He's just outside talking with the foreman. He'll be in directly."

After the other woman left, Sarah waited nervously, looking around at the richness of the room in which she found herself. Old polished oak gleamed around the hearth and on the mantel, and small pieces of bronze statuary stood carelessly about. Some of them were horses, and Sarah studied them with a keen collector's eye, knowing that each of them must be worth a small fortune. Many of the books were calf-bound and looked much read. One paneled wall was empty of books, and the small framed paintings that hung there appeared incredibly old and valuable.

There was no doubt, she thought, that Jim Fleming had grown up in great beauty and luxury. She thought of his apartment as she had last seen it—crowded with baby equipment, messy and cluttered with children's toys and piles of clothing. Involuntarily her throat tightened with sympathy.

Just then the door opened and a man entered.

Sarah gripped the arms of the chair and gazed up at him, wide-eyed and startled. She had known about his appearance, of course, from seeing him in pictures, but the reality of the man was so much more impressive. And Senator Jameson Fleming was the image of his son. He not only looked like Jim, he *was* Jim, miraculously recaptured from some time in the future. He had the same wide shoulders and tall, sturdy build, the same fine, aquiline features and astonishing blue eyes, the same firm jaw softened by that charming, incongruous dimple.

Sarah was assailed by a sudden almost suffocating sense of family, of dynasties and legacies and physical continuity. She realized that this was precisely what she had most feared, the sense of powerful connectedness between father and son and the child in her womb. She had been terrified of the wealth and influence of these people, their sense of family, their possible and quite legitimate claim to her own child.

And yet now here she was in the man's home, having sought him out of her own free will. The whole thing made no sense. Why was she here? Sarah shook her head, trying to clear her thoughts, trying to organize her scattered impressions.

She realized in dismay that the man who looked so much like Jim was still standing near his desk, regarding her with a look of courteous inquiry. Sarah forced herself to meet those piercing blue eyes, feeling faint and confused. Jameson Fleming brought with him an aura of freshness and outdoors, a clean scent of hay and animals. He wore high polished riding boots, worn to a silky sheen, and soft faded denims, and looked every inch the gentleman farmer. Arching one dark eyebrow, he extended a finely shaped brown hand and smiled politely.

"Miss Burnard? My sister tells me you're acquainted with my son, but I doubt that he's aware of your visit here."

"No," Sarah murmured, watching as the senator moved around the desk to seat himself in a high-backed oaken chair. "No, Jim doesn't know I've come to see you. He'd be . . . very upset if he knew."

Jameson Fleming smiled dryly, but when he met her eyes Sarah was struck by the bleak pain in those vivid blue depths.

The older man's glance was so revealing, so eloquent in its unspoken suffering, that Sarah began to recover her poise and concern herself more with the man opposite the desk.

"Jim's in trouble," she said briefly, and wasn't surprised to see an expression of instant alarm on the senator's craggy features. His eyes widened, and Sarah hastened to reassure him.

"Not like that," she said. "I mean, he's not sick or in trouble with the police or anything. But he has a real problem, and none of us has any idea how to deal with it."

Senator Fleming listened in silence, toying with a paperweight made of a huge gold nugget set in black onyx, while Sarah told him about the three children, about Jim's impulsive acquisition of them and his subsequent struggle to keep them together and provide a home for them.

The man across the desk looked so intelligent and sympathetic, so full of humor and understanding, that Sarah found herself telling him a good deal more than she had intended, although, of course, she carefully omitted any mention of the reason she had been with Jim Fleming on that particular evening. After she finished her story, she waited in silence, looking awkwardly at the polished expanse of wood between them.

Finally she glanced up at Jameson, who shook his head and gave her a rueful grin. "I must say I'm completely amazed by what you're saying," he told her slowly. "I just can't believe it's my son you're talking about. The boy I remember was much too self-absorbed to inconvenience himself by becoming involved in the problems of a trio of abandoned children."

"That's just it," Sarah said earnestly, leaning forward. "He's not the boy you remember any longer, Senator Fleming. He's a man well past thirty, and he's probably changed in a lot of ways over the years. And," she added, shocked by her own boldness, "I wouldn't be surprised to learn that you've changed a good deal, too. I think it's likely that both of you have."

She paused, holding her breath while the man's face tightened and looked grim, his blue eyes turning to ice. Then, surprisingly, he smiled.

"You think so, do you? Well, you may be right. You're an interesting young lady, Miss Burnard. I certainly applaud my son's taste in women."

Sarah flushed painfully. "I'm not...it's not like that," she said. "There's nothing romantic between Jim and me, Senator Fleming. We're just friends, and even that is entirely because of the children. And I came to see you today because I wanted...to understand the situation a little better, that's all."

"Does my son want my help with these children?" the senator asked bluntly, his gaze direct and disconcerting. "Is that what this is all about? Does he want to give him the money to provide them with adequate housing?"

Sarah looked back at him, once again a little intimidated by the man's overwhelming air of power and command, the instinctive authority of his manner.

"No," she said. "To be honest, that was my suggestion, but Jim rejects it absolutely."

Once more she saw that flare of pain, that deep, deep hurt in the man's surprising blue eyes. Sarah drew a long breath.

"What happened, sir?" she asked softly. "What really happened between you and your son all those years ago?"

The senator raked her with a sharp glance and then turned his chair a little to look out the window at the rolling acres of his small holding.

"What answer does Jim give to that question?" he asked.

"He says you made his mother very unhappy," Sarah answered quietly. "He says he can never forgive you for the way you treated her."

The older man turned back to look steadily at Sarah, his tanned face silent and drawn beneath the shock of silver hair. He nodded silently, and Sarah watched him, waiting for him to speak.

"Cecile was certainly an unhappy woman," Jameson said finally, gazing moodily out the window once more, his eyes dark with memories. "When I was younger, I felt guilty over it, felt that I had failed her somehow, and if I'd been a better man, she would have been happy with me. In later years, " he added with a small, bitter smile, "I came to realize that nothing and nobody in the world could have made her happy. But by then, of course, it was much too late."

Sarah stared at him, stunned by the pain on his face, unable to find any words of response.

"I could have forgiven her the scenes and the tantrums, the many, many times she hurt me and embarrassed me in public," Jameson went on. "What I could never forgive was the way she used the boy in her battles with me and turned my own son against me out of spite and selfishness."

"Is that the way it happened?" Sarah asked, her mouth dry. "Is Jim really so mistaken, sir, about what actually happened?"

Jameson Fleming regarded her directly, his face intent and thoughtful. "We all have our own versions of the truth, Miss Burnard, and we see things through our own eyes, usually to our own advantage. As a result, truth is often a very difficult thing to determine. But as far as I am able to understand, and believe me, I've given it many years of thought, what I'm telling you is the truth."

He hesitated, toying with the costly paperweight once more, and then looked up at Sarah as if coming to some kind of decision.

She met his eyes silently, her face white with tension, waiting for him to go on.

"Cecile was beautiful," he said finally, "and a woman of rare charm when she chose to be. She was the kind of woman who knew how to arouse all the protective instincts in any male, including her own son. Jim adored her, and she encouraged him, urged him to side with her, appealed to all the gallantry and idealism of a young adolescent boy, convincing him that he was her only friend and I was an enemy to both of them. He had to bear all the burden of her pain and unhappiness—far too great a burden for a sensitive and impressionable young boy."

Sarah stared at the man opposite her. "Was there...was there nothing you could do?" she whispered finally.

He shook his silver head regretfully. "God knows, I tried. I argued with her, pleaded with her, tried to talk with him, get him away into a more wholesome setting, but the damage was too deep. I was the villain as far as he was concerned, and he came to hate even being in the same room with me."

He fell silent abruptly.

Sarah waited, gazing cautiously at his patrician profile as he stared out the broad windows.

"What happened in the end?" she asked finally.

"She killed herself when Jim was thirteen," the senator said tonelessly. "She took a razor and opened her wrists, making sure that Jim would be the one to find her and the note she left in which she blamed me for everything."

Sarah stared at him, appalled. "But..." she whispered. "But she must have known how awful that would be for a young boy. How could...?"

"How could any normal loving mother do such a thing to her child?" Jameson Fleming echoed bitterly. "Is that what you're asking me, Miss Burnard? Well, believe me, I don't know. I could forgive her everything else, because she really was a terribly troubled and unhappy woman. But I've never been able to forgive that final monstrous act of selfishness and cruelty."

He was silent again, his brown, veined hands trembling slightly against the polished surface of his desk. At last he glanced back up at Sarah, trying to smile. "Once again," he said, "I must try to be fair. I don't believe I'm the villain of the piece, but I'm not totally without blame, Miss Burnard. Much of what Jim says *is* true. I was selfish, I was wrapped up in my career, I neglected my family, I was addicted to my work and I didn't spend as much time with him as I should have when he was small. Those things are absolutely true."

Sarah looked back at him, her gray eyes calm and level. "Those are mistakes, Senator Fleming, that many men make. But in my opinion they're not such terrible crimes that you should be cut out of your son's life for the rest of your days because of them."

He returned her gaze in startled silence for a moment, and then his face twisted with sudden pain and he looked away abruptly. "My sister tells me the same thing," he murmured, his voice unsteady. "But you have no idea how good it feels to hear those particular words coming from a woman like you, Miss Burnard, who is also a friend of my son."

Sarah was silent for a moment, looking down and toying with the strap of her handbag to allow him time to regain his composure.

"You really love him, don't you?" she said finally, her voice soft. "I wish he could understand that."

Jameson Fleming sighed. "There's never a day goes by that I don't think of him, wonder what my son is doing and if he's well," he said simply. "The most precious, vitally important thing in my life is gone, and I'll never get it back."

The sadness in his voice, the weary slump to those broad shoulders and the anguish in his blue eyes, so like Jim's, were suddenly more than Sarah could bear.

"There's something I'd like to tell you, Senator Fleming," she said, aghast at herself, unable to believe what she was doing. But she knew she couldn't stop herself.

He gave her a questioning glance, clearly struck by the sudden, taut seriousness of her voice.

Sarah drew a deep breath, sat erect clutching her handbag tightly in her lap and looked directly at the older man. "I'm two months pregnant, Senator. The child I'm carrying is Jim's. It's your grandchild."

He stared at her, thunderstruck, hope and disbelief both showing plainly on his aristocratic face. But when he spoke his voice was harsh. "Why have you come here, young lady? What do you want, exactly? Is it money?"

Understanding the emotions that racked him, Sarah was unable to be angry at his words. Quietly she explained what had happened, how she had decided to have a child, chosen Jim Fleming as the father and managed to get herself pregnant without his knowledge.

Jameson stared at her, astounded. "And he still doesn't know?"

Sarah shook her head.

"But...but why?" he asked, still bewildered. "Why such a calculated, cold-blooded approach? And why my son in particular?"

"I'm a botanical geneticist, Mr. Fleming. I have a doctorate, in fact, and I'm deeply involved in research at the moment. Genetics and heredity are extremely important to me."

His weathered face sparkled with sudden humor and understanding. "And you chose the Flemings as likely genetic specimens. Is that the idea? Good hardy Scots stock?"

"Exactly," Sarah said, smiling back at him.

Jameson Fleming appeared to set aside all of his earlier emotion, throwing his head back and laughing heartily. "Miss Burnard," he said finally, wiping his eyes and chuckling, "you are a rare treat. You are certainly a bright spot in a dull world today."

"I think you'd better call me Sarah," she said calmly. "After all, I'm going to be the mother of your grandchild, aren't I?"

The old man's vivid blue eyes kindled with sudden fire, and he gazed at her, his face taut with feeling once more. "Yes," he whispered finally. "Yes, it seems that you are. Why haven't you told Jim about this, Sarah? Why all the secrecy?"

"I was afraid," she said simply. "I want a baby, more than anything, and I wanted this particular genetic pool for a variety of reasons. But I didn't want Jim or his family to know because I can't bear the thought of anyone making claims on my baby. It's *my* baby," she concluded fiercely, staring at him, her gray eyes blazing. "Nobody else's, just mine. I can't bear the thought of custody battles or joint visitation or that sort of thing. And especially after I saw how involved Jim got with these three children, just after one meeting, I've been so afraid that he might—"

She broke off abruptly, biting her lip and staring down at her hands.

Jameson Fleming gazed thoughtfully at her bent head. "Then, Sarah," he asked softly, "why have you told me? Aren't you afraid of me, too?"

"Yes," she said honestly, looking up to meet his gaze again. "Of course I am. I know how much power and influence you have, and I know I'm taking a big risk by telling you. But I feel—" Her voice broke and then steadied. "I feel so sad for you, Senator Fleming, because of the choice Jim has made, and the way it makes you feel. I just wanted you to know about your grandchild and to make a sort of...agreement with you, I guess."

"What sort of agreement?"

Sarah drew a deep breath. "If you'll promise," she began, "absolutely *promise* not to interfere or ever make any kind of legal claim on my baby or anything like that..."

She paused and cast a questioning glance at the powerful man across the desk. He nodded quietly, waiting for her to go on.

"Under those conditions," Sarah said, "then I would agree to give you regular access to the baby, allow you to be a part of her life. I don't want money from you," she added hastily. "I have a good job, and I'm very secure financially. I can afford to provide comfortably for my child and hire live-in care while I'm working. I guess what I'm saying," she concluded lamely, "is that I just think you deserve the chance to be a grandfather, Senator Fleming.''

When she looked up at him, she was deeply moved to see the expression on his rugged face and the tears that gathered in his eyes. He brushed at them impatiently with his hand and struggled to compose himself.

''Sarah Burnard,'' he murmured finally, ''you've made an old man very happy today. I'm afraid you'll never know just how much this means to me.''

Sarah swallowed hard, feeling her own eyes begin to sting warmly. She smiled at him in gentle silence, and then remembered something. ''Senator,'' she said warningly, ''I still don't want Jim to know about this.''

''About what? About your visit to see us or about the baby or what?''

''About anything,'' Sarah said firmly.

The senator gave her a shrewd glance. ''You're a slender, elegant woman, Sarah Burnard. You aren't going to be able to conceal a pregnancy indefinitely. And I understand that you see my son regularly.''

Sarah flushed, but met his eyes steadily. ''It was just a . . . a casual sexual encounter that we had,'' she murmured awkwardly. ''What's known as a one-night-stand. He thinks . . . he believes that I do that sort of thing all the time. There'll be no reason for him to conclude absolutely that this is his child, if I don't tell him.''

''Well,'' Jameson said with a sudden edge of bitterness to his voice, ''there's not much likelihood that I'll be telling him, Sarah. I don't even see him from one year to the next.''

Sarah got to her feet, looking steadily at the man opposite her. ''Then it'll be our secret?''

''Well . . .'' Jameson hesitated. ''I *would* like your permission to tell my sister Maureen. She's very discreet," he said with a fond smile, "and this news is going to delight her more than anything in the world."

Sarah paused and then nodded. "Of course, if she promises not to tell Jim. You sister seems like a real darling," she added impulsively.

"She is. She certainly is. This baby of yours," Jameson said with another shining smile, "will have the fondest, most indulgent grandpa and auntie in all the world, Sarah. I can promise you that."

Sarah's eyes misted again, and she smiled back at him. She still felt frightened, apprehensive, deeply shocked by what she had done. She could foresee all kinds of problems and complications in the future, all kinds of repercussions that would inevitably arise from her actions this day.

But, gazing into the joyous depths of the old man's wise blue eyes, she still knew absolutely that telling him about her baby had been the right thing to do.

NEAR THE END of the following week the weather changed again. The mercury plunged to the bottom of the thermometer and stuck there until well into March, so bitterly cold that the very air seemed to freeze and crack in the blue-white stillness. At night houses stood silent and withdrawn, glowing faintly behind frost-painted windows like fragile shells protecting their occupants from the icy fury of the elements.

Sarah cuddled in an easy chair by her fireplace, frowning through her heavy-rimmed glasses at the enigmatic symbols of the knitting pattern on her lap, trying to remember if "pss" meant "purl second stitch," or "pass slip stitch."

"I think," she said aloud to Amos, who lay spread-eagled in front of the fireplace like a small furry rug, "that it has to refer to the slip stitch, doesn't it? Otherwise how could—"

The doorbell rang and she glanced up blankly, wondering who could possibly be out soliciting on this bitter night. Then, hastily, she jammed the tiny white jacket she was knitting into her bag, folded the pattern book beside it and padded across to answer the door.

Jim Fleming stood there, holding a couple of laden grocery bags, his blond hair gleaming in the light, his big, solid body filling the doorway while the breath came from his mouth in frosty white clouds.

"Jim!" Sarah said, gazing up at him wide-eyed. "What on earth—?"

"God, you look cute in those glasses," he said, smiling down at her fondly. "Have you had your supper yet?"

"Well, not exactly, just a slice of toast a while ago, but I'm not really—"

"Aha! Just as I suspected," he said cheerfully. "You've been looking awfully thin and pale these days, Dr. Burnard, and I've been fairly certain you're working too hard and not getting enough to eat. Let me in, why don't you, before the wine freezes?"

"Does wine freeze?" Sarah asked, standing aside to let him in and watching while he set the bags carefully on the floor, stamped the snow from his boots and stripped off his heavy down-filled jacket.

"I don't know. I would assume that it does. You're the scientist," he said, picking up his bags again. "Where's the kitchen?"

Sarah gazed at him, still confused by his sudden arrival and the way his big body and his golden masculinity filled her whole house with light and warmth. Her heart began to pound, and she struggled to sound cool and collected.

"May I ask," she said dryly, "just what you think you're doing?"

"You may," he said equably, following her toward the kitchen. "I'm visiting for the evening, and I propose to make you the best omelet you've ever tasted and force you to eat every bite of it. I hope you have a microwave."

"Why?" Sarah asked, still a little stunned by his presence and his cheery air of command.

"Because, dummy," Jim said, setting his bags carefully on the shining kitchen counter, "a microwave is the best thing that's happened to the omelet since the egg. You don't have to flip it, you see. It just cooks through smoothly and perfectly, top to bottom, and makes the chef look extremely professional. I trust you have basic tools like whisks and spatulas? Or is this place just equipped with Bunsen burners and petri dishes?"

Sarah chuckled in spite of herself, showing him her well-stocked cutlery drawer and then watching with interest while he unpacked brown eggs, fresh mushrooms, cheddar cheese, romaine lettuce, a thick loaf of fragrant garlic bread.

Her mouth began to water, and she realized with a little shock of surprise that she hadn't experienced any morning sickness for several days now, and that she was, in fact, ravenously hungry.

"That all looks so good, Jim," she said with a little sigh. "You're right. I haven't been eating much lately, and I'm just starved all of a sudden."

Jim smiled down at her and bent casually to kiss her cheek. Sarah's face flamed at the warmth and spontaneity of his unexpected gesture. She seated herself awkwardly on one of the kitchen stools, looking at the assortment of groceries.

"Just give me a few minutes, my pretty lady," he said cheerfully, "and I'll serve you a repast worthy of the princess that you are."

"You're so corny," she said automatically, feeling absurdly pleased by his words and suddenly deeply happy to be with him. "How did you get away?"

"You mean," he asked, glancing up from where he knelt before an open cupboard, "why am I not baby-sitting tonight and tending to my responsibilities? Do you have a metal mixing bowl, by the way?"

"Next door over, lower shelf. Yes, that's what I mean. I thought you said last week that Billy was getting rather edgy and you were afraid to leave the kids alone for a minute these days."

Jim found the bowl, placed it on the counter and began to break eggs into it, his handsome face darkening with concern.

"He is. He's getting really tense and nervous, knowing how much hassle I'm having finding a place to live in, and I'm scared what he might do." Jim paused in his vigorous whisking of the eggs, added some seasoning salt and looked up at Sarah, his blue eyes troubled. "That place didn't work out," he told her. "The one I was hoping for, remember? There were no schools nearby, and I hated the thought of Ellie riding for an hour on some damn bus. Besides, it was just as cramped and ugly as all the others."

"Oh, Jim," Sarah murmured. "I'm sorry to hear that. I know how much you were counting on it."

She watched as he took a heavy cast-iron skillet from the drawer under the stove, set it on the burner, tossed in a pat of butter and began to slice mushrooms with casual expertise.

"What now?" she asked finally. "What will you do?"

He shrugged. "Not much choice. No place that's halfway decent will take kids, and if they do, there's a six-month waiting list. As soon as I get back, we're moving into a motel with a kitchen and we'll just wait until something comes up."

Sarah absorbed this information in silence and then looked up, startled. "Get-back? Are you going away? Where are you going?"

Once again his face glowed with fondness and he reached out to pat her cheek. "For a bright girl," he observed, "you're really quite slow sometimes, you know that? Yes," he added, slicing green onions in with his mushrooms, "I'm going away. To Europe, as a matter of fact. I hope you like onions."

"Love them," Sarah said absently, still watching his skillful brown hands. "Why are you going to Europe?"

"On a buying trip," he said briskly. "You wouldn't believe it, kid. Athletic clothing these days is as haute couture as evening wear. I have to buy running shoes at fashion houses as fancy as Dior, where they serve little canapés and chilled champagne in crystal goblets."

Sarah giggled at the image, then sobered. "How long will you be gone? When are you leaving?"

"About ten days, and first thing tomorrow morning. That's why I'm able to be here. Maude is staying with the kids, and she moved in today since I'll be up and gone early in the morning. Why do you look so troubled, pretty lady? Don't tell me you're actually going to *miss* me?"

"Of course not," Sarah said firmly. "It's just that all this is going on ... I mean, you're moving into a motel, Billy's all upset, you're going away for ten days, and nobody ever tells me anything."

"It's hard to tell somebody anything," Jim said calmly, "when they shut themselves up in a laboratory for eighteen hours a day and refuse to return calls."

Sarah blushed. "I'm sorry, Jim. It's just that we're on the edge of a real breakthrough. We've developed this incredibly hardy strain, with all the right indicators, but we can't seem to get it to—oh," she added, interrupting herself, "that smells just heavenly! I'm so hungry!"

He paused, holding a spatula and looking thoughtfully at her shining face, her huge gray eyes alight with happiness, her slender, shapely body in a casual sweater and slacks. With a visible effort he collected himself and grinned.

"Then why don't you help a bit?" he said with forced lightness. "Make yourself useful, woman. Set the table, and put out some wineglasses. And salad dressing."

Sarah smiled, hurrying to obey, watching hungrily as he slid the fragrant omelet onto a serving dish and carried it to the table along with warmed slices of garlic bread and a hastily tossed salad.

"Do the kids know you're here?" she asked over her shoulder.

"Are you kidding? If they knew I was coming here, nothing on earth would have kept Ellie from coming along. And I wanted to be selfish just this once. I wanted you all to myself for a little while."

Sarah smiled nervously at this, uncertain how to respond, while Jim paused by the table to admire his handiwork.

"I told them I was working late at the office, getting ready for my trip. A harmless lie, right? Now sit down and eat before this omelet caves in and makes me look bad."

Sarah seated herself opposite him, eating the delicious meal with enormous appetite while he looked over at her placidly. Once again she was struck by the ease and pleasure of his company, the way their conversation sparkled and flowed, the comforting manner in which he seemed to understand her instantly and the way he laughed so heartily at all her jokes.

"Come on," he said, lifting his wineglass as they finished their meal. "You haven't touched your wine yet, Dr. Burnard. Doesn't Riesling go with a mushroom omelet? Did I make a bad choice?"

"Oh, no," Sarah said, suddenly nervous. "It's just that I..." She hesitated, casting about for excuses. "It's just that I...I don't drink," she concluded desperately.

"Not at all?"

"No," she said. "Not much at all."

Not when I'm pregnant and entering the second trimester, she added silently. *Not for anything in the world.*

Jim was frowning, his blue eyes thoughtful. "But..." he began, and paused. "But the night I first met you in the bar, weren't you drinking then? I was sure you were nursing a drink most of the evening."

Sarah gazed at him, wide-eyed, searching frantically for a response. Suddenly she felt an almost overwhelming urge to tell him the truth, to tell him all about the baby. "Jim . . ." she began.

"Yes?"

This was crazy, Sarah thought firmly. All her efforts, ever since that fateful night, had been directed toward keeping her secret, holding him at arm's length. And now, after one pleasant evening, she was considering upsetting months of careful, meticulous planning.

"Thank you for the lovely meal," she said aloud, holding her wineglass up and taking a valiant sip. "Here's to the chef."

He smiled and toasted her silently, then turned to fetch the coffeepot from the counter. While his back was turned Sarah quickly poured the rest of her drink into the potted rubber tree by the table.

Her eyes shone and her cheeks glowed. She was warmed by the fun of their impromptu meal and pleased by the way he deliberately kept things light, tried to keep that disturbing, hard gleam of longing from tightening his face when he looked across the room at her.

They did the dishes together, still easy and companionable, talking about her work and his trip, about the children and the weather and their co-workers, laughing and interrupting each other while they tidied the kitchen.

Sarah found herself growing more and more conscious of him, with a warm, rising excitement and a deep, aching hunger that surprised her. She was sharply aware of his lean, muscular body, his finely molded lips, his firm brown hands. In troubled astonishment she realized that she wanted, more than anything, to feel his arms around her and his lips on hers, craved his touch and the feel of his naked skin burning against hers.

She looked up as they stood in the middle of the kitchen, her lips parted, her eyes full of the emotion she could no longer conceal, and he gazed down at her in wonder.

"Sarah," he whispered. "Oh, Sarah . . ."

Wordlessly she moved into his arms and clung to him, responding with fiery passion when he lifted her face and sought her lips with his. She didn't seem able to control herself, couldn't keep a check on her emotions, couldn't stop herself from burrowing into him, straining into the core of him, yearning with all her being toward the delicious fire and fulfillment she remembered, and knew that only he could give.

Swept away by her passion, he held her, murmuring broken endearments in her ear, kissing her eyelids, her earlobes, her mouth and neck, pulling her sweater aside to kiss the fragrant hollow of her throat.

Still without words, she drew him gently toward the stairs and began to climb silently up to her room while Jim followed her. His hands still caressed her slender, rounded hips as she mounted the stairs in front of him, and his handsome golden face was taut with passion and desire.

CHAPTER TEN

AT ABOUT THE SAME TIME that Jim and Sarah were finishing their mushroom omelet, Senator Jameson Fleming stood in the doorway of his luxurious living room, smiling at his sister. He was dressed with casual distinction in a tweed sport jacket, slacks and polished boots, topped by a leather coat with a wide silver fox collar. His gray hair shone like dull pewter in the firelight, and his tanned, handsome features were cheerful and composed.

He carried a black leather briefcase in one gloved hand and a giraffe under the other arm. The giraffe was enormous, at least four feet tall, beautifully constructed in a patchwork pattern of soft tan suede and white calfskin, with shining blue eyes, a benign, alert expression and long, flirtatious eyelashes.

"Well, I'm off, Mo," the senator said. "I'm meeting Jock and a couple of others at the Cattlemen's Club. One of them," he added, shifting the giraffe into a more comfortable position, "is apparently interested in supplying some party funding. Jock feels that he could potentially be a big contributor if we handle him just right."

Maureen glanced up from the creamy baby shawl she was working on, crochet hook poised, eyeing him thoughtfully over the gold rims of her granny glasses.

"I'm sure," she said dryly, "that they'll all be *very* impressed by the giraffe, Jamie. He's quite lovely."

Jameson shifted nervously on his feet and looked a little defensive. "I'm stopping off at Sarah's on the way to the club," he said. "The other day, when I dropped by the lab to see her, she mentioned that she was ready to begin decorating the nursery soon, and I spotted this fellow yesterday at Abercrombie and Fitch when I was in Edmonton. I just couldn't resist him, Mo. He's handmade, you know, imported from Guatemala."

Maureen continued to eye her brother thoughtfully, trying to control the little grin that tugged at the corners of her mouth. "Jamie," she said at last, "don't you think it would be more practical to give her... I don't know... a crib, or something?"

"To *Sarah?* You think she isn't already busy researching the various crib designs, comparing consumer reports, organizing all the scientific data to determine which crib is the safest and most effective? Believe me, Mo, this is a girl who wants to make that kind of decision for herself."

Maureen nodded, looking down at the soft length of wool on her knees, smoothing it thoughtfully with her calloused fingers. "I guess you're right," she said at last. "I just..."

"What, Mo?" her brother asked. "What's bothering you?"

"I don't know. I just think maybe it's risky, Jamie, you going to her house. What if Jim's there or something? We promised not to give away her secret, and I think we should be very careful to keep that promise as long as she wants us to."

"I agree. You're absolutely right. But I happen to know that he's not there."

"How do you know?" Maureen asked, leaning forward to poke at a blackened, smoldering log that was threatening to roll off the grate.

"I called his apartment, ready with some pretense if he was home. But one of those children answered the phone and said he was working late at the office tonight."

"Which one?" Maureen asked wistfully.

"I believe he only has one office, Mo. Do you really like the giraffe?"

"Jamie, that is absolutely without a doubt the most elegant and expensive giraffe that any baby ever received. I *meant*," she added, "which child answered the phone?"

Jameson stared at his sister in surprise. "I don't know which one, Mo. It sounded like a girl."

"Then it would be Ellie," Maureen said with a fond, private smile. "Billy's voice is already changing, getting quite deep."

Jameson continued to regard the small red-haired woman in astonishment while she shifted a little awkwardly under his gaze. "I've gone over to Jim's place a couple of times lately," she said, "just by chance, you know, and the children are always there, at least Ellie and the baby are. Billy comes and goes. You should see them, Jamie," she added, smiling fondly. "They're all such darlings. That fat little baby, so bright and happy, he's just learning to stand alone and reach for things. And Ellie is a lovely child, so sweet and quiet, and she looks after the baby like a real little mother."

Something in her voice, a subtle, hidden note of pain and yearning, made Jameson give her another sharp, thoughtful glance. But when he spoke, his voice was gentle. "You know that you can go there any time you want, Mo. You could get to know those kids, take them places, even bring them here, be a real auntie to them.''

Maureen looked up, her blue eyes dark with emotion. ''How could I bring them here, Jamie? Jim would never allow it. And as long as he's going to be that way, I know what side I'm going to be on. I don't approve of his attitude, Jamie, and he knows it. We've discussed it many times. And while he persists in treating you as he does, I don't like to involve myself in his life or go to his home when *you're* not welcome. There's such a thing as loyalty, after all.''

Jameson looked at her with affection, deeply moved by her words. ''There's also such a thing as divided loyalties, Mo,'' he said. ''I know you suffer from this whole situation as much as I do. Believe me, if it brings you pleasure, I'd be happy for you to involve yourself with these little waifs of Jim's. I wouldn't mind at all.''

Maureen shook her head sadly. ''Not unless he brings them here to see us. But seeing those children, even for a little while, make me realize how terribly much I've missed, Jamie. I wish I'd been able to have little ones of my own. Sometimes I feel so...''

She choked and looked down, gripping her yarn tightly while she fought to calm herself.

Jameson stood in the doorway, watching her quivering shoulders with helpless concern.

''Anyway,'' Maureen said, looking up finally and trying to smile as she smoothed her length of crochet work, ''we're going to have a baby to play with soon, Jamie. And Jim has no say in the matter at all.''

''None at all,'' Jameson agreed, smiling at her. He turned to go, and Maureen got up to wander over to the window, watching as he backed his big car out of the garage and into the floodlit yard. The giraffe sat in the passenger seat, looking out the window with cheerful alertness, its long, curly eyelashes silhouetted against the frosty moonlight.

The lines of pain and loneliness smoothed from Maureen's face, and she laughed, watching with a fond grin as the elegant, heavy car with its two unlikely occupants circled in front of the house and drove off through the moonlight. Then, still smiling, she returned to her crocheting.

THROUGHOUT THE CITY the same moonlight shone down with impartial radiance on frozen streets and alleys, on snow-covered yards and delicate, frosted shrubbery.

Soft silvery beams filtered through the heavy lace at Sarah's bedroom windows, casting a dappled, shifting glow over the two people on the bed. The room was still and washed with silver, silent except for their breathing and their occasional broken whispers.

Sarah moved above Jim's body, kissing his face and shoulders, lying across him in total abandonment as she felt him move within her, felt his hands caress her body with slow, languorous movements.

She marveled at his iron self-control, almost overcome by his deep, caring tenderness, by his overwhelming concern for her pleasure.

"Jim . . ." she whispered, eyes closed, face raised toward him.

"Shh," he murmured, holding her, stroking her rounded silken hips. "It's all right, Sarah. It's all right."

"But you're—" Then suddenly she fell silent. Overcome with pleasure she felt herself rising and falling, drowning and gasping in rippling waves of delight, felt herself soaring up to touch the sun and falling back to earth, warmed and sated and rich with joy. Beneath her, Jim, too, shuddered as he finally allowed himself the release he'd held back so long.

"Oh, God," she muttered when she was able to find her voice again. "Oh, my God," she repeated helplessly.

Jim laughed beneath her, still holding her and stroking her gently. With great tenderness he rolled her onto her back and cuddled her beside him, burying his face in her hair and holding her close in his big, hard-muscled arms.

"Do I understand you to say, pretty lady, that you found that a somewhat enjoyable experience?"

"Oh, God," Sarah repeated, still at a loss for words.

Jim chuckled again and raised himself on one elbow, gently tracing the line of her cheek and lips in the moonlight with his finger.

"Maybe you should do this more often, pretty lady," he whispered huskily.

Sarah smiled up at him. "Maybe I should," she whispered back. She regarded him with fondness, overcome by warm emotion. He was so tender, so considerate, such a generous and thoughtful lover, such an altogether loveable man.

"Jim," she whispered suddenly, "I want to talk."

"Sure," he said at once, pulling the bedclothes up and tucking them snugly over her shoulders, then his own. "Go ahead."

"Jim, about the kids... I don't want you to have to take them to a motel. I want you to bring them here."

"But, Sarah..." he began, his eyes widening in surprise.

Sarah reached up tenderly and covered his lips with her fingers. "No, Jim. Don't argue with me about this, because I mean it. You've made so many sacrifices already, and it's time you had some help. I don't want you to be forced to leave your apartment and go live in some shabby, crowded motel just so that they have a place to stay. It's not fair, that's all.''

He stared down at her, his eyes dark in the moonlight, his face thoughtful.

''They can come here,'' Sarah went on, ''and Maude can come over during the day to watch them, just like she does at your place, and you can stay in your apartment and have some peace and privacy for a change. And later on when—'' Sarah fell abruptly silent, realizing with a little shock of alarm that she had been on the verge of telling him about the baby.

But Jim didn't notice the break in her conversation. He was considering her words, his face dubious. ''There's no doubt,'' he began slowly, ''that it would be kind of wonderful to have some peace and privacy at home for a change. I certainly can't deny that. But, Sarah, I don't think you really know what you're giving up. It's a full-time job, kid, and it can be pretty wearing when you come home from work to that kind of chaos. You haven't actually experienced it, you know.''

''But you have. That's just what I mean, Jim. You've done your part, and now I think it's my turn for a while. It's only fair. Tell them I'll come over tomorrow,'' she added, ''in the morning after you leave to pick them up. Clarence can help us move their stuff and get them settled in here. He'll do anything if it involves getting to spend a couple of hours with Maude.''

Jim was still leaning on one elbow, absently stroking her hair while he thought about what she was saying. ''God knows, it's tempting,'' he said wistfully. ''But,'' he added with a sudden grin, "after a few days of that kind of that kind of uproar, you may not even be speaking to me by the time I get back, Sarah. That's a big risk for me to take. Especially now."

The tender significance in his tone made Sarah flush with sudden warmth and happiness. "I'll still be speaking to you," she whispered, pulling him down toward her and kissing his lips gently. "I promise."

He drew back, smiling, and looked at her, still thoughtful. "Why, Sarah?" he asked suddenly. "Why, just now, do you make this offer? You always resisted any idea of the kids living with you, even though anyone can see how much you love them. It was like...like something was holding you back, something you didn't want to tell me. Why have you suddenly changed your mind?"

Sarah gazed into his eyes, considering, torn by a deep longing to tell him about the child she carried. He was so good, so kind and generous. She knew, with deep, instinctive confidence, that she had been wrong about him. This man wasn't going to cause any problems to her or to her baby. He would just be overjoyed at her news, full of sympathy and eager to help. And once he knew, once he understood about the baby, then they would be able to make more intelligent long-term plans for the care of the other children while considering the needs of their own child, as well.

But, with the stark honesty of her orderly, scientific mind, Sarah knew that rationality and reasoning actually had little to do with her conflict. She yearned to tell him about the baby simply because she wanted him to know, and to share her happiness.

She loved him.

When Sarah finally realized this, fully and completely, it wasn't a blinding revelation like a lightning flash. It was more like a sunrise, creeping with silent radiance above the horizon and flooding her world with light and warmth. She laughed, almost crying with the sheer joy of the moment, her body trembling with happiness.

"Jim," she whispered. "Jim, darling, there's something I have to tell you."

He heard the depths of tenderness in her voice, and his face softened and glowed. He drew her into his arms again, cradling her, kissing her cheeks and hair. "What is it, Sarah?" he murmured gently. "What did you want to tell me? Because, sweetheart, there's something I want to tell you, too."

Sarah smiled against his chest, thinking how surprised he was going to be, savoring the sweet, rich delight of this special, precious moment.

But before she could say anything the doorbell rang, echoing through the silent lower floor of the house.

They drew apart and looked at each other, their eyes wide and startled.

"Were you expecting anybody?" Jim asked.

"Not a soul," Sarah said. "Not even you, in fact," she added with a smile. She sat up, swinging her legs over the edge of the bed and reaching for her robe as the bell shrilled once more.

"Don't go," Jim protested, grasping the trailing end of her belt. "Just let them go away, darling, and come back to bed. Come on. This is my last night before I have to leave for ten days."

Sarah hesitated, looking down at him, and then shook her head. "I can't, Jim. It might be someone from the lab. We have student assistants on an all-night shift this week, tracking germination rates, and Carl might..." As she spoke, she was tying the belt on her robe, rummaging under the bed for her slippers, running a distracted hand through her hair.

Acknowledging defeat, Jim swung his long body out of bed, stepped hastily into his shorts and jeans and grabbed his shirt, following her down the stairs.

Sarah went to the front door as the bell rang a third time. Jim stood barefoot behind her in the dimness of the foyer, tugging his sweatshirt over his head.

His head emerged and he looked out, grinning cheerfully at the man standing in the pool of light on the threshold.

It was his father.

Jim's smile faded. His chest tightened with amazement and some other emotion, something halfway between shock and outrage, as he stared wordlessly at the other man. His father looked as smug and expensive as ever in his five-hundred-dollar boots and his fur-trimmed leather topcoat. But he was carrying... Jim blinked in utter disbelief.

The old man was carrying a *giraffe!*

Jim frowned, peering at the object under this father's arm as if it just might be an incendiary device or a weapon of some kind. The giraffe smiled blandly back at him, its long, thick eyelashes fluttering in the chill night wind.

"Come in, Senator," Sarah was saying calmly. "We might as well discuss this inside where it's warm. Jim, move over and let your father in."

Blindly Jim obeyed, standing aside while his father passed him in the foyer, maddened even more than usual by the distinctive scent of expensive leather and after-shave that was so uniquely the old man's.

At least, he observed, if it was any satisfaction, his father appeared to be just as dazed and shell-shocked as Jim felt, and was clearly uncomfortable. Besides, he looked completely ridiculous clutching that damn giraffe, which he seemed to have altogether forgotten.

Sarah led them into the living room, switched on a couple of lamps and put a fresh log on the smoldering embers, turning it gently until it burst into a cheery little blaze. Jim sank into a chair opposite his father and watched the calm efficiency of her movements, dazzled in spite of himself by her beauty even in the old terrycloth robe with her hair tumbled around her face.

His mind whirled with questions, struggling to absorb the crushing impact of his father's unexpected appearance. Wildly he tried to devise scenarios, tried to impose some kind of order on what was happening.

His father had been passing and recognized his car out front, stopped to tell him something, he improvised frantically. Maybe there was something important going on in the family that just couldn't wait, and his father had— He shook his head, holding his bare feet awkwardly toward the warmth of the fire and trying not to look at the man sitting quietly opposite him.

Jim realized what he was attempting to do. He was struggling to arrange things so that it wasn't the way it looked, so that his father and Sarah didn't already know each other. He realized that he couldn't bear the idea of Sarah having some kind of relationship with his father. His mind just refused to absorb the possibility, and he was searching desperately for some other explanation.

But this hope was dashed when Jameson said quietly, "I'm sorry about this, Sarah, believe me. I called Jim's home, and the children told me he was working late at the office tonight. I had no idea he'd be here."

"Well, then," Sarah said with a bleak little smile, sinking down on the couch and tucking her feet nervously beneath her, "this is just what he gets for telling lies to children, I guess."

"Look," Jim burst out abruptly, addressing himself to Sarah because he was still unable to look at his father. "Look, just quit talking about me as if I'm not here, or as if I'm six years old, okay? And tell me what's going on, please."

"Jim," the senator began, his deep voice low and concerned. "Son, please don't—"

"Not you!" Jim said harshly, casting a brief, bitter glance at the older man. "I want Sarah to tell me what's going on. I don't have anything to say to you."

His father's hand tightened on the plump leather body of the giraffe.

"It's all right, Jameson," Sarah said quietly. "I'll talk to him. He had to find out soon, anyway. In fact, I was about to tell him."

"Tell me *what?*" Jim shouted. "Goddamn it, tell me *what?*"

He was almost beside himself with outrage and frustration. But even in his agitation he was able to realize that what tormented him the most was the easy air of understanding between Sarah and his father, the way they spoke to each other with the casual warmth of old friends.

Jim felt confused, betrayed and nakedly exposed. But most of all he felt concerned for Sarah. The man across the room from him was dangerous and unreliable, a man who had caused untold suffering and damage to another woman Jim had loved. He just couldn't bear to think that Jameson Fleming had somehow gotten close to Sarah, as well, wormed his way into her confidence, made her believe that he was ...

"Would you like me to leave, Sarah?" Jameson asked quietly, ignoring Jim's outburst.

"I think it might be best," Sarah said. "I'll talk to Jim." She got up, following the senator's large, sturdy figure to the door. "And I'll call you tomorrow," she promised. "Thank you for stopping by," she added with a bleak smile.

Jameson hesitated awkwardly in the doorway as if about to speak, then nodded and reached for the knob.

"Aren't you forgetting something, Senator?" Jim asked bitterly from his chair near the fire. "You seem to have left your toy behind," he added with cold sarcasm, indicating the big giraffe that stood on the floor near the other chair, gazing at the fire on the hearth with gentle interest, its blue eyes wide and cheerful.

"That's for Sarah, son," Jameson said in the doorway.

"For *Sarah?*" Jim asked. "What does Sarah want with a goddamn toy giraffe? It's horses that Sarah likes, isn't it?"

Jameson looked thoughtfully for a long moment at his son's puzzled, angry expression, then smiled sadly at Sarah, squeezed her hand and let himself silently out the door into the bitter night. Sarah gazed at the closed door, drew a deep breath and came slowly back into the room to stand in front of Jim's chair.

"Jim," she began, "I'm truly sorry that things had to happen this way. Please believe me. And believe, too, that I was about to tell you, I truly was, just before your father arrived."

"Tell me what?" he asked, staring up at her, his blue eyes cold and wary. "For God's sake, Sarah, what is going on here?"

Sarah sank down to kneel beside the chair, her hands folded on his leg, her eyes searching his face with a pleading expression. "I'm pregnant, Jim," she said softly. "I'm almost into my fourth month. And it's your baby."

He stared down at her in disbelief, his mind whirling, realizing that of all the things she might have said, these words were absolutely the most shocking and unexpected.

"What did you say?" he asked numbly. "What did you just tell me?"

"I told you that I'm pregnant," Sarah repeated patiently. "I got pregnant that night we first slept together, way back before Christmas, at the Kingston Arms."

He gripped the arms of the chair, his mind still numb with shock, feeling dull and stupid. "Pregnant," he repeated slowly. "You're pregnant. And you say it's my baby."

"Yes," Sarah murmured. "Yes, Jim that's right. I didn't want to tell you at first because..."

Jim caught sight of the giraffe, still gazing blandly into the flickering flames. Suddenly the full significance of the expensive child's toy came crashing into his dazed thoughts. "And—" he interrupted her, not listening at all, still struggling to get his mind to work properly "—and the old man knows about it. You told him before you told me. You told my father about the baby."

He glanced down at her sharply, his eyes flashing cold blue fire while she watched him in silence, still kneeling beside him.

"Right?" he asked, his voice harsh. "That's right, isn't it?"

Sarah nodded.

Jim's handsome golden face twisted with pain, but he kept his voice calm and level. "How long?" he asked grimly. "How long has the old man known about this, Sarah?"

"Jim, please, don't—"

"How long?" he shouted.

"Almost a month," Sarah said quietly. "I went out to the ranch about mid-February, just to meet him and...and hear his side of the story, I guess. I hadn't intended to tell him about the baby—it was the last thing on my mind, actually—but I found that I couldn't stop myself. After I met him, I discovered that I really wanted him to know."

"What are you, Sarah?" Jim asked, his voice dangerously quiet. "Are you a fortune hunter, or what? All this 'I'm just an absentminded scientist,' is that all just a front for the devious, plotting mind of a big-time gold digger? Do you want to get into the old man's bank account? It's big enough, God knows," he added bitterly. "It'd certainly be worth your while, although this really seems like a lot of trouble for anyone to be going to."

Sarah looked up at him sadly, too concerned for him to be angered by his words. "Jim," she began, "things aren't always the way they seem, you know."

He ignored her, staring fixedly at the tall leather giraffe still poised so elegantly beside the chair that his father had recently occupied.

"That night in December," he said slowly, "I was right about that, wasn't I, Sarah? You did seek me out for a purpose. It wasn't any kind of casual pickup, was it? You *intended* to get pregnant."

"Yes," Sarah said quietly. She stood up gracefully, crossed the room and sat down opposite him, leaning forward, her voice low and earnest. "Yes, Jim, it was deliberate."

"And you're enough of a scientist," he continued doggedly, "to have it all planned precisely, right? You knew that was an optimum time for you to get pregnant, so you used me for your purpose."

Sarah nodded again, her face composed.

"Why, Sarah?" he asked quietly. "Why me?"

"I remembered you from college," she began, "and I'd followed your career a little in the press. I knew quite a lot about your family background and your father and all, and I—"

She looked up, startled by the cold intensity of his gaze, and faltered briefly, then went on. "I liked the genetic indicators," she concluded finally. "I wanted to have a baby, and there was nobody in my life that I cared about, and I just wanted to ensure the best possible hereditary factors, since I was in a position to choose."

"In a position to choose," he echoed. "So you picked me," he went on, still staring at her with cold disbelief. "You selected me like a goddamn bull in a pen and said, 'I want that one over there. Bring him into the barn.'"

At the pain in his voice Sarah's composure weakened, and she shifted awkwardly in her chair, her face bleak with unhappiness. "It didn't seem like that," she whispered. "Not at the time."

"Sure it didn't," he said bitterly. "Not to *you*, right? Because you're so wrapped up in numbers and figures and genetic charts that you never think about people's feelings, right, Sarah? To you they're all just statistics."

"That's not true!" she burst out, staring at him, her gray eyes huge and dark.

"I'm not just talking about being selected to stand at stud for you, Sarah," he went on, his voice dangerously soft. "Although God knows that's bad enough. But if you cared about me, cared even a tiny bit about my feelings, you would have told me before you told *him*. That was just monstrous of you, Sarah. It was unforgivable."

Sarah bit her lip nervously and gazed at him, her eyes full of appeal. "Jim," she pleaded, "try to look at it from my point of view. I was afraid to tell you about the baby. I didn't want to get involved with you at all, and you know how hard I tried from the very beginning to avoid any kind of further contact."

"So your intention was to just go ahead, have this baby that's half mine and never, ever allow me to know about its existence?"

"Yes," Sarah said. "That's what I intended. I didn't know what you were like," she went on earnestly, "and I didn't want to put you in a position where you could make claims on the baby, try to seize custody or have some input into the child's upbringing. I just wanted to be completely free of you after I conceived, all alone with my baby."

He nodded thoughtfully. "So what went wrong, Sarah? What happened to all these careful plans?"

"Oh, lots of things," Sarah told him with a sad little smile. "The three kids to begin with. I could have turned my back on you at that time, Jim, just as I'd intended, but it was awfully hard to walk away from them. And then there were your father and your Aunt Maureen. I hadn't expected to feel the way I did about them, either, but I've visited them several times since that first weekend, and your father has come to the lab and taken me out to lunch a couple of times, and I find that I'm growing very close to both of them. And," she concluded simply, "I never expected to feel the way I do about you."

"And just how's that?" he murmured, gazing at her fixedly. "How do you feel about me, Sarah?"

I love you, she wanted to shout. *I love you with all my heart and soul the way I never dreamed I could love a man, and just looking at you, my darling, makes me feel all weak and shivery and melting inside, makes me want to—*

"Sarah?" he prompted, still in that same low, dangerous tone. "You haven't answered my question."

She gazed at his bitter face, knowing she couldn't say it, knowing that now wasn't the time to speak of love to him, not while he was so angry.

Instead, she lowered her head and murmured, "I care very deeply about you, Jim. You're a good, kind, generous person, and also a very good friend. I was going to tell you about the baby tonight just because I believe that you deserve to know."

"But I didn't deserve to be the first to know, right?" he asked coldly. "The old man got *that* honor, didn't he, Sarah?"

Sarah stared at him, wide-eyed, appalled by the depths of bitterness in his voice.

"Jim," she whispered, "why do you hate him so much? Tell me why."

"Because he's a monster," Jim said coldly. "A selfish, egotistical, destructive monster."

"How do you know that?" Sarah asked, forcing her voice to stay calm, knowing all too well the crucial importance of this conversation, and the absolute necessity to proceed with caution, to choose her words with extreme care. "Do you know it through your own observations or just because of all the things your mother told you about him?"

"Leave my mother out of this!" he burst out in sudden anguish. "I don't want to talk about my mother!"

"Maybe it's time you did, Jim," Sarah said gently. "She's been dead for over seventeen years, but she's still at the heart of all this, isn't she? Your mother was always the cause of the estrangement between you and your father, right?"

Jim gazed at Sarah's face for a long time, not seeing her, his blue eyes shadowed with thoughts and memories.

"She was so beautiful," he said finally in a low, choked voice. "So beautiful and so sweet when she was happy, laughing and playing with me as if she were just another kid, telling me all kinds of stories and singing to me."

"You said, 'so sweet when she was happy,'" Sarah persisted gently, treading as gingerly as a person picking her way through a swamp full of quicksand pools. "But don't you think there might, just *might* have been another side to her, too, Jim? A different person that she didn't necessarily show to a young son, but that her husband might be aware of? Did you ever think that things might have been a little more complicated than you always thought, that maybe she wasn't entirely the victim or your father completely the villain?"

Jim looked at the earnest face of the woman across the room, hearing her words but not wanting to consider them, not wanting to deal with what she was suggesting.

"Think of it from your father's point of view, Jim," Sarah urged, leaning forward again. "Think of yourself at Billy's age. That's exactly how old you were when she died, Jim, just about the age Billy is now. I want you to visualize it."

Sarah paused and drew a deep breath while Jim watched her in tense silence.

"Imagine that you and I were married, Jim," she went on, "and Billy was our son. Imagine me telling him the kind of things your mother told you, terrible things about you and about our marriage, burdening him with all that information. As a father, think how you might feel. Think how angry you might be about what I was doing to the boy, and how, from an adult point of view, you might fight with me over it and question my motives."

Jim stared at her, his blue eyes wide and strained. Sarah realized that he had never thought of his parents' relationship this way before.

"And the way she died," Sarah hurried on, pressing her advantage when she saw him waver. "Think of that, Jim. Think how selfish an act it really was, to do that to you when you were—"

But, looking into his taut, passionate face, Sarah realized with a little shock of dread that she had gone too far.

"*Damn!*" he burst out finally, his voice shaking with fury. "You two really had a cozy little chat, didn't you? Talked about everything under the sun, right? Even talked about—" his voice broke, and he dropped his head into his hands, muffling his words "—about how she died."

Sarah looked at his heaving shoulders, her throat tight, aching with love and concern as she thought of the horrors that her words must have unleashed in his mind. But when he raised his face, there was no visible emotion there at all, just a cold, bitter stillness that frightened her. He got to his feet, walked over to the closet and began, slowly and methodically, to put on his jacket and boots.

Sarah watched him in helpless silence, not knowing what to say, bruised by the terrible pain she could feel emanating from him.

"Look," he said slowly, his hand on the doorknob, "I'm going away tomorrow. When I come back, I want it to be over. I know that I can't stop you from having this baby or spending every day with my father if you want to, but I don't want any part of it. I never want to see you again, if that's the choice you're going to make. Do you understand me?"

Sarah nodded, her mind numb with anguish, staring at him with wide, strained eyes.

"And," he continued tonelessly, "I don't want you having anything to do with the kids, either. I certainly don't want you to bring them over here to live the way you were planning."

He gave her a questioning look, and she nodded.

"That's not enough, Sarah," Jim said quietly. "I do have the right, after all, to make certain stipulations regarding the kids. I want you to swear to me that you won't bring them here to live."

"I swear, Jim," Sarah said quietly. "I swear that I won't bring the kids here to live."

Jim watched her face for a moment, then bent his head in acknowledgment, turned and let himself out the door into the night. Sarah wandered to the window, lifted aside the heavy drape and watched him go, her whole body aching with a sorrow so vast that she could scarcely contain all the sadness.

When his car left the curb and he'd driven slowly off into the moonlight, Sarah let the curtain drop, picked up the big giraffe and sank down into an armchair, curling up as if to shield her pain from the world. She hugged the plump, soft body of the giraffe, resting her chin on its back while she gazed with brooding, unseeing eyes at the dying flames on the hearth.

CHAPTER ELEVEN

MAUDE WILLETT STOOD uncertainly in the foyer of Jim's cluttered apartment, looking with some misgivings at the two older children.

"Come on, Maude," Clarence said from the doorway. "Let's go if we're going. I have to go on shift at four, so we'll hardly have time to get down there and get all those groceries back here, especially when the streets are so icy."

Maude nodded absently, barely hearing him. Her gaze turned to Arthur, who stood clinging to the edge of an end table with one chubby fist, stretching his small body toward the inviting lower fronds of a tall, bushy palm in the corner. His other hand just barely missed grasping the trailing greenery, and his small fat face was red with effort and frustration.

"When the baby finally starts walking," Maude said darkly to nobody in particular, "there's going to be hell to pay, let me tell you. Jim's going to have to hire more help full-time just to follow Arthur around and clean up after him."

Neither Ellie nor Billy responded. Ellie was busy at the table, a pencil clutched in her thin hand, writing with great concentration. At Sarah's urging, Jim had enrolled both the children in correspondence school so that they could catch up with their respective age groups before the next school term, and Ellie took her work very seriously, handing in neat, exquisitely detailed assignments.

Billy, on the other hand, disdained the lessons and dashed them off sketchily, if at all. Now, slouched casually in an armchair, he smiled blandly at the two adults over the top of a fishing magazine and then returned to the article he was reading.

Maude glanced at him suspiciously. There was something about Billy today, ever since Jim had left, in fact, something that disturbed her a little, though she couldn't actually put her finger on it.

Maybe, Maude mused, it was just that the boy was being a little *too* cheerful and cooperative, although that idea certainly sounded ridiculous when she thought about it.

Or maybe, she decided, trying to be optimistic, he was just finally coming around, realizing that these really were people who could be trusted and he might as well relax.

"Come *on,* Maude," Clarence urged, interrupting her troubled thoughts. "I'm a busy man, you know. I don't have all day."

"Yeah, right," Maude said with a grin, gathering herself together and starting toward the door. "I know how busy you are, sitting down there all day long playing solitaire and looking so important in your fancy uniform."

Clarence grinned back at her, holding the door open with a flourish.

"We won't be gone more than an hour or so," Maude told the two older children. "Remember now—don't let anybody in, and don't touch the stove, because I've got the oven set to come on automatically. And *watch that baby,*" she concluded, glaring at Arthur who was oblivious to everybody else, still thoughtfully measuring the distance between himself and the tall plant. "He's going to get into that thing before long, you know," Maude predicted with deep gloom, "and then there'll be such a mess." Shaking her head, she disappeared through the outer door, and silence fell.

Billy and Ellie looked at each other, and then at the closed door. Billy tossed the magazine aside with contained excitement, walked over and gazed down at the street, watching until Clarence's car pulled away from the curb. The little car with its two gray-haired occupants eased off down the street, fishtailing slightly on the ice, and vanished around the corner. He kept watching, forcing himself to count slowly to one hundred. Finally he turned back to Ellie, his face blazing with purpose.

"Okay, they're gone. Hurry up, El, we only got a little time!"

Ellie sat behind the table and stared at him, her eyes round and full of pain. "Oh, Billy," she whispered, "do we *have* to? Billy, it's so cold...."

The boy's face darkened angrily. "Come *on,* Ellie!" he shouted. "Don't give me all that crap. You know we gotta do this. You know we got no choice. Now come on! You get your stuff and Arthur's, and I'll get the boxes from the storage room."

Ellie's pale face set with quiet stubbornness. "I won't," she said, gripping her pencil and avoiding her brother's eyes. "I don't want to go, Billy. It's so mean to just run off like this."

"Mean?" Billy echoed in disbelief. "You call it *mean* for us to go off and look after ourselves the way we always did before? What's mean about it?"

"Jim will be so sad," Ellie whispered. "When he gets home and we're gone, he'll feel just awful. You know he will."

Billy's eyes flickered momentarily and then hardened again. "Jim won't be mad," the boy said firmly. "He may worry a little, but we'll call him and tell him we're all right after I find us a place to live. I promise you we'll phone him, Ellie. And then, believe me, El, he'll just be glad. All this mess will be gone, and he won't have to go to some little motel with us, and he can have his life just like it used to be before we came along. He'll be glad, Ellie. And you know it."

"I don't think so," Ellie said staunchly. "I think Jim loves us, Billy."

"Oh, sure," Billy said scornfully. "And how much do you think he's going to love us when he has to move away from here next week and live in a motel? He's going to get sick of it pretty fast, Ellie, and then he'll call in the Welfare, and then you know what'll happen. Goodbye Arthur, that's what'll happen."

At this familiar threat Ellie's blue eyes filled with tears, but she continued to shake her head defiantly. "No he won't. Jim would never, ever do that. He cares about us. All of us."

"Ellie," Billy said in the slow, patient tones of an adult dealing with a backward child, "that may be true, but things are getting too hard for Jim. He can't take much more, and when he cracks, we'll be the ones to suffer. Just wait and see."

He crossed the room to stare at his sister, his face passionate with conviction. Ellie stared back at him, wide-eyed and unhappy.

"You know what happened the night just before he left, El," Billy said softly. "That was just the icing on the cake as far as I'm concerned. We gotta get out of here fast.''

''I don't think it was so bad that night,'' Ellie began loyally. ''I think maybe he was just sad about having to go away on this trip, that's all.''

''Ellie, don't be such a *feeb,* okay? Jim was mad, and you know it. You stayed up on purpose to give him that dumb going-away card you made, and he barely looked at it. He was so mad he could hardly talk to us. Believe me, Ellie, he's getting sick of us. I can tell.''

Ellie thought about Billy's words, remembering how cold and distant Jim had been the night before he'd left on his trip, how he'd almost ignored the card she'd spent so much time making.

He'd gone down to work late at the office, catching up before he left on his trip. That was what he'd said. And he'd seemed really happy when he left right after supper, hugging all three of them, joking with Maude and Clarence, kissing Arthur twice on his way out the door. But when he came home, he was tight-lipped and angry, and even though he tried not to show anything, it was easy to see that he felt like yelling at everybody.

Maybe Billy was right. Maybe Jim *was* getting tired of all of them and ready to get rid of them.

She hesitated, still gazing at her brother while a couple of sorrowful tears slipped unheeded down her pale cheeks.

Seeing her waver, Billy pressed his advantage. ''The only way we can be safe, El, is to be on our own where they can't find us. And I know just the place. I talked to a guy at the arcade who knows another guy who says— *Jeez! Arthur!*''

This last shout was occasioned by a sudden crashing noise that echoed through the apartment. Both children turned to gaze in horror at the plump baby in his denim overalls, who had succeeded at last in grasping the lower fronds of the palm and pulling the whole tall plant over onto the floor.

The mess was awe-inspiring. There was broken greenery everywhere. Bushels of dirt spilled over the carpet and the goatskin rug, intermingled with the shattered crockery of the big planter. Arthur stood wide-eyed and silent in the midst of it all, amazed and a little frightened by the havoc he had created.

"Well, that does it for sure," Billy muttered. "We gotta get out of here, fast. These people can't stand no more of this crap, Ellie. Believe me, we gotta get *out* of here."

Galvanized by his panic and by the dreadful sight of the huge plant lying flat and broken on the floor, Ellie nodded sadly. She got to her feet and began to move around the room in a troubled, distracted manner, picking up articles and setting them down again.

Billy followed her, barking out instructions. "No toys and stuff, Ellie. Just what we can carry. Just some clothes and things, a few diapers for Arthur, something for him to eat later on today, that's all. Now hurry up while I get the boxes."

Blinking back the tears that stung in her eyes, Ellie put together a little pile of clothes for herself and Arthur, tossed in the baby's soft plastic rabbit and then hesitated in agony between Arthur's beloved activity board and her own shellcraft kit.

"Don't even *think* about it, El," Billy said, returning with a couple of cardboard boxes in his arms. "You gotta carry Arthur, so I have to carry both boxes. We can't take much."

"But, Billy—"

"Just hurry up, will you?" Billy said wearily. "Before Maude gets back? For God's sake, Ellie, you'd think you *wanted* us to get sent to the Welfare and have Arthur taken away and all."

At his words, something snapped in Ellie. Her face hardened with sudden decision, and she moved rapidly around the room, a cold, distant look about her while she sorted clothes with quiet efficiency.

A few minutes later they were down on the street, the bitter wind tugging at their clothes and stinging their cheeks as they struggled toward the bus stop.

Arthur seemed to have gained a ton in the months they'd lived with Jim. Ellie staggered a little under his weight. He was slippery and hard to hold in his bulky, metallic snowsuit, and he kept wriggling and whimpering, trying to get down.

Beside her Billy plodded along, shivering in his thin jacket and sneakers, his head lowered into the wind, clutching the two heavy boxes. They waited in the little glass shelter at the bus stop where Arthur stood solemnly beside Ellie on the bench, gripping the back with his red-mittened hands and staring at passersby, his eyes round above his scarf.

An older lady with a sweet, wrinkled face looked dubiously at the shabby teenager and well-dressed little girl, the two big cardboard boxes, the solemn baby.

Billy smiled at her blandly. "Our mom's sure gonna be surprised," he observed in an easy, casual tone.

Ellie stared at him while the woman continued to eye them with quiet concern.

"She's doing some volunteer work down at the Goodwill," Billy went on with that same air of cheerful, informative politeness, "and we decided to surprise her. We're taking a bunch of our old toys and clothes and stuff down there to give to the poor kids. She doesn't even know we're coming.''

''You're sure she's there right now?'' the woman asked. ''It's really awfully cold for that baby to be out, you know.''

Billy nodded. ''She just called,'' he said smoothly. ''She checks on us all the time. She said she'd be coming home around five, so we thought we'd just go down on the bus, surprise her with our stuff and then get a ride home with her later on.''

The woman's face cleared, and she smiled as the bus ground to the curb, its exhaust sending out great clouds of frosty steam into the stillness of the winter afternoon.

''Well,'' she said, ''that's fine, then. It's very sweet of you children to want to share your things with others who are less fortunate.''

Still smiling, she followed them onto the bus, carrying one of the boxes for Billy, who thanked her courteously as he sat down beside Ellie and his baby brother.

Ellie gazed blindly out the big side window of the bus, biting her lip and trying not to cry. She knew all too well what kind of world they were returning to, and she wondered how long it was going to be before any grown-up ever again showed them any trace of kindness or interest.

She lowered Arthur's scarf and kissed his cheek, burying her face briefly in his warmth and sweetness, her eyes bleak. It was starting all over again, the lonely nightmare time that Ellie most dreaded. And knowing what she faced, she didn't really feel frightened or worried or even sad anymore.

She just felt tired . . . so terribly, awfully tired.

THE MEADOW WAS wide and green, silent and washed in early-morning freshness, starred sweetly with drifts of wildflowers that glowed like rainbows. Jim floated over the fragrant grass, his feet barely touching the ground, his eyes fixed on a little glade in the distance where he could hear the soft ripple of running water and see a silvery glimmer through the trees.

He knew that he was dreaming because the place that he moved through was so ethereal and lovely, pure and far removed from anything of real life. And yet the experience was so vivid, so rich in color and texture that he seemed to be completely inside this magic world, living it with all his consciousness.

His heart began to beat faster as he neared the sheltered glade, knowing who waited for him there. He brushed aside the long, trailing fronds of fern that enclosed the green and secret sun-dappled space, peered through and caught his breath in wonder.

Sarah lay on the grass beside the silver stream of water, smiling up at him, wearing a long, diaphanous gown that seemed to be spun from moonbeams. Through the delicate transparent fabric he could see the beautiful, alluring lines of her body, the radiant, pearl-like glow of her skin and the delicate buds of pink that tipped her breasts.

He knelt beside her, suspended in time and space as dreamers often are, and passed an endless age just caressing her, lifting the silky clinging fabric away to reveal all of her loveliness, gazing down at her in rapt stillness.

Slowly, languidly, he stroked the long, curving lines of her body, cupped and touched her soft, full breasts, bent to kiss her lips, her neck and shoulders, intoxicated by the perfumed fragrance of her skin and the gentle, loving promise in her wide, starry eyes.

At last, somehow, his own clothes seemed to melt away, as well. He lowered himself into her arms and felt himself sinking, falling, drowning endlessly in the silken warmth and sweetness of her, groaning and murmuring her name, knowing that he was lost and rejoicing, wanting to stay forever with her, in her, surrounded by her....

Jim was awakened by his own voice muttering her name brokenly as he thrashed and stirred on the lumpy, unyielding hotel mattress. He groaned again and rolled his aching head on the pillow to gaze blearily at his little bedside clock.

Three o'clock.

Still groggy, Jim lifted himself on one elbow and stared at the clock, trying to remember if it was afternoon or early morning. The deep, dark stillness of the room convinced him that it was still the first hours of the day, and he sank back on the pillows, shivering a little, longing wistfully to close his eyes and lose himself once more in the delicious sweetness of his dream.

But sleep eluded him. He rolled over again on the pillow, hands behind his head, staring moodily at the shifting patterns of shadow and darkness that washed softly through the heavy drapes muffling the window.

He was still exhausted and disoriented, suffering the effects of jet lag and the need to compress a month of business into a one-week trip. But when he was completely honest with himself, he knew he was suffering most of all not from this trip, but from the events that had happened at home just before he'd left.

Jim winced, recalling his last evening with Sarah, thinking about the things he'd said to her and the way she'd responded.

He remembered the cheerful, casual intimacy of their impromptu dinner, and then the incredible richness of their lovemaking. That night in her bed had been the first time he'd sensed himself really getting close to her. Somehow he'd managed to penetrate her armor of aloofness and reserve. He'd felt her drawing near to him, finally beginning after all those months to trust him and respond to him.

We were just on the verge of a real breakthrough, he thought in anguish. *She was ready to turn to me, to open up a little, even to love me. And I had to ruin everything.*

He turned over again, restless with pain, and buried his head in his arms, trying to block out the memory of how brutally shocked he had been to see his father standing there on Sarah's doorstep, and the things he had said to Sarah afterward.

But his mind worked as efficiently as a movie projector, playing back the whole scene on the backdrop of his memory in steady, relentless sequence.

Jim remembered every expression and nuance, every word his father had said before he left. And then, still shuddering with pain, he went through all the details of his own conversation with Sarah.

The same memory had been haunting him ever since he'd boarded the plane, gritty and restless with lack of sleep, vaguely aware that Maude and the children were distressed by his behavior. He'd been unable to respond to them at all.

But at last, in the chill black silence of the Parisian night, the murky fog of pain and emotion began to dissipate and things became clearer to him. He could see now how unfair he had been to Sarah, and how hard she had tried to show him the truth.

"You were the same age Billy is now, Jim," she'd said earnestly. "I want you to visualize it."

And he could.

He'd never thought of it that way before, never once questioned what his mother had done or whether she might have been wrong in her actions. He had always just loved her so much, believed that he was her only friend, bitterly hated his father for his cruelty to this poor, helpless woman. And yet now, when Sarah insisted that he look at the past from a different point of view, he wasn't so sure about anything.

Jim frowned thoughtfully against the pillow, his golden handsome face drawn and taut in the dim stillness of the little hotel room.

He thought about Billy, about the boy's touching air of bravado, his sturdy attempt to be a man and shoulder all the responsibility of his little family while he was still only a child himself, with a child's terrors and uncertainties.

The memory aroused a tenderness and hurt in Jim that was almost unbearable. He thought of the way he cared so deeply for this proud and touchy boy, longed to lift all those crushing responsibilities from Billy so that the boy would be free to enjoy his own precious and fleeting childhood.

Then, as Sarah had urged, he tried to place himself in his father's position, watching in helpless outrage as a self-absorbed and thoughtless woman heaped a load of terrible pain and pressure on a young boy's frail shoulders, a burden that he was too young to bear and too gallant to refuse.

What his mother had done, including the manner of her death, had been wrong and selfish. Jim knew at last that this was the truth, and that he had realized it as soon as Sarah pointed it out, but refused to accept the fact.

Now he found that he could face it, and the realization no longer caused him the same kind of agony. In fact, it made him feel washed clean, empty and even a little frightened, stripped at last of the bitter anger that had enclosed him and defined his life for so many years.

Sarah was right, after all. There were two sides to every story.

Jim's father had undoubtedly been far from perfect, but he had probably also not been the complete villain Jim had always accused him of being. Jameson Fleming had merely been a troubled man trying to deal with a woman whose insecurity and discontentment had made her spiteful and unhappy, a woman who had managed, even in death, to take from her husband something of great value.

Jim rolled over again and sat up in the rumpled bed, hugging his knees, racked with a painful, visceral need for Sarah's warmth and sweetness, for her laughter and wisdom and the rich beauty of her womanly body in his arms.

He loved her so much. And he wanted her with him right now, today, this morning as the sun rose over Paris. He wanted to stroll with her through the crowded, snowy streets, enjoying the winter sunlight in her hair and the glow of cold on her cheeks. He wanted to take her into exquisite little shops and buy the kind of beautiful jewelry for her that matched her rare and classic loveliness. He wanted to stop at a street vendor's, buy her a hot baked potato, steaming in the frosted air, and laugh as she ate it, her gray eyes spar-kling at him over the fluted edge of the paper dish.

Jim moaned softly, aching with need and yearning, and finally allowed himself to explore the last, sweetest, most painful memory of all.

Sarah was pregnant. She was carrying his baby.

The wondrous strangeness of this was almost more than he could bear to contemplate. He thought of her grave, lovely face, her awesome, soaring intelligence that contrasted so delightfully with a sort of childlike simplicity, and the adorable sweetness of her in his arms. He remembered, smiling, the matter-of-fact way she had told him of her plans, of her desire for a child and the way she had set out, all on her own, to achieve her goal.

"I liked the genetic indicators," she had said calmly.

Oh, Sarah. Sarah, my love, my darling...

Still smiling, he thought of the generosity that had prompted Sarah to share her secret with his father and his aunt, despite her own fears for her child. It had been the sweetest, most unselfish thing she could have done, and yet, learning of it, he had made all those wild, bit-ter accusations.

Jim's smile faded. He was almost crushed by a sud-den, urgent need for her, by his overpowering longing to tell her how he adored her, to shield and protect her, to surround her and their child with love and safety and endless security. He glanced at the telephone, yearning to call her, and struggled to remember what time it was back in Alberta.

But at last he shook his head and stretched out on the hard mattress again, pulling the blankets back up to his chin.

He had a lot of fences to mend, and Jim knew that he couldn't do any of it over the telephone. It wasn't just Sarah. There was also the memory of Ellie's sad, crumpled little face when he brushed off the goodbye card she'd made so carefully to show her love....

Jim winced at the memory of the little girl's disappointed expression, which she'd tried so hard to hide, and at the wary, angry look in Billy's eyes. Even Maude had seemed quietly disapproving as she stood and watched him leave in silence.

He needed time to make a proper apology to all of them, not just to Sarah. He needed to stand face-to-face with the people he loved and explain how foolish he'd been, too wrapped up in himself and his own angry memories to think very much about anyone else.

Less than a week, he thought. In just a few more days his plane would touch down in Calgary, and he'd be home, back where he could start undoing all the wrong he'd done. Until then all he could do was wait, try to drown himself in work, to push aside all the thoughts and memories that stabbed him with their sweetness and their pain.

He closed his eyes and felt himself slipping back into sleep. Sarah's sweet gray eyes glowed in the darkness, and he drew close to her, yearning passionately to fall back into his dream, to find once again the green sun-warmed glade where she lay smiling, waiting for him.

SARAH WAS in a green sun-warmed place, but it was a botanical laboratory, not an enchanted glade. The greenery was supplied by endless rows and banks of seedlings sprouting in orderly fashion in trays and wide plastic flats, and the warmth came from a fading winter sun filtering through acres of greenhouse glass.

Sarah leaned over one of the flats, frowning in concentration as she studied a row of little wheat plants. Carl was at her elbow, listening for her murmured observations and noting them carefully on a chart attached to a clipboard.

Sarah finally straightened and turned to her assistant with a little teasing smile. He gazed at her with anxious expectancy.

"Maybe," she said finally, still smiling. "A definite maybe, Carl. That's all I'll give you."

"But, Sarah," he protested. "Look at the numbers, Sarah. Look at the test results. There's no doubt. We've got it this time. We've got it, girl!"

"Maybe," Sarah repeated firmly. "But I want to see a lot more test results first."

Carl's round, freckled face registered extreme agitation. He opened his mouth to speak and then fell silent, looking in surprise at Joelle, the pretty front-desk receptionist, who was approaching hesitantly along one of the damp, leafy aisles.

"Sarah?" she murmured. "I'm sorry to bother you in here while you're working, but there's a phone call for you. It seems really important."

Sarah wiped the sleeve of her lab coat across her damp forehead and smiled at the girl. "It *must* be important, Joelle," she said cheerfully, "for you to come all the way in here. I know how much you hate being in the greenhouse."

Joelle shivered, gazing around her with distaste. "It's all so hot and icky and . . . and *green*," she muttered. "Who knows what kind of horrible things you scientist types are growing under there? Pods developing into monsters, and all that stuff."

Sarah chuckled. "You watch far too many of those awful science fiction movies on television. Who's calling, Joelle?"

"Oh," Joelle said, turning away from her gloomy examination of the botanical laboratory with its verdant banks of lush and steaming growth. "A woman named Maude. She said you'd know. She said it was an emergency," Joelle added cautiously, glancing at Sarah. "I think maybe she was crying, Sarah."

Sarah stiffened and stared at the girl, her gray eyes wide, her face suddenly white with shock and fear.

"Sarah?" Carl queried, moving hastily toward her, but Sarah wasn't even aware of him.

Jim, she thought wildly. *It's Jim. Something's happened to him. Oh, God, how can I live if something's happened to him?*

Nightmare images beat like dark wings within her mind. She saw his plane banking and slipping, plunging from the sky toward the cold, enclosing waves of the ocean, heard the muffled screams of the people trapped inside the little silver capsule, saw the golden warmth that was Jim Fleming swallowed up in icy, unforgiving blackness, gone forever.

In the searing anguish of the moment Sarah realized at last just how deeply she loved this man. He was the one, the only man for her, now and always. As long as she lived, she would love him. And if she had lost him now, then her love was gone, everything was gone, and she'd never even had the chance to tell him.

She found herself moving along the aisle toward the front office, walking blindly, unaware of the whispers and anxious glances of the laboratory staff workers. All she could think of was the moment when she would pick up the telephone and Maude would tell her what she dreaded to hear.

Joelle punched the call through to one of the executive offices behind the front desk and then closed the door quietly, leaving Sarah alone.

"Maude," she whispered, clutching the telephone receiver so tightly that her fingers ached. "Maude, what is it? Is it Jim? Has he been hurt?"

"No," Maude said, sounding briefly startled. "No, as far as I know, Jim's fine. It's the kids, Sarah."

The relief was so enormous that Sarah couldn't speak at first. She sagged against the desk, her head spinning, feeling weak and giddy with the floods of joy that washed through her.

"Sarah?" Maude said anxiously. "Sarah, are you still there? Have we been cut off?"

Sarah heard the note of panic in Maude's normally cheery voice, and realized that the woman was, as Joelle had said, close to tears.

Instantly contrite, she pulled herself together and forced her voice to sound as normal as possible. "Sorry, Maude," she murmured. "It's just that when they told me you were calling, I was so sure that . . . that Jim had been hurt or something."

"No, it's the kids," Maude repeated miserably. Sarah finally began to grasp the situation.

"What about them, Maude?" she asked sharply. "What's happened?"

"Oh, Sarah," Maude said, no longer able to control the quaver in her voice. "They're gone, Sarah. I thought there was something strange about Billy today, I truly did, but he's been so nice lately, and Clarence just had a few minutes to take me down for some groceries. It's so much easier when he has the car, and I never dreamed that anything would happen when I was only going to be gone for—''

"Okay, Maude," Sarah said soothingly. "Steady now. Just relax, slow down and tell me what's happened. Nobody's blaming you, dear. You've given so much time, so unselfishly, to help Jim with these kids. Nobody could ever have done more. Now just take a deep breath and tell me where they've gone."

"We don't *know*," Maude wailed. "Clarence is out now asking around the building to see if anybody's seen them, but I know Billy's too smart for that. He must have had this all planned, and he just took them and ducked out of sight somewhere the first chance he got, and now we'll never, ever find them."

Sarah was silent, listening as Maude sniffled and blew her nose firmly on the other end of the line.

"My poor baby," Maude quavered, coming back on the phone after a moment. "Out there in this awful cold. And poor little Ellie, the darling. She was so happy here, Sarah, reading and doing all her hobbies, having good food to eat and all those nice clothes to wear, looking forward so much to going back to school next term. Sarah, just *think* where they probably are right now. I can't bear it, Sarah."

"We'll find them, Maude," Sarah said automatically, glancing with growing concern at the evening sky, already darkening from a livid sunset glow to black and frosty stillness. "Don't worry. We'll find them right away. Maude," she added, "why do you think this happened just now? What made Billy decide to take off today? Maybe if we knew that, it might give us some clues where to look for them."

"I doubt it," Maude said gloomily. "I think he just decided it was too risky staying here because Jim might be losing interest in them and getting ready to turn them over to the authorities or something."

"But," Sarah began, puzzled, "I don't understand. Why would Billy especially be worrying about that just now? I thought things have been going pretty well between them lately."

"The other night, you know, the night just before Jim left?" Maude began. "Well, he told us he was working late at the office, and Ellie waited up to give him this big going-away card she made for him. She worked on it all day, cutting pictures from magazines of airplanes, the Eiffel Tower, all the things he was going to see, you know?"

Sarah nodded miserably. She knew what Maude's next words were going to be and dreaded hearing them.

"And then when he came home," Maude went on, "it was like he was mad at everybody, you know? He hardly paid any attention to Ellie's card at all, and he snapped at Billy. I could see right then that Billy was starting to think about things."

"What, Maude?" Sarah asked, her mouth dry with fear. "What was Billy thinking?"

"Oh, you know, that Jim was getting tired of them all, upset about having to move out of this place, maybe ready to dump them, just get rid of them. Billy's never had much reason to trust adults, Sarah," Maude added. "I guess it was too much to expect that he could change that quickly."

Sarah nodded again, gazing with growing anxiety at the swirling darkness that gathered beyond the window and the thin columns of frost rising straight up from the chimneys into the icy, brittle night air. It was a brutal night for anyone to be out on the streets, let alone three helpless children, one of them a baby.

And it was mostly her fault, Sarah thought. If she'd just offered her home earlier . . . if she hadn't let Jim go away angry that night . . .

"What should we do?" Maude asked, interrupting Sarah's scattered thoughts. "Should I try to call Jim? Should we contact the police, give them a description of the kids?"

Sarah thought rapidly, forcing herself to put aside her emotions and deal logically with the problem at hand. "No, don't do that. I don't think it makes any sense to bother Jim, because there's nothing he can do and chances are we'll find them by tomorrow, anyhow. And I don't want the police involved, either, not at first, anyway. Not till we've had a chance to try on our own."

"But, Sarah," Maude protested, "the police would be able to—"

"Think about it, Maude," Sarah said firmly. "If we notify the police, then they'll know about the kids and their situation. Jim's not even a legal guardian, and besides, he's out of the country. We don't have any assurance that the authorities might not just decide to keep them in their custody when they find them. After all, we can't just lay claim to a group of kids because we happen to like them, as if they were puppies in the pound or something."

Maude began to sniffle again, possibly picturing her beloved Arthur and Ellie trapped in a cage, gazing wistfully through the bars like a pair of homeless little puppies.

"You're right, I guess," she said slowly. "And if that happens, then all Billy's worst fears will have come true, right?"

"Right," Sarah said firmly. "I think you should just stay right there in case they come back, and then we'll have somebody central so we can contact each other. Get Clarence to find anybody he can and start looking downtown, anywhere Billy might be likely to take them, and I'll do the same.''

After a few more hasty words of encouragement, Sarah hung up and stood gazing for a moment in bleak unhappiness at the darkened square of window rimmed with frost.

At last, her face pale and tense with misery, she gathered herself together, hurried out of the room and ran down the hall toward her own office to get her coat and her car keys.

FOR THE THIRD TIME in her life Sarah trudged up the stairs to the room that had once been home to Billy, Ellie and Arthur. Again she shuddered at the dismal poverty of the place, the unkempt squalor, the mingled smell of dirt and hopelessness that hung over everything.

The cold was vicious, knifing through the thin, tacky walls of the building, creeping in around poorly fitted doors and broken windows. Even inside on the upper landing Sarah could feel it. She shivered within the enclosing warmth of her heavy duffel coat, pulling her scarf closer around her face.

There was a new lock fitted on the door, a few tattered bits of paper lying outside, other signs of recent occupation. Sarah's heart leaped and began to pound wildly when she heard footsteps shuffling across the floor in answer to her knock. But the door was opened by a thin woman of indeterminate age with ragged, unwashed hair and a pinched, frightened expression.

"Who are you?" the woman whispered in panic, staring at Sarah's expensive coat and boots, her dark hair that shone softly in the glow of the naked light bulb overhead. "What do you want?"

"I'm looking for some children who've run away," Sarah murmured gently, trying not to frighten the woman who stood poised on the splintered threshold like some timid woodland animal.

"Children?" the woman asked blankly. "No kids here 'cept my own," she said. A sudden scream of anger split the musty air inside the room, followed by a heavy thud and a high, fretful wail. "An' God knows," the woman added wearily, "there's times I'd just give them kids away to anybody who asked. I'm sick of 'em tonight, believe me."

At the note of ineffable, hopeless despair in the poor woman's voice Sarah's throat tightened painfully in sympathy. She was about to speak when a man appeared behind the woman, wearing nothing but faded dirty jeans that hung low on his skinny hips. He looked very young, and as weary and desperate as the woman.

"Is she from the Welfare?" he whispered, as if Sarah couldn't hear him. "Does she have the check?"

The woman glanced at him pityingly. "The check don't come for two weeks yet," she said. "An' it's bread an' water for them kids till then, no matter how hungry they get."

Sarah peeped into the room and saw the children in question, a sad little trio ranging in age from six months to about six years, inadequately clothed against the chill and fretful with hunger.

"The children I'm looking for," she said, clearing her throat nervously, "are a boy of thirteen, his sister who's ten, and a baby about a year old. They used to live here in this room," she added by way of explanation. "That's why I came here first. I thought they might have come back."

"They won't likely come back here," the woman said matter-of-factly. "Not if they know you're lookin' for 'em. Street kids, they know how to stay away from the Welfare if they have to."

"I'm not from the Welfare," Sarah said. "I'm just an ordinary person who's a friend of these children. I . . . I love them, and I'd like to find them before they get hurt or something."

The skinny woman on the threshold examined Sarah's face in thoughtful silence and then smiled wanly, showing small white teeth and a sudden, startling glimmer of the delicate prettiness she must have had just a few years earlier.

"Okay," she said. "If I see them around here, maybe I could call you or something?"

"That would be just wonderful of you," Sarah said fervently. She rummaged in her purse and took out a small business card with her phone number. On impulse she opened her wallet, noted with relief that she had recently been to the bank and pressed two hundred dollars into the woman's thin hand.

"Some cash for the telephone," she whispered.

"Oh," the woman breathed, holding the money up in her shaking fingers so that the man behind her could see it, too. They both gazed in awe as Sarah smiled awkwardly, backed away and started to descend the steps.

All the way down to the street she could feel their eyes burning into her back. The memory of their rapt and wondering faces made her feel like crying.

Sarah stumbled back to her car, unlocked it, climbed behind the wheel and sat silently, trying to control her trembling, trying to think.

She glanced up at the dismal, battered buildings that surrounded her. Shutters banged desolately in the bitter wind, and lights blinked dimly behind torn curtains and window shades. Dark shadows lurked and slithered in the alleys, probably just dogs and cats, Sarah hoped, because it was far too cold, now that night had fallen, for people to be on the streets.

She wondered if Billy and Ellie were huddled in an alley somewhere with Arthur, bent over a little flickering fire in a trash can. Would they know enough to protect Arthur's small cheeks and fingers from frostbite? She thought of Arthur's chubby little hands, his beautiful, tiny, shell-tipped fingers and the dimples at his wrists, and her eyes stung with hot tears.

Surely Billy wouldn't have taken them away in cold weather like this without a place to shelter them. Surely he would be more responsible. And yet Billy was only thirteen and frightened. What if he had just assumed that he would be able to find...?

The endless weary speculations and dark, creeping fears were almost too much to bear. Sarah dropped her head briefly onto the steering wheel, closing her eyes and struggling to block it all out, trying to think logically about nothing but what she had to do next.

After a long time, when the freezing night air began to creep into the little car and chill her body, she raised her head, her eyes enormous and dark with purpose. She put her car into gear, pulled away from the curb and drove slowly along the dirty, deserted street, staring intently into every alley, every doorway, every side street that stretched away beyond her sight, black and forbidding in the chill darkness.

CHAPTER TWELVE

JIM GAZED DOWN through the window of the plane at the dazzling whiteness of the prairie carpeted in snow. He smiled, realizing he was startled by the chill, wintry look of the wide plains beneath him. Accustomed as he was to the changeable extremes of prairie weather, he had half expected, after little more than a week's absence, to find Calgary sunning itself in balmy breezes, lush and warm under a cloudless blue sky amid the first flowers of spring.

But this wasn't the case, not at all. As soon as Jim stepped from the plane, the cold bit into him, seeming even more icy and penetrating than when he had left. And there was an ominous edge to the wind, a threatening, rising whine as it snarled around the buildings and rows of grounded planes on the broad airport grounds. Jim hurried through the terminal, casting a glance through the wide bank of windows at a mass of gray clouds brooding low and dark along the ridge of mountains.

Something terrible was coming, he thought, probably one of the vicious spring blizzards that could strike so suddenly and harshly on the Canadian plains. He thought longingly of his own comfortable little apartment, cozy and warm with its cheery clutter of children and toys. Even their clutter seemed appealing today, after more than a week away from them.

He retrieved his luggage and bundled it into a waiting cab, still thinking longingly about all the people who waited for him in this city, people who had in such a short time grown incredibly dear to him. He gave the cab driver his address and rested his head briefly against the back of the seat, allowing himself, now that he was so close to her, to dream a little about Sarah. He pictured her home with its beautiful sunken living room, the fire glowing on the hearth, the dainty carousel horse poised elegantly nearby, and Sarah warm and sweet in his arms, smiling and kissing him while the storm raged outside.

"Here we are," the cabbie said. "Looks like this weather is getting ugly," he added cheerfully as Jim wrestled his luggage out onto the sidewalk and peeled off a couple of bills.

"I don't care," Jim told him with a grin. "I'd still rather be here than anywhere else in the world."

"Well, you must be crazy, man," the cabbie observed, still cheerful. "Me, I'd rather be anywhere else *but* here."

Still grinning, Jim hurried across the lobby and up to his own floor, fitting the key into the lock with a hand so anxious that his fingers shook a little.

When he stepped inside, the absolute stillness assaulted him like a physical blow and made him almost unsteady on his feet for a second. He felt a clutch of apprehension and fought against it, moving cautiously through the foyer, pausing to hang his tweed topcoat away in the closet.

The silence wasn't just that of a place temporarily unoccupied. It was the deep, settled quietness of a place where nobody had lived for a long time.

Jim stood in the entrance to the living room, staring around, his face white with shock.

The room looked exactly as it had back before Christmas, before Sarah and the three children had ever entered his life. There was no trace of them anywhere, not even a discarded toy or a stray sock. The room was gleaming clean, freshly dusted and almost clinically neat.

Jim moved hesitantly across the living room and into the kitchen, holding his breath, and then edged back out into the other room again.

Everything that had anything to do with the children had been removed. The crib, the changing table, the box where Ellie kept her lessons and her shellcraft kit, Billy's fishing gear and magazines—everything was gone.

Jim's heart began to beat heavily with growing alarm. He looked desperately around the room for something, anything, that would give him a clue about what had happened to them. But all he noticed was a tiny difference in the big palm in the corner, something vaguely strange and puzzling.

Jim moved closer to examine the plant, certain that it was new. The old palm had been taller, the leaves a paler green with less prominent veins. He stared intently at the planter. This was unfamiliar, too, a rough terra-cotta with a frieze of stylized horses painted around its wide lip.

Still gazing at the planter, Jim smiled wistfully, thinking that it looked like something Sarah would like. Suddenly the smile froze on his lips, and he bent closer to examine the big piece of pottery. He was certain, now that he thought of it, that he had seen this same planter at Sarah's house, sitting with a couple of other pots on the tiles at the entry to her living room.

He knelt and ran an absent hand over the little painted row of horses, trying to force his tired mind to work, to sort out this situation and determine what must have happened.

Maybe one of the kids had done something really out of line and the patience of the other tenants had finally snapped. Maybe Maude and Sarah had been told to move the children out of the building immediately and they had packed them up in a hurry and taken them, along with all their things, over to Sarah's house.

Jim nodded in relief and stood up, still gazing thoughtfully at the beautiful rounded lines of the earthenware planter. He remembered forcing Sarah to promise that she wouldn't take the children to her house, and shook his head angrily, cursing himself for being such a blind and arrogant fool.

Taut with anxiety, he went over to the telephone and dialed Sarah's home number. The phone shrilled again and again before he finally gave up and replaced the receiver.

All right, he told himself silently, trying to be calm. Steady now.

He struggled to develop a likely scenario. Maybe the kids weren't at Sarah's. After all, before he'd left on his trip he had required her to swear that she wouldn't take them to her house, and Sarah was a woman who was likely to honor her word no matter who extracted the promise or under what circumstances.

Once more Jim shook his head at his own obtuse foolishness. He picked up the telephone again, this time calling Sarah's office number. But the receptionist told him with her usual dispassionate courtesy that Dr. Burnard was out of the facility for the day delivering a guest lecture at a nearby college, couldn't possibly be

located until much later in the afternoon and would return his call as soon as she was back.

Jim responded with a polite murmur, smiling bitterly at the phone as he hung up.

"Oh, sure," he muttered aloud. "*Sure* she will. We
all know when Dr. Burnard is going to start returning
her calls, don't we? When wheat grows on the moon,
that's when."

It was heartening to hear a human voice, even his
own, disrupting the heavy, enclosing stillness. Jim
looked around, wishing he had something that was
alive, even a hamster or a bird to talk to. He had never
been so lonely.

He sank wearily down on the couch, drew the telephone into his lap and dialed Maude's home number.
Again the phone shrilled hopelessly in some far-off silence, but this time Jim felt a little cheered by the lack
of response.

"Okay," he said aloud once more, just to hear his
own voice again. "Okay, now we're getting somewhere. The kids aren't at Sarah's, but wherever they are
we can assume Maude's with them. That's good,
right?"

But there was nobody in the deserted apartment to
answer his question.

He opened his address book, frowning thoughtfully,
and looked up the name of the only other contact he
had for Maude, which was her son.

This time, miraculously, a woman answered, sounding warm and cheerful against the gathering violence of
the storm outside.

"Mrs. Willett?" Jim said. "This is Jim Fleming. I
wonder if you could tell me how to locate your mother-
in-law?"

There was a brief silence. "I'm sorry," the woman said cautiously. "Maude's not in the city just now. She's gone to Seattle for a few weeks to visit her daughter, my sister-in-law, that is, who just had a baby."

"Seattle?" Jim repeated numbly. "But...what about the kids?"

There was another brief, charged silence, and Jim hastened to explain himself.

"Look, I'm not sure if you know who I am," he began. "Maude's been helping me to look after these three children, and I've been away in Europe for the past week. I got home just a few minutes ago, and there's no sign of the kids or Maude here at my place. Nothing at all. I just wondered if you might—"

"I'm sorry," the woman interrupted firmly, although Jim thought he could hear, deep in her voice, a note of sympathy. "I really can't say anything about that, Mr. Fleming. Maude just told us that she didn't have the baby-sitting job anymore and she was feeling a little lonely, so she thought she'd fly down to Seattle and spend a few weeks with Bonnie. Her baby was cesarean," the woman's comfortable voice added, "and she's having a real hard time getting back on her feet. Poor Bonnie. I just know she'll be so happy to have her mother there for a while."

Most of these medical and family details went completely over Jim's head. All he knew for certain was that Maude was gone from the city, Sarah was unavailable and the children had disappeared.

He murmured something polite and hung up slowly, staring at the new palm tree in the corner.

"She doesn't have the baby-sitting job anymore," the woman had said.

On a sudden inspiration he grabbed the phone again and called the front desk, but Clarence wasn't on duty. It was one of the newly hired younger men, courteous and anxious to be helpful.

"Children?" the young man said blankly. "I don't think so, sir. I mean, it's an adults-only building. There are no children living here."

"But..." Jim began, and then hesitated. "When will Clarence be on shift?" he asked.

"Clarence is on holidays," the young doorman responded. "I think he's gone to Seattle for a few weeks."

Jim silently acknowledged defeat and hung up, troubled by a mounting tide of fear and tension. Something had clearly happened, possibly something terrible. But there was nothing at all that he could do about it now. He could hardly go out and run around in a blizzard, calling their names. All he could do was wait until Sarah got back to the lab and he was able to find out from her just what was going on.

Feeling hungry all at once, Jim wandered into the kitchen, opened the fridge and rummaged inside, looking for something to make himself a sandwich.

He sat at the table, eating, feeling waves of weariness roll over him. All the euphoria of homecoming had evaporated, leaving him numb with fatigue. He wanted to crawl into bed, pull the covers over his head and sleep the day away until he could see Sarah, get some kind of handle on this situation, figure out what to do. He got up to put his dish in the sink and something caught his eye, a tiny ragged corner of pink behind the big refrigerator.

Jim bent to retrieve it, pulling a square of folded construction paper from where it had lodged between the fridge and the gleaming chrome of the trash can.

Suddenly the significance of what he held in his hand dawned on him with harsh clarity.

It was the going-away card that Ellie had made for him.

Jim looked down at the careful printing, the little pictures cut out so meticulously, with so much thought and care. "Have a good time and hurry home, Jim," Ellie had written in her tiny, precise lettering, "because we all love you lots."

His eyes flooded with tears, and he wiped at them unashamedly with the back of his hand, smoothing the crumpled paper between his fingers.

Light-headed and weak with exhaustion, he wandered through the living room again, still carrying his little square of pink paper. He undressed in his bedroom, drew the drapes to muffle the howling of the wind, set the card carefully on the night table where he could see it in the glow of the clock radio and crawled into his bed, dropping like a stone into a dark, bottomless pool of sleep.

SARAH NESTLED on the couch of her living room, an open book beside her, a cup of hot chocolate on the end table next to her, and Amos purring lustily at her feet. She took a little sip of chocolate, lifted out a scoop of melted marshmallow with the spoon, savored it, then picked up her book again. But the print swam in front of her eyes and she set the book aside, drew her knees up and rested her chin on them, gazing at the fire with brooding eyes.

She knew that Jim was back in town, because he had left a couple of messages at her office earlier in the day. But she hadn't returned his calls, simply because she dreaded having to talk to him and still didn't have a clear idea of what she was going to tell him about the children.

Now it was late in the evening, almost time to go to bed, and he hadn't called again. She dreaded the moment when the phone would ring and she would have to pick it up, hear his voice, try to think of something to tell him.

Maybe, she thought hopefully, the storm had gotten so fierce that it already knocked the telephone service out, and she would have a few hours' reprieve.

With this thought, Sarah got off the couch, stepped into her fluffy slippers and wandered over to pull one of the drapes aside and peer out.

The wind shrieked around the eaves of the house, driving gusts of snow that whispered and spattered against the windowpanes and piled in huge, billowing drifts along the roadways and sidewalks. The neighboring houses looked distant and isolated in the storm, looming mistily through the shifting screen of white. Snow was piled around the foundations up to the windows in places so that the houses reminded Sarah of Arthur with his scarf pulled over his face and just his bright eyes peeping out.

The memory made her feel sad and a little lost. She turned away abruptly, let the drape fall and went to pick up her mug, carrying it into the kitchen and rinsing it out carefully before hanging it away in the cupboard. Just as she did so, a bell shrilled through the house, and Sarah jumped a little, thinking it was the telephone, bracing herself for the ordeal to come.

But it wasn't the telephone, she realized almost instantly. It was the doorbell.

Sarah belted her robe tightly around her waist and ran to answer the door, recoiling from the icy blast and the fierce shrieking of the wind around the veranda columns.

Jim shouldered his way into the foyer and took off his sheepskin jacket, handing it to Sarah, who hung it away silently in the closet.

"How did you ever manage to get over here in this storm?" she asked, trying hard to keep her voice casual and conversational.

"With more luck than brains, I'm afraid," Jim said quietly, his handsome face still vivid with cold. "It didn't look so bad at my place when I started out, but the traffic's hardly moving. There are abandoned cars everywhere, some of them blocking the streets. I just kind of slid in here on a wing and a prayer."

"You shouldn't have driven over," Sarah told him severely, terrified as she always was by the thought of something happening to him. "You should have just stayed home and telephoned."

"I didn't want to telephone," Jim said, sitting down by the fire. "I wanted to see you."

Amos roused himself, cast Jim a bitter glance and moved over with an elaborate air of injured dignity to resettle himself near the hearth.

Sarah came hastily across the room and sat down opposite her visitor, drinking in the sight of him. He was so tall and golden and splendid, so masculine and powerful-looking in his jeans and a casual navy blue woolen pullover that accentuated the dull blond gleam of his smooth hair. She studied his face, enjoying all the things she loved the most—the straight aristocratic line of his nose, the startling blue of his eyes, the strong but sensual curve of his lower lip....

"How are you, Sarah?" he asked abruptly. "How have you been?"

"Oh . . . fine," she began. "Just the same as always, I guess."

"Sarah, where are the kids?"

Sarah trembled a little and looked down, pleating the soft fabric of her belt with nervous fingers. Then she met his eyes, looking at him silently.

"Sarah?" he prompted. "I want to know where they are. You *do* know, don't you?" he added, his face suddenly anxious.

Sarah nodded, her eyes wide and strained.

Jim looked at her in growing surprise, his blue eyes flashing with a sudden, quick flare of impatience.

"What's all this about, Sarah? Are you waiting for me to apologize for my behavior the other night? Well, I apologize. I came here prepared to tell you that you were right and I was wrong. And now I want you to tell me where the kids are so I can go see them, please."

"About what?" Sarah asked, her voice low. "What was I right about?"

"About my father," Jim told her wearily. "I know I behaved badly the other night, and the only excuse I can make for myself is that it was just such a terrible shock to see him here unexpectedly like that, you know?"

He gave her a quick, questioning glance, and she nodded, her gray eyes troubled. "Jim . . ." she began.

"It's all right, Sarah. Let me finish my apology. I had a lot of time to think while I was away, lying around in those lonely hotel rooms. I know I've been way out of line, and lots of things I've said and done have been wrong. I want you to know that, Sarah," he went on earnestly, looking up and meeting her eyes.

Sarah nodded. "It doesn't matter who's right and who's wrong," she began in a low voice. "All that matters is getting things sorted out in the end so everyone can be happy.''

"I know. And I think I'm well on my way, Sarah. I want you to understand that. I'm getting my mind straightened out, and starting to look at the past from a more adult point of view, thanks to you. I love you, Sarah," he added, his voice suddenly low and husky with emotion.

"Oh, Jim…" Sarah gazed at him, her lips parted, her eyes luminous. "Then you'll go to your father?" she asked. "You'll go and see him and talk things over with him?"

Jim moved restlessly in his chair and looked away again, staring at the fire. "No," he began slowly. "I don't think so. I mean, there's been too much said and done between us for my father and I ever to be friends, Sarah. I don't actually hate him anymore, but I don't want to be friends with him, either."

Sarah tensed and sat up straighter, her eyes shadowing. "He wants to be friends with you, Jim. He wants it more than anything."

Jim leaned forward, his handsome face taut with emotion. "Look, Sarah," he began, "don't push me so hard, okay? Don't ask more of me than I can give. I'm willing to admit that he wasn't a complete monster. I'll even admit that my mother wronged him in some ways. But I still remember a lot of things from the past, Sarah, and I can't just set them aside and be pals with him. Maybe I'll go there for Christmas dinner next time he asks, and for Aunt Maureen's birthday—that sort of thing. But I don't want to be drawn back into the fold and play all my father's games again. I just don't."

"What do you mean, play all his games? Maybe there aren't any games, Jim. Maybe there's just a man who loves his son and wants to be close to him."

"He was never that simple," Jim said stubbornly. "I'm trying to be fair, but I still happen to believe, Sarah, that he's never done a single unselfish thing in his life. There's always something in it for him, and I just don't want to get drawn into that world again."

"Oh, Jim." Sarah looked at him sadly, shaking her head. "For a minute there I really thought you were making some progress. And I know that if you'd give him a chance, just go and see him and talk with him, you'd change your point of view, because you're too fair and intelligent not to. But you refuse to bend an inch, don't you?"

"I've already bent enough," Jim said stubbornly. "I've told you I don't blame him altogether, and that sometime in the distant future I might even consider going to his house for a visit. But not right away, and not for any heart-to-heart chats. Forget it, Sarah. It isn't going to happen."

Sarah looked over at him, and their eyes locked in a long moment of silent challenge while the wind shrieked outside and the fire crackled cheerily on the hearth.

"Now for our other business," Jim said, moving restlessly under her level gaze. "Where are the kids, Sarah?"

Sarah continued to look at him, emboldened by the anger she felt at his stubborn refusal to give his father a chance.

"The kids are gone, Jim," she said steadily, "and they won't be coming back."

Jim stared at her, stunned and disbelieving. "What are you saying?"

''They ran away,'' Sarah said. ''Right after you left on your trip, Billy seized the first opportunity he could. Maude went out to get some groceries, and he took the kids and a few clothes and headed back to the streets with them.''

Jim continued to gaze at her, his face white with shock. ''My God,'' he whispered. ''In this cold?''

Sarah nodded grimly. ''It took us two days to find them. They were in a horrible little deserted tenement that was slated for demolition, trying to keep warm with an old hibachi they'd found somewhere.''

Jim's face twisted and he searched for words. ''Were they . . . were they all right?''

''They were all starving hungry, and Ellie had a bad cold, just on the edge of pneumonia, but it's better now, and Arthur had a terrible diaper rash. Billy was the worst, with some frostbitten fingers and toes, but he's going to be all right.''

''Sarah . . . why did they run away? Why did Billy do it?''

Sarah looked at him, weighing and measuring his state of mind, wondering how much he could bear. ''They were afraid, Jim,'' she said finally. ''The night you left here and went home, and you were so angry, you remember?''

He nodded, numb with sorrow.

''Well,'' Sarah went on calmly, ''they were sure you were upset because of them, getting tired of them and ready to turn to the authorities for help, and Billy felt he just couldn't risk that, so he ran.''

''Oh, God.'' Jim dropped his head into his hands and sat slumped on the couch, his face hidden, while Sarah looked over at him sadly.

"How did you find them?" he asked finally, looking up at the quiet woman opposite him, his face haggard.

Sarah smiled grimly. "It certainly wasn't easy. We didn't want to call the police in, because we didn't want the authorities to know about them if we could help it."

She cast Jim a questioning glance, and he nodded quietly, waiting for her to continue.

"So," Sarah went on, "we had everyone we could think of wandering around those seamy downtown streets in the bitter cold. Maude's entire family, my lab assistants, Clarence's brother, all looking everywhere for two kids with a baby and a couple of cardboard boxes."

"And?" Jim asked tensely when she paused, staring at the fire.

"We were almost ready to give up and call the police for help when I got a phone call from some people I met the first night the kids disappeared."

Sarah went on to tell him about the couple living in the old room the children had once occupied. Jim listened intently, his face unreadable.

"The woman called," she said, "to tell me that her husband had been out looking for the kids all that night and the next day, and he'd heard about a couple of kids seen going into this certain building. Clarence took Maude and me down, and there they were."

"Thank God," Jim murmured fervently. "Thank God, Sarah." He looked up. "I should give them something," he said. "That couple, I should give them some money, Sarah. You say they live in the room where we first found the kids?"

"Not for long," Sarah said with another fleeting smile. "I got them a job, Jim. We needed a night janitor team at the facility, and I asked if they'd be interested. They've been working several nights already, and you should see the job they do. Everything is just shining when they finish. They bring their babies with them and put them to sleep in the waiting room while they work so they don't have to pay child care, and I got them a month's advance on their salary so that they could move to a better place.''

Jim looked at her, his eyes full of emotion. ''You're a remarkable woman, Sarah,'' he said quietly. ''You seem to have a profound effect on every life you touch.''

Sarah shifted awkwardly under his gaze. ''Hardly, Jim,'' she said. ''Lots of times I just make mistakes and cause all kinds of problems.''

They were both silent for a moment.

''So,'' Jim said finally, clearing his throat, ''where are they now?''

Sarah braced herself, looked up and met his gaze steadily. ''I can't tell you, Jim.''

His blue eyes widened in disbelief.

''I can't tell you,'' Sarah repeated quietly. ''They're with friends of mine, a professional couple who have no children of their own and live in comfortable circumstances. The kids are happy there. That's all I can tell you.''

''But...Sarah, I don't understand. You mean you're not going to let me see them?''

''Not just now,'' Sarah said. ''Not until you've decided to have a talk with your father and give him a chance to tell you his side of the story.''

Jim stared at her, his face tightening. ''That's blackmail, Sarah. Pure blackmail. My relationship with my father is none of your business, and certainly nothing to do with the kids.''

"In a way it is." Sarah took a deep breath and went on with the speech she had been rehearsing all day. "I told you, Jim, that the kids are with friends of mine. I go to see them all the time and have regular contact with them. I want to keep on doing that, but I'm afraid I don't want to have any more contact with *you* until you've repaired the hurts you've caused and restored your own family situation. So I prefer that you don't know where the children are just now. Otherwise you'll go to see them, too, and our paths will be crossing all the time and it'll just be really awkward for everybody concerned."

She stopped, out of breath, and looked away, stung by the hot flare of blue anger in his eyes. "So that's the way it's going to be, is it?" he asked, his voice low and furious. "Either I shape up and do things your way, or I'm cut off from everybody, right? No kids, no Sarah, no baby—nothing."

Sarah nodded, trying to look calm despite the turmoil within her. "That's the way it is, Jim. But I'd prefer to word it differently."

"I see. And how would you word it, Sarah?"

Sarah looked up and met his eyes bravely. "I'd say that the choice is entirely yours. You can do the generous and loving thing, and everything will be fine. Or you can go on being stubborn and selfish, but you'll have to do it all alone."

He stared at her, his glance hardening into dangerous blue fire. "I'm not going to accept this, Sarah. It's been me, not you, who's had full responsibility for those kids for months now, and I intend to go on taking care of them. You can't just step in and push me out like this, because I won't allow it. Tell me where they are, Sarah, right now."

Sarah gazed at him quietly. "The kids are happy and comfortable, Jim. If you truly cared about them, you'd leave them alone for a while to adjust. Besides," she added, "I don't really see what choice you have. Maude is gone, and there's nobody else who can tell you where they are except me. And," she concluded simply, "I certainly don't intend to tell you while you're being like this. You'll just go storming around and cause problems for everybody."

"God, you're a hard woman, Sarah," he murmured, gazing at her. "I just told you a few minutes ago that I'm in love with you. I've been thinking about you ever since I left, longing to see you again, and now I find that unless I do everything just the way you want, you'll go ahead and freeze me out, rob me of everything that matters to me. I just can't believe this."

Sarah was silent, aching at the bitterness in his tone, knowing that if she tried to speak, there was a good chance she wouldn't be able to control her own voice.

"Sarah," Jim went on, leaning forward, his face tight with pain and anger, "do you care about me at all? Do you love me even a little bit? Or is everything just a scientific equation to you?"

Sarah returned his gaze, thinking about the melting sweetness of their lovemaking, of the rich and endless depths of her adoration for this man, of the hungry yearning for him that permeated her whole being through all her waking hours.

"Everything is just a scientific equation to me, Jim," she said.

She stayed on the couch, watched quietly while he got up, crossed the room, pulled on his coat and boots and let himself out into the storm, not even looking back at her as he left.

CHAPTER THIRTEEN

JIM CROUCHED OVER the steering wheel of his car, peering ahead through the screen of white that swirled in a dizzying, wild dance just beyond his windshield. His tires slipped and caught in the hard, rounded drifts banked across the street, and the car was flung sideways occasionally by its own momentum, even though he was barely crawling along through the storm.

The snow was so thick that it took a moment for him to realize that he was no longer moving at all. He got out, hunched deep into his upturned sheepskin collar and waded around by the front fender, seeing the problem at once. Two cars had been abandoned in the middle of the street after a collision. They stood humped and silent under mounds of drifted snow, blocking the whole roadway, with Jim's car wedged solidly up against the rear bumper of the nearest one.

Jim gazed at the scene gloomily for a moment, blinked against the stinging wind and hesitated. Then he locked his car, turned reluctantly and began plowing his way back through the heavy, sculpted drifts toward Sarah's house.

He had come only a few blocks, but by the time he had retraced his steps he was almost frozen, even in his heavy coat. He paused by a street sign, scraped the snow from it and studied the numbers to make sure he wasn't lost, then started trudging wearily up the last block to her house.

While he struggled on into the wind, Jim thought about the recent scene with Sarah, and the fact that he seemed, every time he met her, to go stamping out of her house in a rage. She must think him so childish. No wonder she treated him like that, trying patiently to teach him his manners and manipulating him into doing the right thing, as if he were no older than Billy.

And it *was* the right thing.

He knew that, recognized even through his anger that Sarah was entirely correct in what she said. His father deserved a chance, at least, and Jim was being harsh and unfair by not giving it. But it was just so hard. After all those years of bitterness, all the things he'd said and done, it would almost be impossible to swallow his pride and go hat in hand to make peace, pretending that nothing had ever happened.

Maybe, Jim brooded as he slogged along through the drifted snow, he just wasn't the man for Sarah. Maybe he wasn't good enough, strong enough, forgiving enough. No wonder she didn't love him the way he loved her. No wonder she looked at him all the time with that cool, scientific appraisal instead of the loving, melting warmth and passion that he craved from her.

Like the icy wind that tore at his face, Jim's mood slowly chilled and hardened. He thought of Sarah's refusal to tell him where the children were, her cool assumption that she could force him to do as she wished by withholding that vital information. And his feelings shifted. It was time for him to have it out with her, quit being so easygoing and present her with a few hard facts. He had a case to argue, and he intended to force her to listen to him, no matter what he had to do.

His face tightened with resolve, and his pace quickened as he stumbled forward through the drifted snow.

Soon he was at her door, growing angrier all the time, still without any real idea what he was going to say to her when she answered. Nobody came, and he rang again, wondering if she had gone to bed, if she was asleep already and couldn't hear the bell.

He felt the knob, realizing with a quick twinge of alarm that the door was unlocked. He was almost certain that he'd locked it behind him as he'd left.

Stamping the snow from his boots, he stepped inside into a pool of light in the foyer.

"Sarah!" he shouted furiously, hearing some muffled footsteps from the direction of the kitchen. "Listen, my girl, there's a few things we have to—"

He broke off and stared, his mouth suddenly dry.

Sarah had appeared in the entry to the kitchen. She was as pale as sculpted marble, trembling, clutching her robe around her in shaking hands. Her eyes were wide and vague with anguished depths of emotion.

"Sarah!" Jim said, forgetting all his anger and hurt in a flood of concern. "Sarah, darling, what is it? What's the matter?"

He gathered her into his arms, and she began to sob against his chest, increasing his alarm.

"Sarah," he whispered against her hair. "Sarah, it's all right. It's just me. Did I frighten you?"

She shook her head and leaned back in his arms, looking up at him through her tears with an expression of such abject childlike desolation that he wondered how he could ever have thought her clinical and devoid of feeling.

"Jim," she whispered, "I'm having a miscarriage. I'm losing the baby."

He gripped her shoulders and stared down at her, numb with shock.

"I was going upstairs to bed," she went on tonelessly, "and Amos was with me. He wedged in front of me the way he does, rubbing against my ankles, and I tripped over him and fell sideways on the stairwell. I caught myself on the railing before I went very far, but I twisted my back as I fell, and a few minutes later I realized I was bleeding. Oh, Jim—"

Her voice broke, and she burrowed into his arms again, hiding her face against his chest. Jim held her tenderly, cradling her, feeling the tears burn in his own eyes.

"I'll call the doctor, sweetheart," he murmured. "What's his number?"

Sarah shook her head, sniffling. "I already called. I just hung up a second ago. His service said he was on the way home from the hospital, and I should try him there, but his wife said he hadn't made it home yet. You know what it's like out, Jim. I went to look out a minute ago, and it's so—"

"Did she have any ideas? Did she mention anybody else we could call?"

Sarah shook her head. "She just said...she said I should lie down, elevate my hips and feet and try to relax, and that she'd have him call or come over as soon as he got home. Oh, Jim," Sarah finished in sudden agony, "I can't bear to lose this baby. I just can't *bear* it!"

"Shh," he whispered, patting her back, kissing her hair and her wet cheeks, tasting the warm, salty tears and aching with sorrow. "First, we're not going to lose this baby, Sarah. We're going to do just what the doctor's wife said. Where do you want to lie down? Should I carry you up to your room?"

Sarah shook her head. "No, I'd rather...I think this is fine," she murmured, looking up at him piteously. "You won't leave again, will you?"

"Oh, darling..." He gazed down at her, aching with sympathy, marveling again that he could ever have thought her cold and unemotional. "No," he whispered. "I'm not leaving again, sweetheart. Not ever. Come on, now."

He lifted her and carried her into the living room, settling her on the couch, covering her with a blanket from the big wooden chest in one corner, and a warm knitted afghan. Finally he hurried into the bathroom, folded up a couple of big bath towels and slipped them under her slender hips, then carefully positioned a cushion beneath her feet.

"Is that comfortable?" he asked, frowning as he studied the position of her body. "Not elevated too much?"

"It's fine," Sarah murmured, trying to smile, her face bleak and full of misery.

Jim knelt beside her, stroking her hair tenderly. "Do you have any pain?"

"Some," she admitted. "Just little crampy pains, nothing major. They come and go."

Jim looked away from her through one of the narrow leaded glass windows by the front door, measuring the strength and fury of the storm. He would have been completely willing to carry her in his arms through the blizzard, all the way to the hospital if necessary. But he knew that it wasn't possible. They were stranded here, and she had nobody else but him. It was up to him, whatever happened, to look after her. His face tightened, and he had to force his jaw muscles to relax before he turned back to her.

"Okay," he said cheerfully. "Now listen up, you stubborn woman. The doctor's wife said you were supposed to take it easy, and that's exactly what I want you to do. Just relax."

He settled himself on the floor beside her, holding her, whispering and murmuring to her as he stroked her hair and gently kneaded her arms and shoulders.

"Sarah," he whispered, "you're so tense. Try to relax. Try to fall asleep."

"Jim, how can I relax? I'm so scared. I'm just so scared."

The telephone rang, muffled and distant through the howling noise of the storm.

Jim ran to answer it, his heart beating crazily in his chest.

"Dr. Ian McLellan here. Who is this?" a hearty male voice asked on the other end.

"Thank God," Jim said fervently. "Dr. McLellan, this is Jim Fleming. I'm here with Sarah. I'm...I'm the baby's father," he said, feeling a little flare of pride at speaking these words for the first time. Then, remembering, he was almost overcome by a terrible, desolate wave of sorrow.

"Well, well," Dr. McLellan said thoughtfully. "I really had no idea *you* were on the scene at all, young man, but I'm certainly glad you're there now. Describe the situation for me."

Jim obeyed, carefully repeating the story Sarah had told him, describing her condition and what he had done for her.

"And you say the bleeding hasn't increased?"

"I don't think so. Not since I came, anyway," Jim said.

"Any pain?"

"Little cramps, she says."

"Hmm," Dr. McLellan said. There was a long pause while Jim gripped the receiver anxiously, staring at the archway leading into the living room.

"Listen, son," the doctor said finally, "there's nothing at all I can do. Even the emergency vehicles aren't getting through tonight, so I'm afraid you're on your own. Now this is what I want you to do. Just keep her warm and try to get her to sleep. Either she's going to miscarry or she isn't, and by morning we should know the score. Give her a couple of drinks," he added. "Good stiff ones."

"Drinks?" Jim echoed blankly. "But... she's pregnant. She won't ever take a drink at all. Not even a sip of wine."

"Good for her," the doctor said approvingly. "Sarah's a smart girl, and she knows what careless alcohol consumption can do to an unborn child, but this is an exceptional circumstance. In cases of premature labor, where there's no other medication available, we often find that a few ounces of alcohol can relax the muscles surrounding the uterus, and sometimes even stop the contractions."

Jim hesitated and the doctor chuckled wryly, a warm, cheerful sound above the howling fury of the blizzard outside.

"Trust me, son," he said. "I'm a doctor."

"MORE ORANGE JUICE?" Sarah asked in dismay, propping herself unsteadily on one elbow. "But,

Jim...I just finished a whole glass of orange juice. And half of this one."

"Try to drink another glass," Jim urged, kneeling beside her and holding the glass to her lips.

"But I'm not thirsty," she said piteously, glancing up at him with childlike confusion.

"Come on, Sarah," Jim said. "The doctor said liquids were good for you."

Well, he told himself, that wasn't entirely a lie. The doctor had definitely said *something* like that.

Jim grinned wanly, thinking how lucky he was, just the same, that he'd found that half bottle of vodka in Sarah's cupboard. He was sure, doctor or no doctor, that Sarah would never have taken the orange juice if she could smell or taste what was in it.

"Why?" she was asking, regarding him owlishly with what he recognized as her "scientist look."

"Why what? Here, have another sip."

She gave up and leaned forward to sip obediently at the foaming glass of juice, then looked up at him again with wide-eyed bewilderment. "Why are liquids good for me, Jim?"

Jim floundered, casting about for a plausible answer, remembering how much she knew and how difficult it always was to mislead her. But she wasn't listening anymore. Instead, she was frowning intently at some thought of her own as she traced one hand in the air in slow, dreamy circles.

Dr. Burnard, Jim realized, was getting a little inebriated.

He felt a small stirring of concern, wondering if he might be making the drinks too strong. But the doctor had said "a few ounces," and she hadn't had more than that—just one stiff drink, and now this one.

"Sarah," he said, "did you have any supper?"

She pondered, her eyes narrowing as she tried to remember. "Maybe not," she said finally, and hiccuped.

"What do you mean, maybe not? Either you did or you didn't."

"Can't remember," Sarah said, her voice a little slurred. "Don' think so. Too..." She hiccuped again, then tried to smile at him. "Too scared," she said apologetically.

"Scared? What were you scared of?"

"You," she said simply. "Scared you'd be mad about the kids. And," she added with another sad, smiling glance at him, "sure enough, you were."

Jim forced himself to smile back at her and held the glass for her to sip again. That explained it, he thought. On an empty stomach, and not accustomed to alcohol, it wasn't surprising that she was reacting like this.

She reached out an unsteady hand to stroke his hair. He smiled down at her tenderly, acknowledging to himself that perhaps Dr. Mclellan had been right. At least she seemed much more relaxed now, her cheeks pink, her body limp and flexible.

"Pure gold," she murmured. "Jason's fleece."

"What's that, Sarah?"

"You hair. Pure gold. A treasure beyond price."

She looked at him in silence for a moment, her eyes wide and luminous.

Jim met her gaze in startled silence, thinking that nobody could accuse Dr. Sarah Burnard of being a belligerent drunk. In fact, he was finding her absolutely adorable.

"I'm a cheat, you know," she announced solemnly. "Jus' a big cheat. Even...even cheated myself."

"How, Sarah?" he asked gently. "What do you mean?"

"Pretended I picked you out to be...baby's father...jus' because of genetics." She shook her head vigorously on the pillow. "Not true."

"Then why, Sarah?" he asked, his heart beating fast as he held the glass to her lips again. "Why did you pick me?"

"Loved you," she said simply. "Loved you since the...since the firs' time I ever saw you, way back in school. Didn't even admit it to...to myself. But it's true."

He drew away and gazed down at her, astonished. "What do you mean, dear?"

She peered up at him, looking confused, and then smiled. "There was nobody like...nobody like Jim Fleming," she murmured. "Never. Made my heart stand still whenever I saw you, right from the very first time. Pretended not to care, because there were always so many pretty girls crowding around you."

"Sarah, I never knew that you..."

"Found your timetable on the floor in English class one day," she confessed with a little giggle, her voice growing more slurred. "Kept it forever. I still have it," she told him solemnly. "In my desk at work."

Jim stared down at her lovely, flushed face against the dark fan of her hair, struggling to absorb all this. "And you're saying that you...you felt this way all these years? That's why you wanted me to be your baby's father?"

Sarah nodded solemnly. "That's the truth," she said, and hiccuped. "Pretended to myself that it was all scientific, because of genetics and stuff, but it wasn't. It was just all about...about loving you, that's all."

"Oh, Sarah—" His voice broke, and he gathered her into his arms, humbled by the tremendous depths of his love, and the knowledge of how badly he had misjudged her. She was shy and reserved and intellectual, and she clung fiercely to her own convictions of right and wrong, but she wasn't cold. There were depths of sweetness and emotion to this woman that he could spend a lifetime exploring and never fully discover.

"Sarah," he whispered against her hair, "will you marry me?"

She pulled away and gazed up at him in childlike surprise. "But," she whispered, her face crumpling, "there's no need, Jim. We're not…there's not going to be a baby. No need to marry me."

"There's every need to marry you, darling," he said, smiling down at her, his face alight with tenderness. "I can't live without you, for one thing. And we'll have more babies. Tell me you'll marry me, sweetheart. I need to hear you say it."

She lay on the pillows, her hair like dark wings around her face, her gray eyes shining as she continued to regard him with that same solemn, owlish look. Then she shook her head. "After," she said.

"After what, dear?" Jim asked, puzzled.

"After you've gone and talked to your father," Sarah said firmly, and closed her eyes, falling asleep almost at once.

Jim looked down at her peaceful, flushed face and laughed in spite of himself. Sarah Burnard had to be the most stubborn woman in the world. And he adored her. He put a hand to his face and was surprised to find his cheeks wet with tears.

THE FIERCE WIND finally began to die in the small hours of the night. By morning the world was still and silent, muffled in white and bathed in sunshine, crowned by a wide, arching prairie sky of serene and cloudless sapphire.

Jim stood at the kitchen window in Sarah's house, sipping a cup of coffee and staring moodily out at the massive snowdrifts, sculpted by the wind into fantasy shapes that curved around the houses and across the streets. Here and there he could see the soft, lumpy mound that indicated a parked car was concealed somewhere beneath the snow.

Snowplow drivers and sanding crews were already at work, their big vehicles rumbling through the white sun-sparkled stillness of the morning. A few cars were beginning to labor down the streets, moving slowly in the wake of the emergency vehicles.

Jim thought of his own car, nosed into the other two and blocking the roadway a few blocks over. He knew that he had to walk down there soon and get it moved out of the way, but he couldn't go yet. He was taut with fear, unable to think about anything but what was happening just now in the other room.

Over the dull, muted roar of the passing trucks Jim could hear another sound, softer but closer to him. It was the muffled conversation between Sarah and her doctor, who had arrived a few minutes earlier and was examining her in the living room.

His jaw clenched with anxiety. Restlessly he moved across the kitchen to pour himself another cup of coffee, his movements stiff and jerky, his eyes darkly shadowed. Jim hadn't slept at all the night before, haunted by a terrible, hollow fear that if he fell asleep something would happen to Sarah. He had sat for hours on the floor by the couch, watching the gentle rise and fall of her breathing, and for hours longer in the opposite chair, just studying the clear, classic beauty of her profile as she slept.

And during all those hours of silent vigil, he had been thinking about what he had found, and what he had come close to losing, a loss that he could hardly bear to contemplate.

"Jim," the doctor's voice called from the other room, "could you come in now, please?"

Hesitantly, dreading what he was about to hear and to see in Sarah's face, Jim walked through the archway into the living room where the morning sun lay in soft rectangles on the floor and burnished the rich jewel tones of the little carousel horse.

Sarah lay on the couch with her hair spread all around her in glorious disarray, her eyes huge and dark in her pale, tired face.

"How do you feel, sweetheart?" Jim asked, walking slowly over to her.

"I have a terrible headache," she said. "Just terrible."

Jim turned with alarm to the doctor, who was packing his bag. Dr. McLellan looked up, blue eyes twinkling. "Nothing to worry about, son," he said cheerfully. "I already told her that the headache is just because she's such a lush."

Jim turned back to Sarah, who was trying to smile at him. "You got me drunk last night," she said. "What a dirty trick."

"Now, Sarah," the doctor said, "don't you be so hard on him. He was only following the doctor's orders. I've known you a long time, my girl. I was pretty sure that the only way to get you to relax, apart from a couple of drinks, would have been a firm blow on the head with a blunt instrument, and all in all this was probably the easiest.''

"And you're *sure* it won't do any harm?" Sarah asked, her eyes beseeching, her face anxious.

Dr. McLellan smiled down at her. "Sarah," he said gently, "if you'd gone to the hospital, you'd probably have been given drugs in an attempt to stop the contractions. I don't think a few ounces of alcohol are going to present that much danger under the circumstances."

Sarah nodded uncertainly. The doctor grinned, his face creasing with good humor. "Just don't make a practice of it for the next few months, okay?" he said, winking at Jim as he reached for his coat.

Jim handed the heavy topcoat to the other man automatically, his blue eyes wide and startled. "Then she's..." he began, almost afraid to frame the words.

Dr. McLellan smiled. "I think she is, son. I think you two are still in the baby business. I've got an ambulance coming," he added, "and I'll want to keep her in the hospital for a few days just for tests and safekeeping, but things look fine to me."

"What happened?" Jim asked. "Why did the miscarriage start and then stop like that?"

The little silver-haired doctor plunged an arm into the sleeve of his topcoat, shrugged it on and looked up thoughtfully.

"Could have been any number of things, all of them too complicated and technical to explain easily," he said. "Most likely things just shifted a little in there when she fell, maybe a little tear that triggered the premature contractions, but still minor enough that it was able to repair itself and reverse the process when she relaxed and fell asleep.''

Jim and Sarah listened to him in silence, unable to speak, both preoccupied with the amazing wonder of what they still possessed.

Dr. McLellan met Jim's eyes in silence for a moment. He reached out to pat the younger man's arm. "I must say, Jim," he began gently, "that I'm certainly glad you were here last night. I don't want to be an alarmist after the fact, but these are the kinds of situations that can sometimes lead to internal hemorrhage if they're not stopped in time, and even be life-threatening. And we wouldn't want our little Sarah to be facing something like that all at home alone in a blizzard, would we now?''

Jim's face paled beneath the tan, and his mouth went dry with shock. He stared unseeingly at the doctor's weathered, kindly face, thinking again about his own relentless stubbornness, his refusal to compromise and yield, and what it might so easily have cost him. He marveled at the wonderful, precious gift that life had given him, a gift that he had come so dangerously close to squandering just because of his blindness and foolish pride.

There was a muffled sound of voices and stamping feet on the veranda. The outside door opened to admit a gust of fresh morning air and two ambulance attendants carrying a heavy canvas stretcher.

"She has a list of things she needs," Dr. McLellan said to Jim as the two men lifted Sarah carefully into position, "but I don't want her climbing any stairs for a while. Maybe you can pack them up and bring them over to the hospital later.''

"Of course," Jim said. He smiled at Sarah, who lay on the high-wheeled stretcher, pale and beautiful against the coarse linen pillow. "I'll be there right away, darling," he told her. "As soon as I can get my car back on the road."

She reached up and placed one hand on his cheek, her eyes soft with love. "Thank you," she murmured. "I love you so much, Jim."

He took her hand and held it, glancing over at the doctor, who was waiting nearby with the two burly young ambulance attendants.

"Dr. McLellan," Jim said abruptly, "how soon do you think she'll be able to travel?"

"Travel?" the doctor asked. "You're planning to go on a trip?"

"Just a little drive in the country," Jim said. "Just to pay a family visit."

He heard Sarah catch her breath beside him, but kept his eyes on the doctor's face.

Sensing from their tension that the question was far more important than it seemed, Dr. McLellan frowned, considering. "Well, let's see now. A few days in the hospital to do some tests, and a few more days' bed rest at home . . . I think," he concluded with a smile, "that by about the end of next week you should be able to take her for a little drive in the country."

The doctor turned aside for a brief conference with the other two uniformed men. Jim looked down at Sarah, who was gazing up at him, her gray eyes shining.

"Jim . . . ?" she whispered.

"Shh," he murmured, tucking the blankets up around her face and smoothing back her hair. "Just rest now, Sarah."

"But why...what made you...?"

"I had a lot of hours to think last night," he told her, his blue eyes serious and intent. "I began to get just a little glimmering, Sarah, of what love really is while I was sitting there watching you sleep. It's going to take the rest of our lives for me to learn everything I need to know about loving you, but I think I've finally made a pretty good start."

She smiled at him drowsily, squeezing his hand, unable to speak.

"And," he went on slowly, "all that time, thinking about everything that's happened and what was going on just then, I think I started to realize just what it is to be a father, too. And you can't come to that kind of realization without beginning to reorganize your life a little bit."

"Oh, Jim," she whispered. "I hope you know how much I love you."

He bent forward, kissed her lips gently and then followed as the ambulance men wheeled her out and lifted her carefully into the big van, its sides dark with sand and road salt.

Long after the vehicle pulled away from the curb and ground slowly off down the street, followed by the doctor's Cadillac, Jim stood bareheaded in the winter sunlight, gazing after them. His eyes were dark and thoughtful, his face white and tense with emotion.

CHAPTER FOURTEEN

BY THE TIME Sarah's term of enforced bed rest was over and Dr. McLellan finally allowed her back on her feet, winter had turned to spring.

The prairie beyond the city was dotted with melting patches of snow fringed all around the edges with lacy, delicate crystals of ice. Here and there sloughs of meltwater sparkled and shimmered in the hollows, miniature lakes that caught and reflected the endless blue of the sky. Above the shining expanses of water, occasional pairs of waterfowl circled, chattering raucously to one another, as if they might already be discussing the search for a perfect nesting place.

The air was crisp and sunny, though it still carried a keen, bracing edge of frost in the morning, and the breeze caressed the waving carpet of dried grass that was beginning to show a touch of green near its roots. The whole world smelled damp and rich, fresh and full of promise.

Jim glanced over at Sarah, who was gazing out the window of his car, her lips parted, her cheeks flushed with happiness. Her dark, beautiful hair was loose around her face, and she was wearing maternity clothes for the first time—a pair of soft faded jeans, a white turtleneck and a roomy pale blue denim smock that made her gray eyes look smoky and luminous.

She turned to smile at him gently, and Jim's heart turned over as it always did these days whenever he saw her face. His love for her was growing all the time, developing into something so deep and powerful that it almost frightened him. He felt incomplete when he was away from her, as if he couldn't even talk or walk or breathe properly. He needed her presence like food and water, needed her warmth and her smile and the gentleness of her voice or he couldn't exist.

"I got a letter from Maude yesterday," she said suddenly, interrupting his thoughts. "Did I tell you?"

"You mentioned it, but then the phone rang and you didn't get a chance to tell me what she said."

"Well," Sarah said, turning toward him with another smile, "she said she's having a lovely time in Seattle and she's staying another week, then going to Vancouver Island for a couple of weeks."

"Clarence, too?"

"Certainly," Sarah said with a grin. "I think it's generally understood by now that Clarence goes where Maude goes."

Jim grinned back at her, then returned his attention to his driving. "What about his job?"

Sarah waved her hand in dismissal. "Clarence has a pension from his old job. He never really needed to work. He just had that job in your building to keep from getting bored. And nobody can be bored if they follow Maude around."

"Are they living in sin?" Jim asked cheerfully.

"Certainly not," Sarah said with dignity. "Maude's living at her daughter's place, and Clarence is staying with his brother." She paused, recalling the letter. "Maude says," she added, "that Clarence wants to get married and she might consider it later on, but she just doesn't have time right now."

Jim grinned again. "Sounds a lot like a girl I know," he said innocently. Sensing Sarah's sudden tension, he retreated immediately to safer ground. "What are they going to do on Vancouver Island?"

Sarah chuckled. "It's an Elderhostel thing, just for seniors. A survival course. Maude says you have to go rock climbing and traverse a big, deep canyon, hanging on to a rope strung thirty feet above the ground—that sort of thing."

Jim laughed. "*Maude* and *Clarence?*" he asked. "You're kidding. Let's go and do it with them. It sounds like fun."

"We can't. You have to be over sixty to join."

Jim shook his head in awe. "These are great days to be alive, you know that?" He was silent for a moment. "So," he said finally, treading carefully, "Maude won't be coming back for a long time? She won't be looking after the kids anymore?"

Sarah gave him a quick, sidelong glance and then looked straight ahead at the lacy drifts of cloud along the mountains. "I told you, Jim. The kids are staying where they are. They're quite happy there."

"Look, I might have something to say about that, you know," Jim began abruptly. "After all, those kids are—" But then, seeing the sudden nervous movement of her hands and the way she quickly averted her face, he caught himself and went on in a gentler tone. "I just miss them so much. I want you to tell me where they're living. I need to see them, Sarah."

"I know," she said evasively. "They're anxious to see you, too, Jim. They talk about you all the time, especially Ellie. But I wanted to be with you the first time you went, so we've had to wait until the doctor allowed me up again."

"But we'll go right away?" he persisted. "Tomorrow maybe?"

"Right away," Sarah promised. "As soon as we can." She looked at him, hesitating, as if about to say more, and then gave a little jump. "Oh!" she said, pressing her hand to her abdomen. "Oh, Jim!"

He ground the car to a halt, pulling hastily over onto the shoulder and turning to her, his face white. "What is it, Sarah?" he asked urgently. "What is it, dear? More pain?"

She looked up at him with shining eyes, her lips trembling. "The baby," she whispered. "I felt the baby move. Oh, Jim, this is the very first time."

He stared at her, breaking slowly into a delighted grin. "No kidding? He really moved? What did it feel like?"

Sarah smiled, closing her eyes with a blissful little sigh. "Like . . . butterfly wings. Just the most delicate, gentle little— Oh, there, it's happening again," she said breathlessly. "Feel it, Jim."

She took his hand and held it against the small swelling beneath her smock. He leaned forward intently and then shook his head. "Can't feel a thing."

Sarah smiled. "You will. Just wait a few months till he's big enough to play football in there."

Jim smiled, lifting away a shining strand of her hair and bending to kiss her ear. "Are you sorry that we let them tell us?"

"That he's a boy?" Sarah shook her head. "I'm glad to know in advance. I always sort of assumed it was a girl, so this way I have time to adjust."

Jim grinned. "It doesn't take any adjustment for me. I'm just going to love him."

Sarah glanced thoughtfully over at him as he moved back behind the wheel and pulled out into the driving lane again. "You mean you wouldn't want to have a girl?"

"Sure," Jim said. "I'd love to have a little girl. Especially one that looked like you," he added, smiling at Sarah. "It's just that men are so much easier to understand. When I'm just an amateur, learning all this for the first time, I think I'd rather start out with a guy."

Sarah laughed. "And," she teased, "I suppose you're going to insist on calling the poor child Jameson Kirkland Fleming the Fifth?"

Jim's smile faded, and his mouth tightened involuntarily. "Not likely," he said tersely. "I'd much rather call him Butch, to be honest with you."

Sarah looked at him, troubled by the pain in his voice, and he turned to meet her eyes briefly.

"Jim," she murmured, "this is really hard for you, isn't it? Going to see your father, I mean."

"Sure it's hard," Jim said, staring straight ahead once more. "It's the hardest thing I've ever done. I'm scared, Sarah."

"Scared? Why would you be scared? What can he do to you?"

"It's not what he can do," Jim said, his handsome, sculpted face taut with concern. "It's just that...Sarah, what if I can't stand him? What if I honestly try, but the old feelings are just too strong and I find I can't bear to be in the same room with the man despite my best intentions?"

"What do you mean, Jim?"

"I mean, what happens then, Sarah? Do I lose you, after all, if I find that I'm just not able to make peace with him?"

Sarah looked steadily at his fine, aristocratic profile, then turned away. "We'll cross that bridge when we come to it," she said. "Here we are," she added as they swung into the long, tree-lined drive leading up to the big stone ranch house.

Jim gripped the wheel in white-knuckled hands, stunned by the experience of driving for the first time in more than a decade down this stretch of road that was so familiar and yet so deeply strange, like something from another life.

He parked by the garage, got out and walked around to open Sarah's door, amazed by the smells of the ranch, of wet soil and animals and rich alfalfa bales damp beneath a warm spring sun. The old remembered scents brought back his boyhood with startling vividness. He felt confused and disoriented, like a time traveler moving too swiftly between different ages.

Sarah gripped his hand. Jim squeezed her fingers gratefully, walking beside her up the curving flagstone path to the wide front door.

She pushed the door open with an easy familiarity that surprised him, and they stepped into the foyer. Jim blinked and gazed around, lost in the wonder of returning to this house that he had loved so much, where he had spent all the early years of his life. The rooms seemed crowded with memories and ghosts, and the impression was suddenly heightened by a far-off remembered burst of childish voices and laughter.

Jim started and lifted his head, his blue eyes puzzled. It was so strange to hear the ghostly sounds of childlike voices in this silent, luxurious house. He knew that it was just a trick of his overwrought imagination, a recollection of his own childhood days with his friends. Nevertheless, the distant, muted sounds had seemed so eerily real that he glanced down quickly to see if Sarah had heard anything.

But she was gazing straight ahead, her delicate face pale and tense with emotion. Jim knew how much this visit meant to her, and how vitally important it was, for her sake, that he keep a firm grip on himself. He took a deep breath, squared his shoulders and turned toward the hallway.

A woman appeared in the entrance to the living room. She was a full-blooded Blackfoot Indian, wearing a vivid orange tent dress, her thick graying braids lying on her shoulders. Her body was immensely tall and broad, and she had a slow-moving, massive dignity and an ageless, bronzed face that radiated wisdom and kindness.

"Hi, Clarice," Jim said softly.

The woman regarded him steadily, a light shining deep in her black eyes. But when she spoke, her voice was as brusque and matter-of-fact as if she had seen him only the day before.

"Well, you've certainly turned into a good-looking boy, Jimmy," she said. "Come in. They're expecting you. And mind you wipe your feet before you step on that hardwood."

"How's Eloise?" Jim asked, turning obediently to the mat and scrubbing his feet as vigorously as if he were ten years old again.

Eloise was Clarice's sister, as small and thin and nervous as Clarice was broad and placid. The two of them had been working in Jameson Fleming's household since they were teenagers, and they were a warm, rich part of Jim's earliest childhood memories.

"Eloise is just fine. She's in the kitchen," Clarice said. "With you-know-who," she added to Sarah, rolling her dark eyes eloquently.

Sarah nodded back at her, smiling. Jim cast both of them another puzzled glance and then fell into step behind Sarah, following Clarice's massive orange form down the hallway.

Part of him was busy with surface impressions: how light and graceful Clarice still was on her feet, despite her bulk, how the house still carried that old tantalizing aroma of cookies and furniture polish, how much he had missed the objects and places of his childhood, like the big painted leather globe on its wooden claw feet, and the secret curtained window seat in the morning room....

Bur on a deeper level he was suffering a powerful, wrenching crisis of emotion. He was drawn relentlessly down the hall toward his father's library, pulled along by the power of his love for the woman beside him. Inside, though, part of him was resisting, longing to escape, yearning to run back through the foyer and out the door into the fresh air, far away from this gracious, quiet house with all its painful memories and unbearable conflicts.

Sarah took his arm and squeezed it gently, letting her head rest against his shoulder for a brief moment of reassurance before she smiled at Clarice and walked past her through the open door of the library. Jim drew a deep breath, paused to still the wild beating of his heart and followed Sarah into the room, then stopped abruptly in confusion.

Jameson Fleming sat casually in a big oak chair at the side of the room, wearing slacks and a cardigan, his silver hair carefully brushed. He was leaning back in his chair, smiling as he explained something to Billy, who sat beside him, frowning intently at the figures on a computer screen.

Jim continued to stare at the two of them, his blue eyes wide with disbelief, his face stunned.

"Hello, Sarah," Jameson said, his voice gentle with affection. "It's so good to see you back on your feet, dear." Then he turned to Jim. "Hello, son," he said as casually as if Jim was in the habit of dropping in every day for lunch.

Jim was saved from having to respond by Billy, who glanced over his shoulder with a cheerful grin, his thin, freckled face alight with happiness. "Hi, Sarah," he said. "Hi, Jim. Good to see you."

Jim gazed back at him, his throat tight with emotion. Billy looked so different, so easy and relaxed. Jim realized in amazement that this was the first time he had ever seen the boy give him a real smile instead of that customary streetwise, sardonic grin. He grappled with his own feelings, beginning to understand at last the tremendous strain that Billy must have been under during all those months.

Billy was finally wearing some new clothes, too— jeans faded almost white, a tooled leather belt with a big shiny buckle, a clean, soft white shirt and fine suede moccasins. Jim realized that somebody had at last gotten Billy into a new wardrobe, and they had managed it simply by taking the trouble to find out what kind of clothes the boy really wanted to wear.

One of his hands was still lightly bandaged, and he kept it in his lap. The other played idly over the keyboard of the computer.

"This boy's a marvel, you know," Jameson was saying proudly to Sarah. "A genuine mathematical genius. A few basic accounting courses, and I could probably turn my entire business over to him."

Jim still felt a little dizzy, staggered by everything that had happened, by the strangeness of actually being in this room again and the incredible implications of Billy's presence. He cleared his throat and tried to smile at the boy.

"I thought you weren't all that interested in school, Billy," he said.

"Not *school*," Billy said. "Not dumb essays and stuff. But this..." He waved his hand at the figures on the screen, his eyes shining. "This stuff is just so *neat*."

Jim turned to Sarah, still groping to understand. She watched him quietly, her gray eyes gentle with love and concern.

"Sarah," he began, "why didn't you tell me they were here?"

"I couldn't, Jim," she said, returning his gaze steadily. "We were all afraid that if we told you when you first got home, you'd come charging out here and insist on taking them away. And that would have been terrible."

He was silent, thinking. "You're probably right," he said, giving her a wan, mirthless smile. "That's probably exactly what I would have done, considering the way I was feeling back then. How long have they been here?"

"Ever since we found them," Sarah said quietly. "They were in pretty rough shape, Jim, and we knew they were going to need full-time care for a while. And we were all too worn out to take it on, so we just brought them out here and turned them over to Clarice.''

Jim grinned faintly at Billy. ''I remember Clarice's medical remedies,'' he said. ''Did she burn bits of rabbit fur over your bed and dance around in a circle?''

Billy laughed, a sound that Jim had never heard, warm and infectious in the quiet, book-lined room. ''Not exactly,'' he said, ''but she ground up some kind of root into paste and put it on my hands and feet, and it took the pain away just like magic.''

He smiled at the memory, and the adults in the room smiled with him, forgetting the tension of the moment in his easy, boyish spontaneity.

''Arthur, too,'' Billy added as an afterthought. ''She put the same stuff on his diaper rash, and he quit screaming right away. Poor little guy,'' he added, his face shadowing briefly.

As if in response to the mention of his own name, Arthur appeared in the doorway in the arms of Maureen. Both of them beamed at the assembled group.

If the baby had suffered recently, he showed no signs of it now. He looked clean and plump, grown-up and splendid in emerald-green corduroy overalls and a dark green plaid shirt, and his round face was blazing with excitement.

''Da!'' he shouted, catching sight of Jim. ''Da da! Da!''

''Listen to that,'' Jim said, grinning foolishly. ''Arthur's calling me Daddy.''

''No, he isn't,'' Billy said. ''It's the only word he knows, the dummy. He calls everything Daddy.''

Arthur struggled in Maureen's arms and demanded to be put down, but she held him firmly, covering his face and neck with kisses.

Jim, who was studying the baby with fond attention, suddenly gave a little start of surprise. "I'll be damned," he murmured in awe. "Arthur's wearing the Fleming clan tartan."

"Indeed he is," Maureen said serenely. "We had a small bolt of fabric left, and Eloise made up a few things for our baby. Three shirts and a kilt," she added with satisfaction.

"A *kilt?*" Jim asked, choking a little. "Arthur has a *kilt?*"

"Aye, he does," Maureen said, overdoing the Scottish accent and grinning at Sarah, "and a fine wee mannie he looks in it, too."

Arthur twisted to pat her cheeks and plant a damp kiss near her eye, then began to squirm once more, clamoring to be released.

"Watch this," Maureen said proudly, setting him down on the floor and holding him briefly to steady him.

She lifted her hands away carefully. Arthur took three wobbling steps across the floor, his eyes wide with awe at his own daring. He lurched forward into Jim's hands, and Jim swept him aloft, laughing and kissing him while Arthur patted the big man's cheeks with a complacent smile.

Jim held the baby and turned to his father, his face growing taut and serious. The others in the room fell silent, watching.

"How long are they staying?" he asked Jameson, his voice rough with emotion.

"What do you mean, son?" Jameson said.

"Just what I said. What do you plan to do with them? How long are you going to let them stay here?"

"This is their home, son," Jameson said quietly. "They live here."

While Jim stared at him in amazement, Jameson turned to Sarah with a gentle smile. "I did what you advised, Sarah, and used my political leverage shamelessly to expedite things. The papers for legal guardianship arrived yesterday by courier. Now we can begin adoption proceedings."

Jim held Arthur, his eyes wide, his face pale with shock. "You're going to *adopt* these kids?" he asked his father. "All three of them?"

"Well, we certainly hope so," Jameson said while Maureen smiled mistily and reached over to place a gentle hand on Billy's shoulder. "Except...well, son, I was hoping to talk it over with you first."

Jim looked at his father in amazement. It *sounded* as if he was asking for Jim's blessing. Jim stood speechless, then turned aside, briefly distracted by Arthur, who was burrowing energetically under his sweater, searching for his shirt pocket and the soft felt pen that Jim always carried.

"The other pocket, Arthur," he murmured. "Try the other pocket."

He glanced into the hallway behind Maureen, his face reflecting a sudden, wistful anxiety. "Where's Ellie?" he asked.

"Where she loves to be best of all—in the kitchen with Eloise," Maureen said. "That child prepared the entire main course for our luncheon today all by herself. And anybody who doesn't praise it to the skies," she added sternly, "will have *me* to answer to, let me tell you."

Maureen's red hair sparked fire, and her blue eyes looked so fierce that the others in the room were startled, then amused.

Maureen moved across the room, pausing to give Sarah a fond little hug and exchange a few murmured words before she stopped beside Jim and gazed up at Arthur, who was clutching the pen triumphantly in his hand. Smears of color already marked his face, and a number of experimental strokes trailed over his fat fists and onto his shirt cuffs.

"It's washable, Aunt Mo," Jim said humbly.

Maureen ignored him, still glaring at Arthur, hands on hips. "Look at you," she said with mock outrage. "All bathed and dressed not twenty minutes ago, and now we need to do it all over."

Arthur beamed, holding the pen out to her. Maureen's face softened, and she smiled at Jim, her flower-blue eyes shining with rich depths of happiness and contentment that he had never seen in her before. She lifted the chuckling baby from his arms.

"I'll just tend to this little man," she said, moving briskly from the room, "and then we'll eat. Billy, come help me for a minute, would you dear?"

Billy smiled at her with warm affection and followed her from the room, murmuring something in an undertone that made her throw her bright head back and laugh heartily.

The laughter lingered in the air when they were gone and Jim stood alone with Sarah and his father in the quiet room.

Jim's mind whirled. Part of him was outraged by everything that had happened, by the way circumstances had somehow slipped so far beyond his control. They had taken charge of everything, these people around him.

But even in the midst of his anger he recalled that rich look of sweet fulfillment in his aunt's blue eyes—Maureen, whom he had always loved, and who had never looked as contented as she did today. He thought of the aura of security and happiness that shone in Billy's eyes and brightened Arthur's plump baby face, and the wonderful life that the three children could have growing up in this big comfortable house in the country.

Most of all, he thought of his father standing quietly opposite him, of the kind of family love and warmth that had been denied the older man through all these years and that was now, incredibly, in Jim's power to give back to him.

It was too much to ask of any man, Jim thought in anguish. He knew in his rational mind that leaving the children here was the best solution for everybody else, but it was wrenching for him. He still didn't know if he had any feelings at all for his father, if he could even bear to have anything to do with him. What if he walked out of this house, leaving the children behind, and then wasn't able to come back again? How much did he have to sacrifice to make amends for the past?

His chest tightened with nervousness. He gripped the edge of the desk to steady himself while the other two watched him silently. At last he turned to Sarah.

"Could you leave us alone for a minute, please, Sarah?" he said. "I'd like to talk with my father."

SARAH SAT with the others in the morning room, smiling automatically at the warm chatter all around her. But she felt tense and awkward, and her eyes kept turning anxiously to the closed door of the library. She knew, without really framing the thought, that whatever was happening behind that broad oak door was of vital important to her. Not until the door opened and she saw Jim's face would she really know what her future was going to be.

She couldn't live with a man who nursed the kind of bitterness Jim had carried around with him all these years. Sarah understood too well that people who nourished that kind of unforgiving anger tended sooner or later to sour the lives of everybody close to them. And yet the thought of a life without this man had become intolerable, almost unthinkable.

She sighed involuntarily and put an arm around Ellie, who was nestled beside her on the couch, cuddling the little girl warmly. Across the room from them Maureen and Billy sat opposite each other over a chessboard on a big drum table, their faces alight with fierce competitiveness.

"That game's been going on for three days," Ellie whispered to Sarah. "They both take forever to decide what they're going to do next."

Sarah smiled down at her. Of all the children, Ellie had changed most dramatically, Sarah thought. Ellie had always been the mother in her little family, the one who worried about everyone's welfare and wanted them to be happy and safe. Back in Jim's apartment her concerns about the future had often shadowed her thin little face, giving her a wan, pinched expression even in the midst of happiness.

Now, though, in a spacious, warm house surrounded by people she loved, secure at last in the knowledge that she was loved in return and never had to leave, Ellie had blossomed. Her face was pink with happiness, her eyes sparkling with a new confidence and a shy, sweet joy that brought a lump to Sarah's throat.

But as she gazed down at the little girl, Sarah saw a look of sudden tension appear on Ellie's face. Ellie was gazing through the broad archway into the dining room where Eloise moved silently around, putting the finishing touches on a festive, beautifully decorated luncheon table.

Sarah followed Ellie's eyes, seeing at once the source of the child's concern. Arthur had crawled up onto one of the chairs near the dining table and was standing on it, one fat hand gripping the chair back as he studied the big centerpiece of spring flowers that Ellie had just arranged with such care.

"He's going to try to get into those flowers," Ellie muttered darkly. "I just know he is."

Sarah glanced at Arthur, recognizing the look of thoughtful sweetness that invariably appeared on the baby's face just before he did something especially terrible.

"I think you're right, Ellie," she murmured. "He's about to make his move."

Ellie got up swiftly and crossed the shining hardwood floor to grasp Arthur by his plump corduroy middle and lift him down. He shouted in protest and began to drum his heels on the floor, causing the chess players to look up in surprise.

But before anyone could speak the library door opened and the two men emerged, their faces still and silent. Father and son paused in the hallway and stood a little apart from each other while the others glanced up at them nervously.

Only Arthur failed to recognize the tension in the room. He crowed when he saw Jameson, turned over to brace his hands on the floor and raise his small posterior into the air, then pushed himself erect. With cautious, wavering steps he crossed the floor, grasped the older man's trouser leg and tugged, raising his arms to be picked up.

Jameson smiled and lifted the baby into his arms, reaching into one pocket to give him a red jelly bean. Arthur chuckled and examined the bright candy for a moment with deep satisfaction before popping it into his mouth.

Ellie came over behind her little brother, smiling shyly up at Jim and leaning with total lack of self-consciousness against Jameson's side. The senator gazed tenderly down at the little girl, stroking her shining hair with his brown, veined hand.

Sarah felt a lump in her throat at the sight of the tall, dignified statesman with those two bright-haired children. She was still afraid to look at Jim, but she glanced anxiously into Jameson's blue eyes, hoping to read something there about what had happened between them.

Jameson smiled at her, his craggy face warm and tender. "Sarah," he said, clearing his throat awkwardly and reaching out to touch Jim's arm with a gentle hand, "I believe my son has something to say to you."

Sarah looked over at Jim then, realizing as soon as she saw his face that she was probably never going to learn exactly what had happened behind that closed door. But it didn't matter anymore.

Jim looked washed clean and completely at peace, his handsome face almost transparent with relief and a new, gentle strength that had never been there in the past. Sarah caught her breath as she gazed at him, thinking that he looked both younger and more mature than he had just a few hours earlier.

He met her eyes, his blue gaze steady and unwavering. "I love you, Sarah," he said quietly. "Will you marry me?"

Sarah got slowly to her feet, awed by the way he looked. Jim Fleming had always been larger than life to her, a wonderfully handsome golden man, but just now he seemed rimmed and suffused with gold, burnished with a glowing aura that touched his face and hair with fire and set him somehow apart.

Maybe it was a trick of the spring sunlight pouring through the tall windows of the morning room, but Sarah had the feeling that he was standing just beyond her at the edge of a wondrous, enchanted world where the air was richer and warmer and the rivers flowed with happiness, and he was inviting her to come and join him there.

She smiled, her eyes misty, and crossed the room toward him, oblivious to everyone else. Jim took her in his arms, and she could feel the warmth that flowed between them, feel his body rejoice in the tides of rich, womanly love that she didn't have to hold back any longer.

His lips finally found hers. They clung together, wrapped in stillness, bathed in sunshine. The warm, sweet fire of their kiss filled Sarah with overwhelming joy, and a deep, rich certainty that all the lost and wandering years were finally over.

Her family man had found his way home at last.

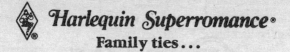

Harlequin Superromance®

Family ties...

SEVENTH HEAVEN

In the introduction to the Osborne family trilogy, Kate Osborne finds her destiny with Police Commissioner Donovan Cade.

Available in December

ON CLOUD NINE

Kate's second daughter, Juliet, has old-fashioned values like her mother's. But those values are tested when she meets Ross Stafford, a jazz musician, sometime actor and teaching assistant . . . and the object of her younger sister's affections. Can Juliet only achieve her heart's desire at the cost of her integrity?

Coming in January

SWINGING ON A STAR

Meridee is Kate's oldest daughter, but very much her own person. Determined to climb the corporate ladder, she has never had time for love. But her life is turned upside down when Zeb Farrell storms into town determined to eliminate jobs in her company—her sister's among them! Meridee is prepared to do battle, but for once she's met her match.

Coming in February

Take 4 bestselling love stories FREE
Plus get a FREE surprise gift!